# ORCHARD

# The Marble Orchard

## A NOVEL

### ALEX TAYLOR

BROOKLYN, NEW YORK

Printed in the United States of America
10 9 8 7 6 5 4 3 2 1

Ig Publishing
392 Clinton Avenue
Brooklyn, NY 11238
www.igpub.com

Library of Congress Cataloging-in-Publication Data

Taylor, Alex.                    2/2015
  The marble orchard / Alex Taylor.
      pages ; cm
  ISBN 978-1-935439-99-8 (softcover)
  1. Young men--Kentucy--Fiction. 2. Rural families--Kentucky--
Fiction. 3. Domestic fiction. I. Title.
  PS3620.A92M37 2015
  813'.6--dc23
                              2014045522

*This book is for my brother, Brian Taylor, and dedicated to the memory of Keri Beth Taylor*

# PROLOGUE

Beam could believe all of it now.

Standing beneath the sycamore tree in the warm shade as it spilled over the thick wind-loomed grass, he watched the rowed and white-clothed picnic tables steeped with dishes and casseroles—deviled eggs, meats and gravies, baskets of rolls and cornbread wedges, bowls of soup beans, fried fish and fried turkey and fried deer tenderloin, the tables curving up the slight hill and beyond it to disappear into the old tobacco barn gone unroofed and useless these many decades before reemerging out the barn's rear door, the entire dinner swarmed by gnats and black flies that appeared like frenzied dust against the white haze of the sky—and he could believe what he'd heard rumored for years but had never thought possible: that he was not a Sheetmire because some other blood yet howled fast and hot within him.

He stood with his mother and father. No one had spoken to them since they arrived in the family truck, a rusted two-tone beige and olive green GMC his father called Old Dog. Now they waited beside the pickup, Clem stroking the worn bed panel and brooding while Derna leaned against the passenger door, her arms folded over her breasts. Beam held quiet, one sneaker propped against the truck's slick front tire, staring out at the line of kin as they moved down the row of tables to fill their plates, each Sheetmire a mirrored replica of the others: squat and neckless head with the flat broad cheeks and full lips and bald unbearded chin that suggested a few errant drops of Cherokee or possibly Chickasaw blood. The eyes, sharp and mystical, showed

the squinty wrinkles of those given to hard grim laughter and
the teeth, once unleashed, were jarringly white. The women were
plain, but not dowdy, and they wore calm Sunday dresses of
mute blue or floral print, their handbags riding the crook of their
elbows when not in the care of their husbands, who were sedate
and loyal in all weathers, men suited to the slow sweaty work of
the land and who tried to love the quiet patient women they'd
wed, and there stood in their eyes the circumspect gaze common
to all survivors of trouble.

Not a one resembled Beam. He saw that plainly. All mirrors
showed him the same gaunt face with its sleep-hollowed eyes
and the thick blonde hair whorled about his head like a broken
hay bale. At nineteen, he'd grown to a height of well above six
feet. Straight and thin as a lodgepole pine, he seemed an odd
and unlikely child of the stocky and swart Clem who, but for his
dingy and unkempt appearance, would fit easily into the line of
Sheetmires now feeding at the tables. He more closely favored
his mother, Derna. Though she wasn't tall, she owned the same
lean cheeks as Beam, the same drowsy eyes. Her form, though
slack and softened by age, still gave rumor to her past beauty, the
dress fitted snug and shapely about her hips.

"It'd be something nice for one of them to say hello or ask
us how we were doing," she said. She leaned hard against the
truck. Its drab double-tone paint flaked off onto her brown dress
and the bondo drummed hollowly when she shifted her weight,
though she was still a slight woman. Her black hair appeared
scorched and blazed with gray and almost like burned foil as she
smoked a menthol cigarette, her white vinyl purse crouched in
the grass between her scuffed black slippers like an attack pup
she'd sic on anyone fool enough to spit a cross word her way.

"Who was it called and invited us anyhow?" Clem asked.
He'd turned away from the potluck and leaned against the truck's
bed panel, facing a glen of green that led into locust trees before
it rose into older hardwoods.

"Alton invited us," said Derna. "I told you that already."

Clem picked a napkin-covered dish of fried chicken livers out of the truck bed. "Well, it don't matter," he said. "I'm going ahead and getting in line and not waiting for them to talk to me."

He walked to the tables and settled the dish of livers amidst the rest of the spread and then retreated to the end of the line, his hands stuffed in the pockets of his blue cotton Dickies. A few of the Sheetmire women gave him curious stares, but he only nodded and smiled at them in return.

"I guess he's right." Derna sighed and dropped her cigarette in the grass, wiping a slipper over it. "We got invited. Might as well go ahead and eat."

Beam gave a tiny shake of his head. "I'm not going to," he said.

"Come along now. It's all right."

"No. I don't want to. You go on."

"It ain't no way to be, just standing there sulking."

"I ain't hungry. You go ahead. Just leave me alone here."

"You ain't hungry?"

"No. I'm fine."

"How is that true? What have you had to eat today?"

"I had a Snickers bar this morning."

"A Snickers bar."

"Yeah."

"That won't do you. Come on over here and get a plate."

Again, Beam shook his head. He watched the slide of faces moving along the table to fill their plates, their soft features licked with afternoon sunlight and glossed with sweat, all of them apparently nothing of his kind, and a cold nausea seeped into his guts.

"I just want to stand here a minute," he said, wiping his lips on the back of his wrist.

Derna gawked at him. "What?" she asked. "Do you think they're going to eat *you*?"

"No. I don't think that. I just want to stand here for a spell."

Derna scratched the dry chalky skin on her elbows. "Well, all right, Beam. I won't make you eat. Just stand here and sulk all you want to. But don't start your bitching on the way home because you didn't get a plate when you had the chance."

She walked away toward the tables, the wind gusting up and roving through her hair and the folds of her brown dress, the sycamore's shade jarring loose and withery over the grass so that she strode through flexing light and flexing dim. Beam watched her fall in line. Taking her plate, filling it with stewed tomatoes and macaroni, nodding and small talking with some of the folk. Her cheeks rouged with cheap dollar-store makeup and her hosiery striped with runners, the late sun whetting her shadow so that it fell sharply in the grass, her own body in its worn wash-faded dress like the last recovered remnant of a time gone to legend as she moved through the throng of gibbering kin. He saw her shapeliness. What others had named "her lustful ways." The slouch of hip, the drip of painted mouth. Even into late middle-age she maintained it.

Beam looked away from her and let his eyes stray over the strangers once more. For years, he'd imagined the stories his folks told him about the Sheetmires—how they turned clannish and tribed up into mere flickers of the old, original blood—as straight lies. Now he remembered how few uncles and aunts had ever come around to visit. How he knew perhaps two cousins well enough to speak to in a county where most kept an acre of memory reserved for family lines. He'd heard a few tales. The stories were mostly grim and unfinished—the drunken ravings of distant grandfathers and the misering of tiny bit-lipped women. He knew a few ghosts as they lurched through his dreams before being swallowed back into the catacombs of forgetting. Beyond this, he figured himself mostly unmoored from history. As hardly any relatives visited, he often wondered if any blood flowed through him at all.

He'd asked his folks about it many times. Standing on the failing porch, his father Clem propped in a peeling rocker and his mother Derna drifting in the swing, the river below smelling muddy and sour as the wind cut over the trees like a currycomb, he'd taken to wondering large thoughts about blood.

"Hell, they're just uppity," his father spat, suckling an unlit cigarillo. "Don't like to associate with folks who run a ferryboat for a living. That's all there is to it."

So it was the ferry then. His father had operated it for the past quarter century, toting people and cars back and forth across the Gasping River for long hours and short pay. The boat had a two-car capacity and a small tug motored by a Cummins diesel engine scuttled it across the waters. It rode on a pulley and cable system, the steel hawsers strung over the river keeping it in place against the current. The fare was five dollars. In past years the traffic had been steady, but these times were leaner. What patrons there were came down the Gasping River Trace from the town of Micadoo, which lay due west of the river. These were travelers bound eastward into bottoms sown with corn and soybeans and then the higher country of hills and limestone bluffs. A few fishing villages survived upstream in rickety shantworks, but little brought travel this way anymore other than the occasional fit of slow wandering, the Sunday drive or the visit to an elderly relative. But for the small salary the state paid him to keep the ferry open, Clem would have been sore put to survive. He had his ways, though. Rumors of drunks who rode the ferry at night and awoke slumped over the wheel of their car in some distant field without a dollar in their wallet and a knot swelling on the crown of their skull snaked up from the black boggy woods. Most chocked it up to dumb overindulgence and drove home, happy the maiming had been negligible. Those who returned to the ferry to question its pilot were dismissed with a smile and an offhand joke.

"Why sure," Clem would say, "you rode up here sauced to the

gills. I'm surprised to see you again. Thought sure I'd be reading your obituary by now."

So maybe that was the reason the rest of the Sheetmires kept their distance. More than the scorched stink of diesel buried in Clem's clothes, it was the legend of his violence that made them wary.

"I take it you ain't eating."

The voice startled Beam. He turned. His cousin Alton stood propped against the pickup's tailgate twisting a toothpick between his lips.

"I ain't hungry," said Beam.

Alton shrugged and lifted the tailgate down. "Suit yourself," he said, settling himself onto the rough metal. He wore khaki trousers and polished loafers and a collared short sleeve yellow shirt, though his chin was barbed with thin bright-black whiskers and he kept glancing down at himself as if surprised and somewhat disgusted by his current state of dress.

"I'm glad y'all could make it anyhow," he said, his voice a deep baritone. "Even if all you're going to do is sit over here by Old Dog and not take one bite of the blackberry cobbler I fixed."

"You didn't fix no blackberry cobbler," said Beam.

"The hell I didn't. Baked on it all morning. You better go get a piece."

"You didn't fix no cobbler."

Alton craned his neck and looked at Beam. His jaw hung open, the toothpick balanced on his bottom lip. "Shit. What kind of feller you think I am? You think I got so little sense I just go around telling lies about cobblers?"

"That sounds about like what I think."

Beam looked past the picnic tables, but felt Alton come sidling along the edge of the pickup. A bright and piney stink of cologne wafted off him.

"Hey, there's something else I got," he said. "Follow me on up to the cemetery and I'll show you."

Beam turned to him. Alton's cheeks were dried and blazed with pale dust from his job hauling rock for the crusher out at Dundee, and his skin seemed to always keep a ghostly film of powder. He was married, a father of two small daughters, and he'd grown paunchy.

"What have you done? Stole a car?" Beam asked.

Alton waved at the air. "Just follow me and you'll see what it is."

He paced away from the potluck and on through the thorny locusts and then up into the beginning hardwoods, red oak and scaly bark hickory that cast a cool murk over the ground.

Beam followed him. Up into the trees, he found loblolly pines grew here as well, the earth carpeted with their soft brown straw, the air honeyed with their sap, and he heard the clatter and talk of the potluck fading to distant drowned murmur as he followed Alton deeper into the woods.

The cemetery sat on a side of the hill in what had once been a clearing. Sapling cedar and dogwood grew amid the stones now, and the tangled grounds were ferny and sown with jagged weeds and an undercover of nitric green moss. The markers were crumbling, the names faded, and lichen spread over the broken marble and granite that appeared as fissured bone in the stark light pouring through the trees.

"What is it you got up here?" Beam asked.

Alton smirked and put a finger to his lips, shushing him. Then he strode off down one of the cemetery rows, the weeds sighing against his legs. At the edge of the cemetery, near what had been a wire fence, he squatted over a midden of soiled plastic lilies and Styrofoam saddles. Briefly, he dug through the refuse and then produced a tall vinegar bottle of green glass corked with a wad of sandpaper. A clear liquid jostled inside. "Come take you a pull of this, Beam," he said. He dug the sandpaper cork out and lifted the bottle. A long chain of bubbles flickered up. When he finished, he gasped.

Beam went to him and immediately smelled the fumey sweetness of alcohol.

"What kind is it?" he asked.

"Honeysuckle." Alton handed him the bottle. "Go ahead and take a yank on it."

Beam held the bottle under his nose. It smelled nothing like honeysuckle. It smelled like pure grain swill and it made his eyes water.

"You know I can't have that," he said. He tried to hand the bottle back but Alton stepped away grinning.

"Oh, go ahead. It won't hurt to just have a taste," he said.

Beam stared at the bottle. It wasn't his age or even deep Protestant guilt that kept him glued to sobriety. Though Clem had taken to prayer of late and was often seen reading in the Bible, his folks were not churchy and he'd been to but a handful of services his entire life. It was his affliction, a mild form of narcolepsy, that made him leery of drink. Without warning, a sudden sleep could come upon him, and he would drop as if felled by an ax. The doctors had told him that with such a disease the right level of drunkenness could kill him, and that it might take hardly more than a shot of whisky or half a six pack of lukewarm Coors to do the job. Beam suspected this was largely bluff, though. He'd been drunk a few times and had survived.

"Where'd you get this?" he asked.

"Don Eddy Ramsey. Makes it himself. You should see his cellar. He's got three refrigerators full of those little bottles."

Beam shook the container and the alcohol beaded against the glass. In one motion, he slung the bottle up and took a long healthy pull and then gasped when he finished. The liquor reached its fire far down into him and left a taste almost like warm iron on his tongue, and he felt his head steady and lighten until he could no longer hear the picnic in the glen below.

"How's that grab you?" Alton asked. He took the bottle from Beam and grinned.

"It drinks pretty good, don't it?"

Alton took another sip and then passed the bottle back to Beam and they spent perhaps a half hour that way, trading drinks and remarking on the bald hurt inside the liquor, the burn and scald of it tempered with only the slightest hint of honeysuckle. They talked and drank until finally Alton declared he was hungry.

"I need a wedge of cornbread to soak up all this whisky I'm drowning in," he said.

Beam remained silent. He drank deeply again, the bottle lifted to his lips as if he were bugling a reveille to the cemetery dead, the liquor pounding loud and brassy between his ears.

"Hey, Beam," said Alton. "Maybe you shouldn't take so much of that stuff. It's pretty stout."

Beam slung the bottle from his mouth and grimaced at his cousin. He leaned against a crumbling headstone to steady himself. Then he put a finger to his lips.

"Ssshh," he said.

Alton jerked the bottle away from Beam and stoppered it with the wad of sandpaper. He replaced it in the mound of cast away flowers and saddles, then covered it with an arrangement of red and mildewed nylon chrysanthemums.

"Look," Alton said, turning to Beam, "you're just going to have stay up here until you get sober enough to come back down again and that's all there is to it."

"I ain't sitting up here," Beam said, shaking his head.

"If you go down there they'll smell the liquor on you."

"I don't give a goddamn. They don't like the smell they should just hold their noses."

Beam stood up from the headstone and walked down the row toward the potluck, but he had to stop and spell himself against another grave marker as Alton came trotting up behind.

"See, you can't even hardly walk right," he said. "You just need to sit here and rest a spell."

Beam looked off through the trees and his head swam.

"Maybe you're right," he mumbled.

"Yeah, I am," said Alton. "You wait right here and I'll go down and get you some water and bring it up to you, okay?"

"All right. That'd be fine."

"Now don't move. Just stay put right there."

Alton walked out of the cemetery, through the sunlight and on into the shady trees until the sound of his footsteps was covered by the quake and jostle of the heat.

Beam braced himself against the gravestone. It crumbled some in his hands and he wiped his fingers against his jeans and then closed his eyes and leaned his head back. The blood throttled through him. His tongue had gone dry and brittle and felt swollen, but when he opened his eyes, he saw the trash heap where Alton had hidden the bottle.

A blue jay screamed somewhere in the pines.

Beam woke to full night, not knowing where he was. The ground under him felt soft and damp with moss. He rolled onto his back and then lifted himself onto his elbows, his head wobbling loose and ugly. The drink gurgled back into his throat and he spat raw bile and then wiped his mouth and remembered.

At one corner of the cemetery burned a low campfire. Two men were seated before it on feed buckets. They smoked cigarettes and shared a bottle. Each wore a patchy beard and cradled a rifle in his lap. Far off in the darkness, a pair of foxhounds bayed. When Beam staggered into the hem of firelight, the men looked up at him.

"Where's the homecoming?" Beam asked.

"You mean the Sheetmire homecoming?" the larger of the two men said.

Beam nodded.

The man who'd spoken scratched at his black whiskers and lit a cigarette. "You're a mite late if that's what you come here for."

Beam wiped the dirt from his arms and then pressed his

palms against his eyes. "I must have fell asleep."

The larger man grunted and adjusted himself atop his feed bucket. He wore a tan hunting jacket and stone-washed blue jeans, his great belly propped on his lap, and his eyes glinted lucent and tiny like bits of feldspar. The other man seated beside him wore faded Carhartt coveralls the color of grocer's paper. He picked up a stick of kindling and began poking at the coals in the fire.

"Are you a Sheetmire?" he asked.

Beam stroked the back of his neck. Looking through the night at the paling of trees faintly illuminated in the firelight before they faded into blank darkness, he recalled the line of faces at the potluck stretched in a cambered row beside the tables like a procession funereal and gaunt.

"Yeah," he answered. "I'm a Sheetmire."

"Which one?"

"I'm Beam Sheetmire. Clem and Derna's boy."

Both men nodded at this. The large one threw his cigarette into the fire and leaned over and lifted a bottle of Old Grandad out of the dust and uncapped it and took two short pulls before screwing the cap on and settling the bottle in the dust again.

"I believe I know them," he said, a bit breathless from the whisky. "There's a lot of Sheetmires around and it's hard to keep track of all the different bunches. I don't even mess with keeping up no more. Now, it used to be a lot of the older folks was good at that kind of thing. Kept it all written down in the front of their Bibles. Didn't just write it down, though. They studied on it. Got it down like an oath they had to say. My Uncle Esker could talk the name of ever half-aunt and cousin on back to when they first left England. Shit. Ought to heard him talk in the night by the fire. It was like hearing the roll get called up yonder. I never could do that. Course I never tried awful hard. Just couldn't see the point, I guess. All those folks were dead and gone long before I ever come to be."

"There was a spot where even the old folks lost track though, wasn't there?" said the smaller man.

"There was. Even Uncle Esker couldn't recollect much past two hundred years. That's nothing. A drop is all. And I'm not sure I'd want to go on past that even if I could."

"I might," said the other man. "I might like to know past what them old folks knew and could tell."

"Well, I don't see any kind of good it'd do you or them."

The smaller man rested his chin against his chest and watched the fire. "Well, maybe not," he said. "I still might like to know it anyway."

Beam squatted in the dirt. His head felt warped from the liquor Alton had given him and now he felt a bit dizzy from sleep. He didn't want to hear the talk of family names or bloodlines, and his guts churned a bit from the memory of all the families at the potluck gawking at him in mute surprise as if he were a guest unexpected and unwelcome.

He sat on his haunches and listened to the men talk of things distant and long forgotten. They seemed to speak with the pulse and rhythm of his own blood as it wandered lost and vagrant inside him and he recalled the faces of the Sheetmires at the potluck again, and heard the dogs hunting in the far wilds beyond the fire. He could see it: the long slick hounds flaming in the pines as they sought the red fox, the great billows of their lungs roaring, their hearts booming like the drum of the wind as it beat against the trees. He could see it all. The drop of paws in the dirt. The fox's burnished eyes like fine tumble-shined stones flared with cold light. He could see it, and a rush of air surrounded him so that he felt he sat in the doorway of a tomb, the gust swifting in from the trees to chill him until he shivered and clutched at his knees.

"Get up closer to the fire here," said the large man.

Beam scooted forward and the heat grazed his arms.

"Said you fell asleep?"

Beam nodded. "I guess I did."

"How you plan on getting home?"

Beam picked at the dirt between his sneakers. He hadn't considered this and now it dawned on him the way Alton had abandoned him in the cemetery. "I don't know," he said, finally. "Walk I guess."

"That'd be quite a hike."

Beam picked a chunk of bark from the ground and tossed it into the fire. "Maybe y'all could give me a ride."

The larger man stuffed his hands into the pockets of his hunting jacket. "I guess we might could," he said, turning to the smaller man. "Let's run this boy home and by the time we get back maybe the dogs will have come in."

The other man bobbed his head in agreement. "That sounds good," he said. He stood up from his bucket, holding his rifle in the crook of his arm. He smiled at Beam. "Truck's down this way," he said, and then moved out through the cemetery.

The larger man stood up and hoisted his rifle over his shoulder. "Come on. It ain't no trouble for us to give you a ride."

Beam stood and dusted himself off and then hitched at his jeans. The large man looked him up and down.

"This old boney ground here don't make much of a bed, does it?" he said.

Beam shook his head. "No, sir."

"I aim to have them throw a mattress down before I get in the grave. Maybe even a nice quilt or blanket."

Beam looked at the man. He expected to see a grin, but the man was stern and serious, his lips a pale seam in his black whiskers.

"I wouldn't want to think about it," Beam said.

The man snorted and pulled at the rifle strap on his shoulder. "Reckon nobody does," he said.

# I

# TUESDAY

Someone called to Beam from the far bank of the river through the darkness. He heard the man's voice as it dropped to him dismal and slow.

"I won't run you for less than five dollars," Beam yelled in answer.

Spasms of moonlight fell through the rearing trees. The moon itself was mirrored in the river, a doppelganger moon trembling on the black water, and everywhere hung a stillness seemingly permanent, a quiet that gave form to the night's own immensity.

Beam walked to the bow of the ferry. Moths whirred in the hull lights and he swatted them away. On the landing opposite stood the man who'd called to him, the moon dusting him with a weak and diffuse light.

"You got five dollars?" Beam hollered.

The man picked up a small duffel and hoisted the strap over one shoulder. He turned and began walking away from the river as if in disgust, rising up the landing until his form receded under the locust boughs with their elongate seedpods hung like dead lanterns in those grim and thorny trees. Beam watched him go.

Since sundown, he'd only given passage to a sulking farmer in a rattling tractor, and the want for company had settled on him a lonesomeness that shivered up through his hands as he gripped the flatboat's railing. He was used to the feeling. It seemed to follow him wherever he went, though he rarely strayed much beyond the ferry and the surrounding bottom country. On nights his daddy let him off duty, Beam might drive Old Dog into the town of Drakesboro to shoot nine ball at The Doe Eyed Lady, a cramped diner that sold fountain drinks and burgers on Wonderbread, the meat so rare and bloody it turned the buns the color of velvet cake. He shot quarter games when money was tight, dollar high when he'd managed to come by extra dough. He had loose friends who joked and ogled the waitresses with him. But even in those times, when the swell of the diner's clanging noise shrank down and all the billiards slowed and stilled, Beam yet felt a deep loneliness stagger through him, its footsteps heavy and ominous. He felt it again as he watched the man trek up the landing away from the river.

Beam unhitched the keeper chains from the jetty cleats and piled them on the flatboat, then crossed the stern and stepped into the tug. He goosed the throttle and the engine gurgled up and a froth of water boiled from the prop as the ferry crept slowly into the current, and the pulleys screaked along their cables. Driftwood bobbled on the river and the soured reek of mud and locust blossoms rose sharp and hot above the charred stink of diesel. When he was close, Beam cut the engine and let the ferry coast into the landing, the aluminum hull grating on the concrete, and then he fastened the chains to the bollards.

"Five dollars is good money if all you got to do to earn it is run across this river here," said the man with the duffel. He'd walked back down the landing and now stood just out of the hem of the ferry lights.

"You got a boat to row yourself across with?" Beam asked.

"No," the man said.

"Then I guess you ain't got room to complain about the fare."

The stranger made no reply. He was a broad man and his scalp showed under a thin crew cut. He wore a pale blue collared shirt creased with filth and the corduroy trousers withered against his legs were also dirty and too small for him so that his bare ankles shone white and boney below the cuffs, and when he stepped aboard the ferry Beam saw the broken tennis shoes he wore were caked with cow manure. A red mustache seeped out of his nose and curled around his lips.

Beam looked him over once and then returned to the tug. As he worked the throttle, the man stuck his head into the cabin and said, "I ain't got five dollars."

Beam cut the engine. "What'd you say?"

"Said I ain't got five dollars." The man's breath smelled of whisky. "I ain't got no money at all to give you."

Beam left the cabin so that he and the stranger stood together on the deck of the ferry. The boat drifted a bit in the current and then steadied as the cables tightened and caught in their iron grommets.

"I ain't got nothing at all but this here duffel bag." The man nodded to his luggage slouched in a corner of the deck. "Ain't nothing in there but extra clothes."

"You might want to think about changing into them then," Beam sneered. "Less maybe those in that duffel are worse off than the grimy shit you're wearing now."

The man smiled thinly, his eyes cinching into a squint. "How old are you?" he asked.

"Old enough to take this boat back to the side you come from and not give your sorry ass a ride nowhere."

"I can walk to a bridge."

Beam threw his hands up and returned to the cabin. He started the engine and began moving back toward the eastern landing. He had no patience for this sort of dawdling. Clem had told him that folks would likely try to bull him over on the ferry on account of his youth and that he couldn't tolerate such behavior, and so he didn't, but in truth he hated the gruffness it took to get by in this world, the brute and angry scowling at life that gave a man the upper hand.

The man stuck his head back into the cabin and leaned against the metal door frame. "Hey, man. I was just shitting you. I got five dollars."

Beam cut the throttle and turned to him. "Let's see it."

"Sure, man. Here." The man dug a wallet of cracked brown leather from his back pocket and produced a wad of singles and handed them to Beam, who counted and then folded them into the plastic Tupperware till sitting on the control panel. Then he ground the starter to life and reversed the prop so the ferry scooted along toward the western landing on the other side of the river.

"I hope that little joke didn't hurt your feelings none," the man said. He still hung in the cabin door, his face pale and slick in the feeble light.

Beam steadied the engine and stepped back on deck. The man moved aside to let him pass. For a time, they studied one another in the glum shadows.

"Are you a Sheetmire?" the man asked.

Beam nodded. "Yeah, I am," he said. The man didn't look familiar, but plenty knew which family ran the ferry and there rested no surprise in a stranger saying his name.

"I don't remember you," the man said. He wiped at his mustache and squinted at Beam, as if trying to fix him in his mind amid a myriad of others. "You don't look like any Sheetmire."

A chill rushed in off the river and Beam zipped up the green nylon racing jacket he was wearing. "What do I look like?" he asked.

The man smiled. "Now there's a dangerous question." He leaned back against the boat railing and folded his arms across his chest and regarded Beam with a look of snide ridicule. "I hate to tell you this, but I don't believe Hollywood's gonna be calling you anytime soon."

Beam eyed the man curiously. He stood close to the duffel and his entire form seemed to rise from the bag as if he were but some séance trick, a jester's prank with his shaven head and mustache, the flesh of his face slick and daubed with harlequin light from the cabin and running bulbs of the ferry.

"Who are you?" Beam asked.

The man shook his head once. "You wouldn't know me," he said.

Beam spat over the railing into the water. The hull groaned against the current and the river drifted through its own blank darkness, and there came an utterance of depths against the underside of the ferry.

"Where are you going?" Beam asked.

The man looked downstream to where the moonlight rode jagged and broken on the river like mishandled glass.

"Just across," he said.

"There ain't much to go to on this side of the river," said Beam, nodding to the shore as it slowly emerged out the dark. "Just dirt and corn mostly."

"Way I like it," said the man. "I like the open air where it ain't crowded. A man can't disappear in a city." He waved a hand at the night and all its distance. "But out here, a fellow can just... be gone."

The man turned and leaned over the railing like a drunk slouched against a bar. Beam went inside the cabin and cut the throttle back to let the ferry coast. When he reemerged onto the deck, the man was still watching the river tremble along below him.

"Where are you coming from?" Beam asked.

The man looked over his shoulder, his face utterly blank and calm. "Where I come from," he said, "is a place a boy like you don't never want to see."

A fire of anger rushed through Beam and then blew out, a cold crater left in its absence. He didn't like the way the man had called him a boy, or the way his smile had wormed its way from his face to leave a look empty and unreadable. Beam did not consider himself a boy. He was nineteen, full of bull piss with his own portion of meanness lurking in him, the kind of youth who'd grit teeth at shop windows and bathroom mirrors, at stolen hubcaps and snatched silverware, anything fool enough to throw his own mug back at him. But this stranger had come out of the night teetering with drink to gibe and prod him, and he felt the bite of something old and fierce in his blood. Watching the stranger on the ferry deck, Beam had a sudden vision of throwing the man overboard. The river would take him. There would be a brief plunge, the water broken in a garland of dingy spray before it settled again. It's what Beam's father Clem might have done, in his early years. Lurching and cruel in his youth, a frequent thief, Clem had aged into a soft routine of diet soda and bran flakes. But he had been right, in his time. Flash lightning through his veins every Friday night, he slid through those early years on a highway of blood. Beam could barely believe the stories he'd heard, the ones told to him by old loose-mouthed men who rode the ferry, about how a man might wind up broke or broken if he rode the deck after taking too much drink. The years had left a few drift scraps of recollected violence in his memory—waking in the night to the sound of gunfire and then running down to the ferry to find his father bowed over a prone stranger on the deck, looking up at Beam on the landing to say, "No worries. He ain't dead." Because Clem had never been a killer. Gruff and lean, he'd been a drinker and a taker of easy money, a schemer at backroom poker games and a parking lot brawler, and the worst crime he'd dipped his hands into was yanking dollars off the drunks who rode the ferry at night. Caution was the word he preached to Beam now, slipping country wisdom into dinnertime conversation. "Don't get dizzy when the fists go to flying," he would say. "And don't throw no punches unless it's worth a good amount of dough. You don't want to pull a jail term for short pay."

"The Gasping is a deep river," the stranger said, pulling Beam away from his thoughts. The man had turned back to regard the water, his arms folded over the metal railings.

Beam didn't say anything. He'd stowed an Igloo cooler beside the cabin for his shift and he opened it and took out a bottle of lemon-lime Gatorade and drank from it and then put it away again and closed the cooler.

"They say it's so deep that it just don't have any bottom in some spots." The man turned and put his back to the railings so that he stared at Beam. "You believe that?"

Beam shrugged. "I don't know," he said.

"Somebody told that the Army Corp of Engineers is going to come down here one day with sonar equipment and find the bottom," he said. "But I don't think they'll find it even then because I just don't think there's any bottom to find down there. What do you think about that?"

"I think there has to be a bottom," said Beam. "Somewhere. Things just can't sink forever."

"Maybe so." The man looked out over the water. "They say a man that jumps off the highest mountain has ten minutes to fall before he hits the ground."

"No."

"That's what they say. But what I want to know is who's the dumb sonuvabitch they got to jump off that mountain?"

"Maybe he didn't jump. Maybe he was throwed."

"Could be." The man shrugged and folded his arms. "Either way, he sure had a spell to think about what it was going to be like once that rocky ground slammed against his head."

The man suddenly went quiet as if weighing the subject at hand with cautious attention, his eyes squenched into the look of one at grave counsel with himself.

"Believe I'd try and jack off," he said, finally.

Beam stared at the man. "I don't think I could do that," he said.

"Ten minutes not long enough for you, huh? Well, I never had that problem. Every circle jerk I ever was in I finished first *and* third."

Beam expected the man to end such a thought with a laugh and when he didn't, his lips set grimly under the red bristles of his mustache with a look of definite affirmation, Beam shook his head and looked away into the night.

"Oh, well." The man shrugged. "It's some folks out there would pay to jump off a mountain. All you'd have to do is tell 'em there was pussy and birthday cake waiting at the bottom and they'd dole out a hundred dollars and just be tearing to get over the edge."

The man turned back to the railings. He lifted one shoe to rest it on the bottom rung. Beam saw the outline of the wallet in the back pocket of his jeans and wondered suddenly how much cash a dirty stranger like this might carry and if there was a way to take it from him. And the canvas duffel slouched in a corner of the deck? Who could say what a traveler might be bearing through the foggy dark?

"You smoke?" the man asked over his shoulder. He turned and produced a pack of Kenyon cigarettes from his jeans and took one out and then offered the pack to Beam.

Though he wasn't a smoker, Beam slid a cigarette out and lit it with the man's proffered matches. The tobacco crackled as it burned and a thick bower of smoke grew about them, singeing Beam's lungs until he coughed and spat.

"Smoke," said the man, grinning. "But not too much, huh?"

Beam threw the cigarette overboard and it hissed in the river.

"Who is your mama and daddy?" the man asked.

"Clem and Derna," Beam said.

The man repeated the names and then shook his head. "I don't believe I know them." He drew on his cigarette. "What's your mama look like?"

Beam put his hands in the pockets of his jacket. He tried to think of his mother. He wondered what she would be doing at this hour and then knew she would be asleep, and then he tried to think what a woman like her, roughed and filed down by years, would dream of, or if she even dreamed at all anymore.

"I don't know," he said. "She's older."

The man flicked the ash from his cigarette. "How old?"

"She's up in her forties."

"That's older?"

"I don't know. I guess so. Her hair is getting gray."

"I bet she's a real good woman," the man said.

Beam's hands grew cold and numb in his pockets. A breeze swept in off the river and rattled against his jacket and the sweat cooled on his cheeks and then he remembered his mother again, and what he'd heard said about her, even as a boy when what was said was spoken by other boys who didn't know truly what it meant to say things such as that. And the smell of the locust blooms, ghosting white and flurried over the black wind-folded river, lifted hot and sweet to him again, and he heard the branches shaking, the leaves a-shiver like rain in the dark.

"I bet she's just about the best woman a man could ever hope to mama him," said the stranger. "What'd you say her name was before she married?"

"I didn't say."

The man drew on his cigarette and then tossed it into the river. "Well, what was it?"

"Kurkendayll."

"Kurkendayll?"

"Yes. That's what I said."

The man put his head down, the smoke running out of his nostrils and blowing away in the wind.

"You don't know her," Beam said.

The man looked up. His eyes were red with whisky and appeared beleaguered and mournful in the lights of the ferry. "I don't know her," he said. "I don't know anything, bud. You just got to ignore most of what I say."

Beam felt a sudden weariness descend on him. For a moment, he thought one of his sleeping spells might be about to overtake him and he braced himself against the aluminum wall of the tug cabin and squeezed his eyes shut until the blood boomed in his head. He pressed his cheek to the cold metal and it stung him and roused him further. When he opened his eyes, the stranger was looking at him.

"You sick or something?" he asked.

Beam dragged a hand over his eyes. "Just a little," he said. He lifted his head and drew a long full breath and then exhaled.

The man had walked just out of the ferry lights now and stood in the dark shadows, his body outlined by the moon.

"You don't look like any Sheetmire," he said. His voice sounded thick and slurred, and Beam felt it slide through him. He closed his eyes and steadied himself against the cabin and in a sudden gust all the faces from the Sheetmire homecoming arose from the blank river, but when he opened his eyes only the night was there, black and swirling with cold wind.

"What are you talking about?" Beam asked the stranger.

"I'm saying how you don't look like any Sheetmire I ever seen." The man hooked his elbows around the boat railing and licked his teeth. "Wasn't there a Kurkendayll girl from over around Leachville that married a Sheetmire?" he asked.

"I don't know," Beam answered.

"Well, is your mama's family from over around Leachville?"

"I don't know that either."

"You don't know if your mama's folks are from over around Leachville?"

"No." Beam felt his head begin to ache and pressed his palms against his eyes. "I don't know any of my mama's family."

"You never met your mama's folks?"

"No."

"Well, you don't really know what you are then, do you? You could be an eighth nigger or three quarters sonuvabitch and not have any clue."

Beam took his hands from his eyes and stared at the man. He looked pale and sickly with the moonlight at his back, his frail arms bowed over the boat railings. Beam wondered suddenly what it would sound like to hear a man drown. To hear it and know you had done it.

"You look like somebody done pissed in your Cheerios, bud," said the man. He laughed a little and then stopped. "I'm just goofing on you. You ain't got to act all hard. I never met no Kurkendayll's or Sheetmire's in my life."

The wind cut off the river and Beam shook inside his jacket. What he'd told the man was true. He didn't know his mother's family, had never met a single one of them. She claimed they were all long dead, but now Beam wondered why she never traveled to any of the cemeteries to place flowers on their graves or to at least show him where his ancestors were buried. She never spoke of them at all. It were as if they didn't exist, and Beam knew it was only bad trouble in someone's past that made them not want to talk about it. Good times and happy days were recounted so often the stories became dried out and useless. But bad times were left untold about, as if to speak of them would call down all the old despairs once more.

"Ain't you ever had nobody goof with you, bud?" the man asked.

Beam stared at the man a moment, then nodded to the tug.

"I got a bottle in there," he said.

The man snorted. "That's the spirit, bud," he said. "Get us a drink and we'll swallow down any hard feelings."

Beam moved into the unlit cabin. He leaned over the throttle lever, looking out the port at the sky spilled with stars. He fumbled in his pocket and found the bottle of caffeine pills his doctor had prescribed and ate three of them hurriedly, washing them down with water from a cup on the control console. His head felt cold and empty.

"Hurry up there, bud," the man called from outside. "I need to get a drink before I step off this jollyboat."

Beam leaned down and searched through a hickory wood tool box that held a tire iron, a pipe wrench, an assortment of claw hammers. When he brought his hand back up, it stank of rust, and cobwebs drifted from his fingertips like puppeteer strings. He looked at himself in the port glass. His cheeks narrow and clean and one eye like a burned hole. His hair smoothed and sculpted by the wind. His lips twisty and wormish. He reached into the toolbox again and found the pipe wrench and stuffed it into the back pocket of his jeans.

"Come in here," he grunted. "I need a light."

The man shuffled into the small cabin. Beam put his back against a tin wall and pointed below the console. "It's down there somewhere," he said. "Light a match and see if you can find it."

"Ain't you got a flashlight?"

"Batteries went dead on me."

"Lord help," the man said, striking a match. "I just don't see how somebody like you ever gets by without somebody else. You're just about like an old goat, ain't you? Don't care if your ass is in the sun so long as your head's in the shade. That right?"

The man was stooping now, guiding the match under the console, throwing light into the webby shadows. His neck was bare above the collar of his shirt. The hairless knuckles of his spine showed a peeling sunburn.

"You don't know me," Beam said. "You don't know who I am."

The man went on rummaging through the boxes, the match lighting a small corona in the dark.

"Forget it, okay bud?" he said. "I told you I was only goofing."

"No. You act like you know me, but you don't."

The man turned on his haunches and looked up at Beam. The match flame halved his face, the fire splitting the cheeks into red and black, and his eyes were two glass bells to hold the flame.

"You're right," he said, finally. "I don't know you."

The match went out. "There ain't no bottle down here," the man said.

Beam backed toward the cabin door. He put his hand behind him and felt the wrench in his back pocket, then took his hand away and leaned against the cabin wall.

"My old man must've finished it off," he said.

The man stood up slowly, his form silhouetted by the moonlit window at his back. In the dark, he seemed much larger than he had in the lights of the ferry, and his breath rustled loud and grating in his chest.

"I see you got a till here," he said. He gestured toward the Tupperware bowl that sat on the control panel, then turned back to Beam. His lips cut into a dim smile. "How much it got in there?"

Beam put his hand into his back pocket and gripped the handle of the wrench again. "I don't believe that's any of your business," he said.

For a moment, the man didn't move. Then he took the till from the console and held it under his arm.

"How'd it be if I just took this?"

"You're not going to take it," Beam said.

"You talk like you got some say in it."

"I do got a say in it."

The man shook his head. "No," he said. "You don't."

He made to move toward the door and when he did Beam pulled the wrench from his pocket and hit the man across the top of the head, opening a gash from the top of his brow to the bridge of his nose. The blood spilled down his face like a veil and the man stared at Beam a moment as if in shocked recognition before he fell forward onto the deck, the aluminum bonging hollowly beneath him.

All of time seemed to have fixed itself on this point so that Beam felt he could not move from where he stood on the deck. Before him lay the body of the stranger, a damp black pool spreading from his head. Somewhere, the chug of the diesel could be heard but dimly so it might have been only imagined. His hand throbbed from the blow he'd dealt the stranger.

So frozen was Beam he didn't notice the ferry had reached

the shore until it was too late and the prow crumpled against the concrete landing and sparks shot off the torn metal until the boat finally came to rest with half its hull beached on the muddy ramp. The impact knocked Beam to his knees. When he recovered, he quickly turned the engine off and leaned against the control console, sweat dribbling off his scalp into his eyes. He wiped them, then turned and saw the man had rolled onto his back on the ferry deck. Blood spilled out of his ear and covered his face. His eyes were drowsy and half closed. As the breath ran in and out of him it made small brushy sounds like a creature building a nest, readying itself to lie down and be still forever.

Beam found the pipe wrench again and picked it up and then squatted beside the man.

"What you got to say now, you sonuvabitch?" said Beam.

The man coughed and then managed to whisper the name "Loat" and then the breath left him.

Beam stood up. He dropped the wrench onto the deck, the metal droning out long and shivery. For a time he felt he would pass out. Then a breeze swam out of the locust trees and his breathing evened and he knew that he would not. Somewhere off in the night, a catfish rolled on the surface of the river and then the chiseling talk of crickets sounded in the dark.

Beam staggered from the ferry and then up the landing toward the house that soon rose before him dim and quiet beneath the smeary vexed moonlight.

He came and stood on the porch. Through the window, the vampish light of the television jerked eely blue and he knocked steadily on the blank unpainted door. As if this were not his home, as though he were but some traveler adrift in a country he did not know.

"Wrecked her pretty good, didn't you?" Clem said. He kicked the torn prow of the ferry and the metal boomed hollow and empty. "Where's the fella you hit?"

Beam nodded toward the body of the stranger. Clem hoisted himself aboard and then Beam followed, their boots clomping on the hull as it listed and swayed.

Clem turned on the wheat light he carried. The beam lit a pair of ragged tennis shoes and two pale calves going up into mired corduroy slacks. The light went higher. Up to the pink nostrils. The stubble on the man's neck aglint like filings of metal. The blood drying on his face.

"Say he's dead?" Clem asked.

"Yes," said Beam. "I believe so."

Clem went forward a step, then stopped. He turned back and walked to the duffel lying on the deck. Squatting, he tucked the light under his arm and moved the zipper down, his hands riffling through a bundle of clothes, old shirts and jeans. A tube of Crest toothpaste. A disposable razor. One canister of Barbasol shave foam. The remains of a tuna sandwich. Implements of hurried travel.

"Say he tried to steal the till?" Clem asked.

"He did," said Beam. "He picked it up off the console and said he was taking it."

"What the hell was he doing in the cabin?"

Beam stammered and then wiped the sweat from his cheeks. "He just come in," he said, finally.

"That so?"

"Yeah," Beam nodded. "That's what happened."

Clem zipped the duffel closed and then stood and entered the cabin. His light washed up the interior wall. The he came back on deck and stooped over the man's body, cupping a hand under his nose. Then he took his hand away and brushed it clean against his thigh. Then the light went out.

"He said a name," Beam said. "He said the name Loat."

"Did he?"

Beam nodded. "You think he meant Loat Duncan?"

Clem paced to the other end of the ferry where the man's

ALEX TAYLOR

duffel sat and he looked down at it for a time, his huge chin resting on his chest. A slight rain had begun falling and thunder kettled in the west.

"That's the only Loat I know," he finally said.

Beam dragged his hands through his hair. "What are we going to do?" he asked. "He's dead, ain't he?"

Clem turned and looked at him. "Yes," he said. "He's dead."

"What do we do?"

"Not exactly certain." Clem cracked his knuckles. "Was there no other way to have done it?"

Beam moved closer to his father. In the darkness, he smelled the soured reek of the shirt Clem hadn't changed since yesterday, and he heard Clem's aged bent hands twisting together in the night.

"He just come at me," Beam said. "He said he was taking the money and there was nothing I could do about it. I never meant to do him as bad as I done."

Clem looked at the river. In the cast of the hull lights, tiny motes of dust blew around his face and turned in the glare. As if he were exhaling ash, as if some yet inextinguishable fire quarreled with his guts.

"Well, maybe he's carrying a few dollars," Clem said.

"Maybe."

"Did you look?"

Beam shook his head.

"Well, why don't you look and see. He paid his fare didn't he?"

"You want me to get his wallet out?"

"That's most likely where he's keeping his money."

"I don't want to."

Clem put his hands on the boat railings. "You already killed him, Beam. Get that straight. You already killed him so stealing ain't near the worst thing you've done."

Beam curled his fists up. His stomach tossed around. He felt a bruised sleep coming on, and he knew he'd have to move to stay

35

awake, and so he went and squatted beside the dead man. This close, he smelled the whisky again, and the manure and mud, and something older and stronger, and then he knew what he smelled was blood.

He slid the man's wallet free from his jeans. He wiped his hands clean against the man's chest, his fingers leaving a black trident of bloodstain on the man's shirt. The wallet smelled rough and dusty like the inside of a barn.

"Twenty dollars," Beam said, plucking a bill out. He turned and showed Clem the money.

"Keep it," he said, jerking his chin. "He got a license in there?"

Beam paused. "Why are we taking his money? Won't that look strange to the cops?"

"We're not calling the cops."

"But it's self-defense. They can't fault me none for that. He was trying to rob me." Beam's voice pitched high and windy and he was about to speak again when Clem gave him a look so hot and wild it silenced him.

"You do like I say," he said. "Now put that money in your pocket and see if there's anything else in his wallet."

Beam stuffed the money into his jeans and searched the wallet. A rubber, some coins, an address in St. Louis scrawled on a piece of hotel stationery. This was all.

"Nothing?" asked Clem.

Beam shook his head.

He coughed and stood and moved back onto the deck beside his father. Both of them looked at the body lying there, each wordless and stalled, hearing the river and the night buzz around them, the small shaft of light from Clem's lantern falling sheer and clean against the dead man's limp cheeks.

"What are we going to do?" Beam asked. He raked the hair back over his head and swallowed.

"I'm still thinking," said Clem.

Beam felt his stomach go sour. "You say you don't know him?"

"I don't believe so." Clem went to the body again, dropping the light flush into the man's face.

"I don't know what to do," Beam muttered. "I don't know what to do."

Clem stood up calmly and it seemed he hadn't heard his son. He kept his head bowed, staring at the body before him, as if a man attending services grave and doom-kindled, and his own shadow leapt out into the light like some crepuscular rake jarred up with nethering prayers.

Slowly, he said, "You got to leave this place and you got to go tonight."

# II

## WEDNESDAY

A damp morning. Rain had begun in the deep of the night and fallen steadily until dawn and at sunrise scraps of mist lay in the bottom country like shorn husks. The Gasping flowed quick and sudsy, its brown churned waters carrying driftwood and other debris downstream, crossties and bridge timbers, stray john boats and car doors, milk jugs and paint cans. There were strange catches in the locust trees, tires and saddle blankets and other such garbage, and a lacy negligee like a bawdy ghost dripped from a thorn bough and from some lowland grave a rosewood casket unearthed by the deluge floated downstream and spun in an eddy before the current took it on, and in the darker woods beyond the roar of the river was the slow ping and drip of water so that this world seemed cold and cavernous and in unceasing plummet.

Sheriff Elvis Dunne drove the cruiser slowly along the river road, the brake discs steaming as the tires pushed through the ponded rainwater. He was a small man with clean hands. In middle age, his face had acquired the grooved, vaguely scuffed look of old furniture, though his hair had grown to a dark chestnut brown that gave credence to the rumor that he had it dyed. However, he was otherwise known as a man without vanity.

He was fond of antiques, a collector. Those who called on him at home usually found him stowed in a room of urns and carafes, tapestries and gilt mirrors, his hands working linseed oil into the stained wood of a footstool, and though he had a fondness for the aged and dusty, he wasn't a man opposed to progress.

"In ten years," he said to his passengers, "I'd like to see all the county paved."

The two riding beside him were state troopers by the names of Donaldson and Pretshue. Water dripped from the clear plastic rain ponchos they wore. Both men kept still and quiet, giving each other brief sideways glances at the lilting rasp of the sheriff's voice.

"Ten years," Elvis said. "There won't be any gravel roads left around here by then. No more washouts and hang-ups. People will have a lot easier time of it then."

Donaldson pushed a cigarette between his lips and lit it with the cruiser's lighter. Beyond the windshield, the world was a dim smear. On the north side of the road were bottoms filled with white cattle, some standing belly-deep in sedge grass. On the south side was the Gasping River.

"That's all fine and good, Elvis," Donaldson said. "But what I want to know is when you plan to fix people from winding up drowned in your rivers. Believe this is the third one this year."

Elvis kept his eyes on the road. The wipers squelched over the dirty windshield. "I'll guess we'll fix that long about the time the boys down at Eddyville figure out how to keep their cons from going AWOL," he said.

Donaldson gnawed the butt of his Winston and chuckled, but Pretshue said nothing.

"There's not much way to fix folks doing each other in," said Elvis. "What I've found anyway. I talk to a lot of these old timers around here and they say it's worse now than before, but I don't believe it. Ask me, they're all just sorry they can't get out and do awful like they used to." He wiped a finger over his teeth, scratched the plaque away with his thumbnail, then wiped his finger against his trouser leg. "They just don't like being benchwarmers," he said. "That's all it is."

"Old timers," Donaldson said, slinging water from the brim of his hat. "You're about to be one yourself aren't you, Elvis?"

"If I live long enough."

"Old timers," repeated Pretshue. "What the fuck do they know?"

Elvis cracked his window and the rain flitted in. "One thing I do know is how much I hate this weather," he said.

The cruiser topped a rise and Elvis let it coast to the bottom before pulling under a stand of cottonwoods where several other cruisers were parked already. An ambulance idled there also, as well as the county coroner's burgundy Buick. Beyond the trees, the Gasping rolled by, its waters swollen from the recent rain. Men stood on the shore. Elvis' deputies, shrinkwrapped in raincoats. At their feet, a body bound with logging chain.

"Reckon that's our boy wrapped up in those?" Donaldson asked.

"I hope to hell it is," said Pretshue. "That fucker has been trouble and I hope he's drowned. That'd solve my headaches."

All three men exited the cruiser. Elvis went first down the steep bank, followed closely by the two troopers. The deputies nodded to him as he approached, but only gave cold glares to Donaldson and Pretshue.

When Elvis reached the river bank, he squatted beside the body. The fishes and turtles had been at it and some of its fingers were missing and a wet reek like carpet left too long in a cellar hung in the air.

"Whoever did it, Elvis, they weighed him down with this." The coroner toed a three foot section of railroad track lying in the mud. He was a tall thin man with a dark complexion and under the blank sky he seemed like a streak of ink running out of the clouds. He spoke with a deep wet croak. "It wasn't enough," he said. "Two old boys out running trot lines come on him this morning. Just floating. I'd say he's been under for a day at the most and probably not even that long." The coroner propped his boot on the section of track and wiped both hands against his trousers and then through his hair. He wore no raincoat. "What I mean is, I'd wager he was put in there last night."

Elvis nodded and scraped at his chin. "Looks like somebody gave him a swat to the head there," he said, pointing to the puckered wound on the dead man's brow. "This your boy, Donaldson?"

The trooper stepped closer and leaned in, stowing his hands on his knees.

"I don't know. Hard to tell from what the river's done to him." Donaldson stood up, running a thumbnail over his belt. "I thought you would know him, Elvis."

"Me? Why would I know him?"

"Well, this is your county. You run him in when he had the wreck and killed that woman. I thought you'd know him."

Elvis sighed. He dragged his hat lower on his brow. "That," he said, "was nine years ago."

Pretshue pushed his hands into his pockets. The plastic poncho rattled around him, and his nostrils flared as a green tint rose under his cheekbones. "Hell," he said. "If you don't know him, then who does?"

Elvis stood up and looked at the covey of deputies. "Where are those old boys at that found him?"

Someone pointed downstream.

Under a red gum stood two men, each dressed in ball caps and shiny rubber hip-waders. They drank coffee from Styrofoam cups. Their johnboat was hitched to a sycamore root jutting from the bank, and they watched it closely as if it were a nervous horse they expected to bolt at any moment.

"He was out there," one of them said when Elvis and the troopers approached. The man raised his coffee cup and pointed to the river with his pinky, but the world before his finger was unmarkable and without definite origin, an empty spill before windbraided trees, and he might have meant any place in all that wide coursing surge. "We brung him to shore then called you boys down." He looked past Elvis at the body lying in the sandy mud. "Dead as a drownt cow."

"Yes." Elvis nodded. He took a small steno pad and pen from

his shirt pocket and began running the pen nervously over the notebook wires. "He is."

The man who'd spoken snuffled and drew a sleeve under his nose. His friend, features honed like a hatchet blade, put his hands in his pockets and rocked on his boot heels. "You know who it is, don't you?" he asked.

Elvis flipped the steno pad open, holding the white page under his hat out of the rain. "No. Do you?"

"Course. That's Paul Duncan. The one stole that car and hit that Cliver lady about ten years back. The same one busted out of Eddyville a few days ago." The man drained his coffee cup and swallowed. "That's Loat's boy."

# III

## WEDNESDAY

From his porch, Loat watched the cruiser slip under the awning of hackberry boughs and then climb the slight rise of his driveway, rocking over the washed out ruts in the gravel before it came to a stop in the muddy yard. He held a neon orange hardhat in his lap and sat spooning soggy cornflakes out of it, milk slipping off his chin onto the porch boards. As the sheriff and two state troopers came through the yard, he stowed the makeshift cereal bowl under his chair, folded his hands over his belly and snorted. Behind him, Presto Geary came through the screen door. His weight made the wooden floor groan, and Loat smelled his stink, a mixture of underarm and motor oil.

"What do they want?" Presto asked.

Loat leaned back in the nylon camp chair he was sitting in. "Same thing they been wanting all week, I'd guess," he said.

Elvis and the two officers crossed through the yard's scant grass. When they reached the porch, the sheriff put a boot on the bottom step and looked up at Loat and Presto as they were paired under the slanted roof of the house with its peeling blue paint, their faces creased and turned by the early gray light to a hard bruised color.

"Morning," said Loat.

Elvis nodded, then gestured to the men behind him. "Loat, this is Officer Donaldson and Officer Pretshue," he said. "State boys."

"I can see what kind of uniforms they're wearing." Loat wiped a hand over his mouth and snorted again. "Y'all come looking for that one you lost out of Eddyville, the story's same now as it's ever going to be. He's not been here and I ain't heard a thing from him."

Elvis scraped the water from his cheeks and dried his hand against his trousers. "We think we found him," he said. "In the river."

Loat leaned forward, propping his elbows on his knees. His light gray hair was spackled like grout to his forehead and he brushed it back over his scalp and sat drawing thin breaths through the tiny slits of his nostrils. Many had remarked on the smallness of his nose, which was no more than a pink bump beneath his putty-colored eyes, and at times it caused his breath to emit a high adenoidal whistle that sounded like the grate and squeak of old water piping. Now, as he sat staring at the sheriff, his nostrils dilated and flexed as if he'd caught the aroma of something unpleasant in the air.

"You think you found Paul?" he asked.

Elvis nodded. "Just this morning." He rested a hand on the stoop railing, the sleeve of his poncho dripping strings of water over the wet footstones.

With his poncho and flushed cheeks, Loat thought the man resembled a shrink-wrapped cut of butcher's work. "Y'all come on up here out of the weather," he said. "Then you can tell me the rest of it."

Elvis moved on up the stoop and the two troopers followed and they all clustered under the eaves. The water dripping from them made a dark halo on the porch boards.

Loat studied the troopers closely, as he'd not seen either of them before. The one named Donaldson was older and once on the porch he lit a cigarette and stood smoking, his rheumy eyes watching the rain spit and shatter in the yard weeds. He seemed almost drowsy, and Loat figured him not far from retirement. Pretshue was younger and kept staring at Loat as if in direct challenge, his chapped lips pressed tightly against his teeth, which Loat imagined were quite straight and white. He pictured the man with all his teeth smashed out by a ball-peen hammer, his mouth only a bleeding hole, and winked at him. The trooper blinked and his lips jerked oddly before he composed himself and resumed his staring.

"Say you found Paul?" Loat asked, turning to Elvis.

Elvis nodded. "We need you to come down to the morgue, make an I.D. on the body."

Loat resettled the hardhat in his lap and looked at the three policemen. Wrapped in their plastic raingear, they appeared hapless and bungling, and he felt a bit embarrassed for them. Especially Elvis, whom Loat had known for years, ever since his election to county sheriff. He'd always struck Loat as a dainty kind of fellow not suited for the rough work of law enforcement.

Whatever shame he felt for these lawmen and their ineptitude soon grew into ripe disgust, though, and he raised his leg and let a long loose fart ripple out.

The lawmen gazed at him in mute shock. None of them moved or spoke.

"You hear something?" Loat said, turning to Presto, who was leaning against the front door of the house with his arms folded over his chest. Presto's wide gray lips broke into a flabby grin and he slowly swayed back and forth, scratching his back against the wooden doorframe.

Loat turned back to the lawmen. "I believe I heard something," he said. Again, he farted, the bottom of the camp chair flapping beneath him. "There it went again," he said, in mock surprise. "What the hell is that?" He looked about him as if searching for the source of the noise and then put his eyes back on the lawmen. "Whatever it is, it stinks," he said.

"Smells like genuine pig shit, don't it?" said Presto.

"I believe you're right," Loat said, staring coldly at the three men. "I believe there's been a few pigs rooting around and shitting on the place here lately."

Elvis took a step back and rested his hands on his hips. Donaldson and Pretshue exchanged brief glances until Pretshue came forward, slinging his poncho aside so that Loat could see the revolver that rode his hip. "Listen," he said, "if all you're going to do is sit up here and fart all day then we need to be getting on. But if you want to come to town and identify the body of your son, then we'll give you a ride."

Loat stared at Pretshue. His cheeks were ashen, which likely meant he was afraid, but Loat knew he was also young enough to call the fear something else and not recognize it for what it truly was, and this made him dangerous. Paul had had the same careless streak in him. If tempered by age and circumstance, Loat knew it made a man into a lethal being who strode over the earth at will and brooked no compromise because none was required. Left unchecked, it usually led one down a dim path of ruin.

"I bet you still remember what your mama's titty tastes like, don't you?" Loat said.

Pretshue's spine straightened as if he'd just be struck in the face. His cheeks flushed and he was about to offer some kind of retort when Donaldson stepped forward and placed a hand on his shoulder.

"Go easy on us, Loat," the older man said. "We ain't here to arrest you. All we want is you to come down to the morgue and tell us whether or not it's your son we pulled out of the river."

Loat sighed and placed the hardhat beneath his chair once more. Then he stood and brushed the front of his shirt and looked past the men at the rain.

"Do you want a poncho?" Elvis asked.

Loat looked at the sheriff as if he were a bit touched. "I don't mind getting wet," he said. He turned to Presto standing behind him. "Mind the dogs," he said. Then he walked down the stoop and out into the rain, moving through the muddy yard toward the idling cruiser, Elvis and the two troopers following behind him.

# IV

## WEDNESDAY

They woke late to the baying of hounds in the nighttime. The howls of the dogs rolled against the windows, then fled down the chimney, ceaseless and somehow resolute against the darkness through which they came until the sound seemed to have neither source nor limit but grew to be the very rage and roar of the night itself.

When Clem looked out the bedroom window, one finger pulling at a gauzy curtain, he saw the pale blue Cadillac parked in the yard and his chest tightened.

"What is it?" Derna asked.

He turned to her. In the blank moonlight filtering through the curtains her hair sprawled scalloped and silver on the pillow beneath her head. He knew she hadn't slept. Since bedding down, he'd been awake himself, listening as she wept quietly beside him. The sheriff had been by that afternoon to deliver the news of Paul's body being found in the river and she'd waited until sundown to begin mourning. Her people were ruddy Irish and Dutch stock and they retained customs such as that, believing it improper to shed tears for the dead in daylight.

"It's where I figured him to wind up," she'd said when Elvis brought her the news, her eyes stern and dry. Now she sniffled and wiped her face with the backs of her hands, and Clem reckoned all women strange and beyond his understanding. She had not seen Paul since he was a toddler and but for a slight written correspondence they'd exchanged in the past few years, had had no dealings with him at all. Yet here she was crying over him.

"What is it out there?" she asked again.

"It's Loat," Clem said. "We knew he'd come." He bent down and picked his jeans up off the floor and pulled them on, then took the .32 snubnose from the bedside drawer. He left the room shirtless, and kept the lights off as he went through the house. When he reached the front door, he placed his forehead against it. The hounds had bounded onto the porch, their claws scraping at the wooden boards.

"Loat," Clem called, and the dogs went quiet. "Loat, I'm here. What do you want?"

A dizzying silence. Behind him, Derna crept to the edge of the hallway, the dry cracked heels of her bare feet scuffling through the dirt on the hardwood floor.

Clem heard a click and when he turned, he saw she cradled his twelve gauge pump-action Mossberg.

"He won't talk unless you open that door," she said.

Clem nodded at the gun in her hands. "What you aim to do with that bear killer?"

She shook her head and the gray sleep-kinked curls of her hair swung around her face, casting erratic shadows over her cheeks. "When something like Loat comes in my yard, I want to be ready," she said.

Clem was accustomed to this from his wife. A vein of stone filled the cleft in her soul and through that rough obdurate part of her there was no path that led to softer footing.

He turned back to the door and placed his hand on the cold brass knob. "I'm going to open this door Loat," he said loudly. "I don't want nothing to happen unless it has to." Clem opened the door a crack. "Loat," he said.

Someone whistled and the dogs bounded from the porch into the yard. Clem watched them scuttle to the Cadillac and then settle in the grass beside it, a half-dozen Dobermans, their sleek coats glinting in the moonlight.

"I'm right here," said Loat.

Clem made him out. He was leaned against the grille of the

Cadillac, the dogs seated before him. He wore his straw hat and the moonlight spilled from the brim and onto his chest before dripping into the flecked tweedy lawn. He was bare-armed in a sleeveless shirt, tall and splay-legged and thin, all of him as skeletal and illusory as a scarecrow.

"Come on out here on your porch, Clem," he said.

Clem opened the door and stepped onto the boards, keeping the pistol hidden behind his thigh. Squinting from beneath the eaves, he saw another man stood beside Loat. That would be Presto Geary, Loat's driver. He was a large man, his head naked and bald as polished marble, and in his belt rode a pair of .44 hog leg pistols.

"Wake you up?" Loat asked.

"I'd say so." Clem stretched and feigned a yawn.

"Well, it's not many folks left that keep the hours I do." Loat jerked his chin and Presto passed him a cigarette. The flame of a match scurried out of the dark, briefly lighting Loat's cheeks and nose until he waved it out. "And besides," he said, "you know me. I like to get out and ride around after a rain when the sky's cleared off." He raised a hand and pointed toward the moon where it hung in the sky like a white ring of bone. "Let's me breathe better," he said.

Clem laid his pistol on the porch railing. "What do you want?" he asked.

Loat drew on his cigarette. "Heard tell my boy's gone."

"Which boy would that be?"

"Don't act ignorant."

Clem spat into the grass growing beside the porch steps. "Paul never was your boy," he said. "All you ever done was run him off when he got to working on your nerves. He got more raising from the drunks and whores out at Daryl's than he ever did from you."

Loat thumped his cigarette into the yard, the orange tip tracing through the dark before it shattered in the grass. "I didn't come out here to get a lesson on daddying from you," he said.

"Paul was mine by blood and I did a damn sight more for him than Derna ever did."

"Well, it don't matter one way or the other now," said Clem. "He's gone and that's all there is to it."

Loat propped a boot on the Cadillac's front fender and folded his arms over his chest. "Who did it?" he asked.

Clem shrugged. "Couldn't tell you."

"He was bringing me something."

Clem picked a few splinters from the porch railing and flung them into the yard. He stared at Loat where he stood in the full moonlight. He'd make an easy target, and doubtless knew this, but Clem could tell the man was unafraid and that whatever fear there was in the night stood with him underneath the porch eaves. "Derna ain't heard nothing out of him going on three years," he said. "Elvis and those state boys been coming by this week, ever since Paul walked off the yard down there at Eddyville, but we hadn't heard a peep out of him. That suited me just fine. I never did want to know nothing about Paul. Whatever kind of souvenir or good luck charm he was bringing you, I don't want to know nothing about that neither."

Loat and Presto looked at one another. One of the Dobermans began to growl steadily, until Loat told it to hush and it went quiet.

"It's something he's got to have," said Presto, his voice scratching like rusty gears.

"Sounds like y'all got a bit of looking to do," said Clem.

Everyone remained quiet for a spell. Somewhere in the trees along the river a screech owl called and the wind stirred the pampas grass edging the lawn and then went still. Clem knew the men standing in his yard well, had even run with Loat for a time in his youth. Memories of the wild drunks he'd gone on, of poker games with fifty dollar antes where sometimes the pot contained not only cash but the affections of a particular whore at Daryl Van Landingham's dance hall rummaged through his mind, and he nearly smiled until he recalled the man Loat had become. He reached out and gripped the pistol on the porch railing.

"Ferry's down," Presto said, breaking the silence. "How come?"

"She run aground the other night," Clem explained. "Got her hoisted on the shore for repairs."

"Run aground? Was you drunk?"

"Course I was. Drunk as Cooter Brown in his underwear."

Loat licked his dentures, then spit into the grass. "You don't usually run it of a night. That's mostly Beam's job."

"Beam's been sick here, lately," Clem said. "I've been taking his shift, letting Derna run it of the morning."

"Say Beam's been feeling poorly?"

"Yes, he has."

"What's the matter with him?"

Clem cleared his throat, but didn't spit. "I don't know why I'm standing out here at such an hour letting you question me this way, Loat," he said.

"You're listening because there ain't another thing you can do. Whatever's wrong with Beam, I'll find it out one way or the other. Same as I'll find out who done Paul in. Anything you know, you best go ahead and say it now because you know how I hate to find a man hasn't been playing square with me." Loat reached a boot out and scratched one of the Dobermans under the chin with it, soliciting a low grumble from the dog.

"Beam's not here," Clem said quickly.

Loat smiled. "Thought you said he was feeling poorly."

"He was, but he's better now."

"So where's he gone off to?"

Clem's guts rumbled and he grimaced. For years, his ulcers had forced him to keep a box of Arm 'N Hammer baking soda and a spoon close by, the chalky powder being the only antidote for his pained innards, and he longed for it now. "He's off tomcatting, I guess. You know how they are at that age," he said, the sting in his stomach shortening his breath.

"I reckon you never told Beam he had a half-brother?" Loat asked.

The trees beyond the yard trembled in the breeze, shivering like naked dry bones, and the wind crept down from the branches and slithered through the grassy yard and up the porch steps to swirl about Clem, drying the sweat from his cheeks.

"That's what we decided, me and Derna," he said. "We'd had our druthers, Paul never would've been told Derna was his mama, either. But you fixed that, didn't you."

"He remembered her."

"That don't seem possible."

"He was four when she left," said Loat. "That's old enough for a boy to remember someone and Paul damn sure remembered Derna. He started asking questions once they hauled him off to Eddyville and I decided to tell him. It's no surprise he wanted to know. Man's mother has a special pull on him. Even if she is an old worn-out whore."

Clem lifted the pistol and held it at his side, keeping the muzzle down. "You can't talk like that. Not in this yard," he said.

Loat took his cigarettes from his shirt pocket and lit one. The smoke bunched beneath his hat and then clouded and dissolved in the cool night air. "Thought I might ought to mention I told Paul about Beam as well," he said. "Man's brother has a special pull on him, too. Why I figured he might come this way if he ever got out."

"I already told you I don't know anything about Paul and neither does Beam."

Loat drew on his cigarette. "That's what you're telling me now." He nodded slowly. "I hope the story don't change any."

"The way I tell it ain't going to change."

"Then you don't have anything to worry about. The farther a man has gone from the truth the harder it is for him to get back to it, but you say you never left it and so there's nothing to trouble your mind." Loat shrugged. "People don't like the truth very much, though. They want it to be a way that would suit them, but the truth can only be one way."

"What way would that be?"

"The way it is." Loat dropped the cigarette into the grass and slid his boot over it. "The way it's always been and is always going to be." He turned and walked back to the Cadillac and opened the passenger side door. He then whistled and the Dobermans scrambled into the backseat, their claws scratching on the vinyl. Presto sat down behind the steering wheel and cranked the engine and sat waiting while Loat stood beside the open door, the moonlight falling damp and slick over his body.

"I'll be going now," he said. "I know you have a lot of prayers to say before the sun comes up." Loat got in the car and pulled the door shut. Presto clicked the headlights on and then turned the car around in the yard and they drove off on the road leading away from the river.

For a long time, Clem stood on the porch listening to the Cadillac's tires bicker over the gravel until the sound receded and no noise was left in the night but the crickets and the wind preening at the trees.

When he came back inside, Derna was sitting on the couch. She kept the shotgun propped between her thighs, clutching the barrel with both hands as if it were a broom.

"Where is Beam?" she asked.

Clem stuck the pistol in the waist of his jeans. "Gone is all I can say. I don't know where to."

Derna shook her head absently. Her gaze lay on the front window, its curtains silvered to a frosty glow from the moonlight. "I can't see why it would be both of them to go at the same time," she said. "Both my boys."

"Beam's out getting drunk and he'll be back by good daylight," said Clem. "You don't need to worry over him."

Derna kept her eyes on the window. She pulled her hair over

her shoulder and began running her fingers through it. "Get my vacuum, Clem. I feel like doing a little cleaning right now."

It was what she was prone to do during hard times. She would mix buckets of suds to mop with, or run a dust cloth over all the furniture if certain dreams chased her from sleep, no matter the hour. It was her way to draw the filth out of the corners of the house whenever life tilted toward disaster, as if polished floors and ironed sheets could bring a timid peace to a place where death or ruin had touched its hand.

Clem was suddenly struck by the memory of Derna back when she'd lived with Loat. He'd dressed her in sleek fitting summer dresses of bright pastel and gave her the duties of cleaning house. Called her "Dollbaby."

"I like to watch Dollbaby push that broom," he'd say, grinning as Derna bowed to guide a few dust kittens into a scoop. Then he'd let his eyes drift shut and nod his head back. "Sometimes, I just close my eyes and listen to her moving in her dress. Sounds slow and easy enough to put me straight to sleep."

When only one or two men were visiting Loat, Derna seemed a bit laggard in her duties, slow to empty the slop jar or to feed dinner scraps to the dogs. But when the house bucked and shook with a wild humid fury, the air charged with the electric hum of men bent in grudge and anger toward one another, Derna came alive. Clem remembered coming over for games of seven card and watching Derna creep into the room full of men where the smoke vined up the newspapered walls and the chips clinked on the baize table, her look cautious but simpering, as if she'd undertaken a great dare by entering the midst of these drunken gamblers. She tended to linger about, her rouged lips cut into a thin smile while she bussed drinks or swept cigarette butts from the tongue-and-groove floor.

Other than to sneak quick glances or give flirty winks, most of the card players ignored her. This changed one night when a liquored tobacco planter named Boyce Hazelip took umbrage toward Derna's loitering in the smoky shadows.

"Loat, that woman a yours makes me nervous," he said, running a yellow fingernail over his chips, his gray beard dripping from his chin like mossy slime. He was an older man, and often deferred to or at least humored because of his seniority, but as the night wore on he tipped his cup more and more and his eyes often went darty and mean toward Derna, especially as his losses began to tally up.

"I say, Loat, do you not have a keep to put that woman in?" he asked. "She's staring at me like a cat."

It was long summer, and the jar flies bumped and whirred against the window screens. Derna stood with her back to the dead woodstove just behind Loat, feeling the cold iron against her rump through her sheer cotton dress. Yes, she had been staring at Hazelip, but only because she found his bald, peeling head a wonder, so warty and livered with moles it appeared like a globe of some reddened world with all its scars and rifted valleys.

"I can see how having a woman look your way would make you nervous, Boyce," said Loat. "It likely don't happen too often to an ugly sonuvabitch like you."

Hazelip chewed his bottom lip and glared at Loat, who didn't look up from his cards. "What if I was to say I think she's been tipping hands to you all night?" he said.

The rest of the gamblers, Clem included, hushed their idle chatter. Loat raised his eyes to the old man and laid his cards face down on the table. He folded his hands calmly over one another. "You're not happy with the way things are going?" he asked.

Hazelip bobbed his chin toward the towers of chips that sat in front of Loat like a city in miniature. "You take all the honey and don't leave none for me," he said.

Loat straightened in his chair. He addressed the table at large, but did not look away from Hazelip. "Any of you other boys think Dollbaby's been tipping hands to me?"

Including Clem, there were six men at the table, and they all looked at their cards or up at the uncovered bulb burning on its wire in the ceiling and said nothing. In later years, Clem wondered what would've happened if he hadn't been the one to speak, if things would have been different if he'd been able to hold to his quiet, to let someone else answer Loat's question. But after nearly a minute of silence, he broke and declared that the thought of Derna tipping hands had never entered his mind. Everyone at the table but Hazelip seconded this, some with grudging whispers, others with eager nods.

"Looks to be nobody but you thinks the game's rigged, Boyce." Loat unfolded his hands and placed them at either side of his stack of chips. "Maybe you better take back what you said."

Hazelip's eyes goggled about the table, searching the gaze of his fellow gamblers, but none would meet his looks. In the thatch of his beard, the old man's lips began a slight tremor and his damp yellow whiskers twitched as if something were trying to burrow into his face, and then he settled his stare on Derna who stood still and gape-eyed against the stove.

"I can't take it back," Hazelip muttered. His eyes clocked upward to the lone light dangling from a ceiling joist and then drifted down again to look at Loat. His hand was creeping slowly toward the pocket of his Dungarees where everyone knew he carried a .25 caliber pistol, but Loat remained steady in his chair as his breath whistled over the flange of his tiny nostrils.

"If you can't take it back, then I guess you'd better leave," he said.

Hazelip's hand suddenly stopped and lay like a flattened crab on the tabletop. His mouth opened a bit, the small worn kernels of his teeth just visible behind his cracked lips. Slowly, he scooted his chair back and stood. A sheen of sweat glossed his brow. He patted his beard down against his chest and grunted. "You know as well as me that woman's been tipping cards to you."

Loat looked at his hands. He drew a Case knife from his trousers and began paring the blue earth from under his fingernails with the blade and then wiping it clean on the edge of the baize. "If that's the story you want to tell there's nothing I can do for you," he said.

"It's not a story," replied Hazelip. "It's the truth."

Loat closed the knife and laid it on the table. He watched it for a moment as if he expected it to spring off the table at his command. "I think you are an old man who has had too much to drink and whose mind isn't what it used to be," he said. "But if you keep talking, these facts won't help you."

He then raised his eyes to Hazelip, and the two locked their stares. What Clem remembered most, however, was the look of expectant joy that rode Derna's face, her eyes bright and hungry as a girl in the throes of her first ravishing. She fumbled with the collar of her dress, revealing the milky flesh of her cleavage, and her lips were soon flushed. Though he was no greenhorn, Clem had never seen a woman actually swoon, but this seemed to be what he witnessed, as Derna's eyes fluttered and a slow groan of ecstasy rolled up from her belly. Her knees buckled and she braced herself against the stove, her head bent so that her black curls dangled in the drafty air, and she gripped the edge of the iron stove with such force her knuckles whitened.

All of the men turned toward her. Even Loat, his mouth now gaped in slack surprise, craned his neck.

"Dollbaby," he said. "Is the heat in here getting to you?"

Derna raised her head. Her eyes had a drowsy cast to them and her open mouth burned a bright ring of color in the center of her powdered face.

"Yes," she said, almost gasping. "I think maybe I'd better go lay down." She stumbled out of the room and clomped down the hall to the room where Loat kept her bedded. For a time, the men stared after her, a bit dazed by what they'd seen. But whatever it had been, true bliss or performed rapture, it had diffused the simmering violence in the room so that Boyce Hazelip raked his chips from the table into his black-banded hat.

"I'll cash these leavings with you at a later date, Loat," he said.

Loat gave no reply as Hazelip exited the house. The other men around the table listened to the cough and grind of his ancient Ford pickup, the engine giving grate and snarl as it descended the grade from Loat's house to the main trace that led back to town. When the noise had diminished, Loat ordered that the game be finished. His gaze was calm and serene as he dealt the final hand.

A week later, Boyce Hazelip's wife found him in his burley patch with his throat slit. Loat was brought in for questioning, but the sway of his influence extended into lofty pockets, and the police soon turned their inquiries elsewhere, and when the trail went cold, the matter was mostly forgotten.

For Clem, this seemed but a footnote to the larger story. What he'd seen that night was a woman throttled by the scene of two men paired against each other, the smell of their building blood hot in the close dingy room. It was the first time he looked upon Derna as something more than just another woman. Her back arced against the iron stove, the sweat dribbling from the crease of her hairline—it all gave her the appearance of a woman being inhabited by forces larger than herself, and the gruff moan as it slid from her throat made it clear the forces were welcome, that her body longed to house them.

"Go on, Clem," she said, bringing him back from memory. "Fetch the Hoover so I can run it over the carpet here. You've dropped cornbread or something all through the house." Her hand darted at invisible crumbs.

Clem retrieved the vacuum, plugged it into an outlet, then sat it before her. She laid the shotgun beside her on the couch and turned on the machine, its brash roar rattling the windows as she wheeled it over the carpet, soft plumes of dust rising about her. Her look was empty and calm, as if this were an action as somber and driven of anger as church.

Clem watched her for a spell, then went to fetch his baking soda.

# V

In the morning sometimes, a white vintage Cadillac would coast into town and lurch to a stop in the gravel parking lot of Steff General Merchandise, the car rocking on its chassis as the motor sputtered and died. In the backseat rode a band of six Doberman hounds posed in various attitudes. At the wheel was Presto Geary and beside him sat Loat Duncan, his face shaded under the straw hat that marked him to folks from a distance. The men on the porch of the store would nod or hello him, but Loat rarely spoke, passing on into the cool dark of the mercantile, bent upon his own mysterious business.

The dogs waited in the car. These were not jolly hounds, but had the look of beasts borne up from some uncharted desert, their lean tapered forms resembling those of jackals, though they were much larger and coated in the black and tan pattern of their breed. When Loat and Presto emerged from the store bearing their brown-bagged groceries, the men on the porch were glad to see them go as the dogs made them nervous because they were clearly bred for hunting and the hunting they were bred for was the hunting of men.

Once the Cadillac drove away in a fog of bone-colored dust, the men on the porch would resume their talk, the appearance of Loat directing the conversation toward grim memory.

"He was around twenty or so I guess when it happened with him and Daryl."

"He was young I remember."

"Young, but mean already."

"Who else was with them the night it happened?"

"Clem Sheetmire. You know that."

"Oh. I recollect now."

"The three of them run out to the Peabody mines. Course the mines had been shut down for a year at that time and that was the summer when if a man had any copper laying around he better sit on it if he didn't want it stole. Folks would leave for church and come home to find the wiring tore right out the walls of their house that copper was going at such a price."

The sun had shifted to fall slantwise beneath the porch eaves, and the men moved in tandem to the cooler shade of the concrete steps.

"It was Daryl climbed that transformer pole out at the mines. All three of them thought the power had been shut off and I guess anybody would have thought the same, seeing as the mines had pulled out a year before."

"The power hadn't been shut off though, had it?"

"No sir. Daryl climbed that pole with a set of bolt cutters and when he laid into the line it exploded. Blew his arms clean off at the elbow."

A collective nodding of heads.

"Electricity cauterized him, didn't it? That's why he didn't bleed to death?"

"That's right. Only, I bet there's been times he wished to hell he had of bled to death. It can't be no easy life without your arms."

"No, I suppose not. But he up and sued Peabody and raked in a hell of a settlement, didn't he? And he was the one stealing from them."

Heads shaking in mute disbelief.

"Another thing I heard told, and it may not be right, but that it was Loat made Clem and Daryl throw dice to see who'd climb that pole. Daryl threw low was how come it was him to climb up there instead of Clem."

"Is that what happened?"

"What I heard. Heard Clem always carried a set of dice in

his pocket he loved to gamble so much and that he rolled them with Daryl that night to see who'd go up. I also heard those dice were loaded."

"Well, I guess that explains why Daryl never had much use for Clem after that, don't it?"

One of the men took a thin carpenter nail from his shirt pocket and began to pick his teeth with it. When he was done, he leaned over and spat off the porch into the dust.

"Ask me, Daryl's been laying for Clem ever since."

"Well, he's taking his time, ain't he? That all happened twenty years ago or better."

"Don't matter. He'll take care of Clem when the time comes. You wait and see."

The men mumbled begrudged dismay at this, the breath swarming out of them in long gusts as they palmed the sweat from their faces. They spoke of other things for a little while, and then, after a time, became very quiet.

# VI

## WEDNESDAY

The dark descended over the game trails Clem had told him to follow, and the hard scarring of stars and moonlight slowly erased the last hints of daylight so that the shadows fell in grainy showers like soot crumbling from a chimney flue, and the night thickened gradually until there was no sound but that of his boots as they swept through the dry tinder of leaves and fallen hickory limbs.

Beam waited until full evening before clicking on the Maglite his father had given him. He knew it was unwise to travel with a light, as the glare could direct any search party or snooping stranger to him, but he was a bit fearful of the dark and of traveling through it.

Occasionally, when he grew tired and stopped to rest, he would pull the duffel from his shoulders and rifle through the clothes and bagged sandwiches as if taking inventory of what meager provender his father had given him, which was now contained within the canvas bag that had belonged to the man he'd killed aboard the ferry. Growing up, Beam had shot squirrels with his .22 rifle and clubbed catfish with a hammer, and he was surprised that taking a human life had been as simple as killing these other lowlier creatures. But people were caged in much the same frailty as any animal. It only took a measure of force to assign a man to his grave, to loose him from this world.

Before that night on the ferry, Beam hadn't known there were things a man could do that he couldn't take back. When he'd gotten in cursing fits with Clem, he would stomp off to sulk in the woods for a few hours, but he always came back. Sometimes he was meek and full of apologies; sometimes he clutched to his defiance through weeks of gritty silence, but he always came back, and Clem always held the door open for him. You couldn't come back from killing a man, though.

When Beam closed his eyes, he saw the stranger tumbling from the tug cabin, his face coated with blood, the damp red bristles of his mustache twitching like the legs of some insect he'd eaten. He heard again the dead drum of the steel wrench striking the man's head, saw forever his eyes as they walled white in the darkness, and then felt the boom as the body fell against the aluminum hull of the ferry. The entire night of blood and death beside the river returned to scream at him like an imp crouched in the glare of oncoming headlights just before it rose on the thin pale staves of its legs and ratcheted into the roadside bracken again, the brief flare of its eyes aglow in a rainy slash of wind that tore at Beam until he forced his eyes open and found himself sweaty and breathless on the trail. His narcolepsy had the potential to cause hallucinations and he reasoned the phantoms away with this explanation, but knew he couldn't do so with the man on the ferry. He was dead and Beam had killed him and that was the stone truth of it.

In a ravine between two hills he stopped again and rested on a mossy rock. He clicked the flashlight off and listened. Trees creaked and wheezed in the breeze and the tremolo of crickets shivered all about him. There was no chill in the night and so he made no fire. He eased down from the rock and pillowed his head with the duffel so that he lay on his back staring at the deep of the sky and waiting for the sudden blow of sleep to come.

He didn't know exactly how it happened, or what caused it. Doctors had informed him, but their jargon was bland and technical and Beam understood little of his condition. If asked, he'd simply shake his head and look at the ground and say, *I just go to sleep sometimes.* As if that was any kind of accounting for the way he fell out while walking along a dusty road ditch or stumbled to one knee without a moment's warning while running the ferry. He did know that when it came, the swift ax-fall of slumber, it was heavy and absolute enough to leave his mind cleared and empty for a few brief minutes after he awoke, and that was something he hoped for now, especially with the brute ghost from the ferry shuttling out to greet him from every knurly tree and coil of briars.

Now, though, when he longed to sleep, it wouldn't come. Pitted with his head against the duffel and his back on the ground, the trees jostling in the wind, he remained dazed and wakeful. Time seemed to bend and flex, to elongate and then contract like a spasm, until he heard movement in the leaves behind him.

In one motion, Beam sat up and turned and flicked on the Maglite. Revealed in the light was a spotted bobcat, one paw lifted in mid-step, the gray tufts of its muttonchops giving it the look of a magistrate who gazed upon Beam with scorn and contempt.

Beam remained crouched and frozen. The bobcat's eyes gleamed in the light, and the animal sniffed the air a few times before bounding away into the trees, traceless and gone as a vapor.

For a time, Beam sat in mute shock. Bobcats were numerous in these woods, he knew, but rarely seen. Some childish fear drove him to wonder if this one had sought him out, if it had meant to glare at him with that smoldering cruelty in its eyes, but he soon shook that thought away and pulled the duffel onto his back and began walking on through the wilderness, the flashlight sprayed before him on the trail.

Eventually, the trail led him to a dirt road that seemed to amble either way toward nothingness, and he followed it until he came upon a culvert. He squirmed into the structure and spent the rest of the night in a whorl of mosquitoes so thick it seemed to fill his lungs like hot cinders.

At dawn, Beam crossed a wide mown field, the dew wetting the
cuffs of his pants as the sun rose above the far poplar woods.
When he reached the trees, he slid the duffel from his back
and rested against a white oak log, sweat draping over him as
he caught his breath. There were birds crying in the forest. For
a moment, he tried to think what kind of birds they might be
and he thought he might know, but he didn't. He thought it was
something he'd forgotten, or maybe never known at all, the way
to name a bird by its song. He wondered if killing the man on
the ferry had taken him farther and farther away from the world
he once knew as he staggered lost and unbidden through a land
solitary and alien.

Unzipping the duffel, he found the last bits of a ham sandwich
wrapped in wax paper and ate it quietly with a motion almost
involuntary, like the simple rise and fall of his own breath. Out of
a mayonnaise jar, he drank some water he'd trapped from a creek.
The water tasted silty and bitter, but he still finished it all, until
only a milky skim remained in the bottom of the jar. He held the
jar to his eye like a kaleidoscope and the world captured in the
glass was blurred and smeary as though made at the behest of a
God harried and suspect.

When he was done, he screwed the lid back on the jar
and returned it to the duffel. He then shut the bag and scooted
from the log so that he rested with it to his back. The birds still
screamed in the trees, and beyond them he heard the faint cawing
of crows, but Beam barely listened. A slow drowning repose came
upon him and he soon slid into a dismal kind of rest.

The scrape of a screwdriver against the white oak log woke him.
Beam didn't know how long he'd slept, but when roused by the
noise, he found the sun stood blank and white overhead. An
old man was on his hands and knees digging at some plant
beneath the log, using the screwdriver to prize the roots loose
from the soil, his hands groping through the black humus, sweat

darkening the blue pearl-snap shirt he wore.

Beam lay motionless and watched the old man. He worked quietly, levering the screwdriver into the hole he'd dug until the plant emerged, its pale hag-wig of roots dripping wet soil. Then he took a plastic Sunbeam bread sack from his pocket, snapped the leaves and stems from the plant, and placed the roots inside. When this was finished, he groaned into standing and wiped the dirt from his pants and breathed deeply.

"Best place I ever seen to get some rest," he said, looking off through the trees, "was in a bed under a roof somewhere." He drew a red spotted rag from his pants pocket and tugged it over his forehead, then balled it in his fist and winked his filmy blue eyes at Beam. "Anyway, I sure wouldn't be one to take a nap in the woods like you're doing. Man's liable to wake up dead."

Beam raised himself off the ground and sat on the oak log. He rested his palms on his knees and watched as the old man toed the dirt back into the hole he'd dug. "What is that you're digging?" he asked.

The man glanced at the bread sack and then hoisted it up higher so that Beam could see it better. "Sang," he announced.

Beam scratched a mosquito bite on his elbow until he felt the warm blood between his fingers.

"This sang in through here is kindly puny," said the old man. He lowered the bread sack and knocked it against his leg. "Course, I'll take what all I can get. These days you got to look awful hard to find any sang whatsoever. Why? Cause everybody's damn greedy, that's why. They snatch up all the sang there is and don't leave none to bear on the next year. It's like they think another year ain't even coming."

Beam knuckled the sleep from his eyes. "Maybe it ain't," he said.

The old man did not remark on this. He propped a boot on the log, and stood staring off through the trees. His form was lean and cut by years of labor, Beam could see, and the hands dangling from his arms were large and crossed with blue varices, his face brown and dried as an apple core.

"I've dug sang most my life," he said. "Dug it in times when it was thick as carpet under the trees. Look on a north hillside where there's plenty of shade because sang likes shade. And digging it after August is best because it's got the berries on then. And where you find sang you'll find bloodroot and goldenseal, though those don't bring a dollar the way sang does."

Beam yawned. "Where are we?" he asked.

"You're right about that," answered the old man, mishearing him. "You can't hardly raise sang from seed. Not if you want quality. It's a tender plant that's careful about where it takes root, but once it finds ground it likes it'll be there forever if some damn fool don't dig it all up. I've always thought folks would fare a sight better if they behaved a little more the way sang does. But they don't. They'll just root in one spot for a time and then be gone with scarcely a trace if they think there's better ground somewheres else."

The day was warming steadily, and the light sliced down from the poplar boughs overhead in sharp obliques that stood amid the trees like corbels of fresh blown glass. The hay field Beam had crossed at dawn colored quickly, the shorn fescue turning a stubbly blond as the dew burned away. There was no wind and somewhere, very distant, Beam thought he heard a highway.

"What is this place?" he asked.

The old man turned and regarded him, his eyes like two holes awled in leather. "This place don't really have a name," he said.

"Well what's it close to then?"

"The Opins farm. Their old home is just over this rise here. Course there ain't been no Opins round these parts for thirty years."

"I think I hear a road."

The old man nodded. "You would. Can't hardly stand nowhere in this country anymore without hearing one. People are always after it, ain't they?" The old man looked at the soil beneath the oak log and shook his head. "Whatever *it* is," he added.

Beam strained to listen. He heard a truck, the steel belts of its tires coughing on the road's rumble strip. "What road is that I'm hearing?" he asked, pointing through the woods.

The old man wiped a hand over the log, clearing a place for himself, and then sat down with a grunt. The slight paunch of his belly pouted over his belt. "That'd be the Natcher Road," he said. "It goes on many a several mile between here and wherever it is you're going to."

Beam stood and hoisted the duffel onto his back. "I got to get on to that road," he said.

"What's your hurry?" The old man's eyes gaped at Beam, as if he couldn't believe what he was hearing. "It'll still be there in the morning. You can sit a spell, can't you?"

Beam shook his head. He sensed that the old man was lonely, as he knew most old people were, but he didn't have time to chat. It was impossible to know who might be looking for him and he wanted to put as much distance between himself and whoever it was as he could.

Beam cinched the duffel's straps tight over his shoulders.

"I best get on," he said quickly.

"Well, you might be back around sometime," the old man replied. Beam gave a slight nod and then tramped off through the trees that stood still and quiet in the vaporous light, his shoes snapping over windfall branches and crackling leaves. He did not look back.

Reaching a clearing, Beam came to a house that must have once been the Opins place. The peaked roof reared through the branches of blight-killed elms, and the tin peeled back in spots to reveal the black rotted joists and rafters underneath. Jonquils grew in green clutches of stems beside the footstones, their yellow petals long wilted away for the year. Beyond the house was a barn with a gambrel roof and slouching walls, and at the far edge of the grounds sat a crumbling smokehouse.

Beam crossed through what once had been a yard. Rusted paint cans and food tins were strewn in the sorrel, and pokeweed grew beside a stoop rock limed with bird shit. Sections of the porch boards were splintered or missing. Water plinked somewhere and wind flumed through the windows that stood glassless and black. The sky grew suddenly overcast so that the abandoned farm appeared like a landscape charcoaled and grim.

Beam took hold of one of the chicken-leg support posts on the porch and pulled himself onto the boards, which grieved his weight with a low moan. The hinges were empty of a door and he walked through the front entrance, his boots knocking against the dusty puncheon floor.

Save for mounds of dried possum scat, the house was empty. The fireplace held brass andirons and cold ash. The large hearth had been built from smooth fieldstones, and water had leeched down the chimney to draw finger streaks in the soot. Beam stood beside the hearth and ran his hands over the rocks, listening to the wind tremble in the flue. He imagined what it would be like to be lord of this manor, the fire crackling on cold evenings as he stood sipping straight bourbon from a highball glass, musing quietly on wealth and the wild straying ways of life and how easily a man could descend from the height of joy into the chasm of misery like a spider falling on a single thread of silk.

He was running his hand along the ridged slope of the fieldstones when he heard the hissing. A kind of gravelly snarl leaked to him from one of the back rooms, and he followed the sound down a hallway into what had perhaps once been a bedroom. In a corner of the room, two vulture chicks lightly downed with white fuzz sat on the floor blinking their black leaden eyes at him. They lifted their wings and hissed raggedly when he stepped closer into the room, but they were still fledglings and could not fly. A stink of putrefied meat suddenly rushed at Beam so that he staggered back to the doorway clutching a hand to his nose.

And then a huge shape fluttered into the room's empty window. There was a brief stalled moment of shock as Beam stared at the buzzard, and then it launched itself at him, its wings buffeting his head as he ran down the hallway, the bird vomiting on him until he fled from the house and sprawled face down in the dry grass of the yard.

Beam rolled onto his back. The sky was a white patch of rain clouds. He began to drag the puke from his hair so that he appeared like a strange creature birthing itself, the vomit draping him in a foul amniotic sheet. He sat up, and the smell caused him to retch violently upon the ground. When the spasm passed, he managed to stand and spit.

The buzzard looked down at him from its perch in one of the blighted elm trees, its wings spread in black cruciform, its feather tips glistening in black dihedrals so that it appeared in the pose of one gifting silence unto the world, its red nodulose face jerking wildly.

Beam stared back at the bird for a few moments. Then he wandered away into the trees again. When he stopped to look back, he could see nothing of the house. A halo of vultures circled above him in the blank sky.

# VII

## THURSDAY

For close to an hour, Beam had waited in the rain at the edge of the Natcher Road, a few cars and cattle trucks the only traffic that had passed by, all of them ignoring him. His hair dripping, his clothes damp against him, he had nearly fallen asleep when a Peterbilt with a blown tire slumped onto the shoulder a quarter mile down.

Beam raised himself from the guardrail where he'd been sitting and hurried to meet the driver as he stepped down from the cab. Strangely, he was dressed in a tailored three-piece suit of navy blue, though he wore a pair of scuffed steel-toed boots. When he moved to inspect the blown tire, he had a slight limp that caused him to list to one side, the thin blades of his shoulder bones scissoring under the taut fabric of the blazer.

"I guess you picked up a nail or a screw there, didn't you?" said Beam.

The trucker spun and glared at him. His face was puckered slightly, and he wore a coating of pomade in his blonde hair, which was flung in a loose marcel over his scalp, a few curled strands hanging in dirty ropes over his ears and down his neck.

"Now see, that's not it at all," he said. His eyes were a dim blue color and they seemed to jump around a bit inside his skull when he spoke. "These tires are too bald to be driving on." He reached a boot out and kicked at the blown radial. "I've been telling Lawrence to put another set on, but he don't listen to me."

Turning to Beam, he said, "What happened to you anyway?"

Beam pushed his thumbs under the straps of the duffel. He

was suddenly unnerved by the trucker, who seemed to pay the rain no more mind than if it were a slight breeze. He didn't even blink as the water collected on the thick batts of his eyelashes and dripped onto his cheeks.

"Ain't nothing happened," Beam said. "Not to me."

"You sure don't look like somebody that ain't had nothing happen to them."

"Other than getting rained on, I'm fine."

The trucker adjusted the lapels of his blazer and sniffed the air. "Do you smell something?" he asked.

Beam thought of the vulture that had spewed on him. He'd hoped the rain had washed some of the stink away, but it hadn't.

"No," he said. "I don't smell anything."

The trucker turned back to regard the limp tire again. "I smell something," he said. He kicked the tire and the rubber flapped loosely on the alloyed wheel. "Can you hoist a jack?"

"Sir?"

"I asked if you could hoist a jack. If you can fit my spare on, I'll give you a ride to wherever it is you're going."

"I didn't say I needed a ride."

The trucker spat through a space in his teeth. "Oh, I guess you just enjoy standing on the shoulder of the highway with that canvas bag in the rain."

Beam looked up the highway to where the rain passed in wind-tossed swarms over the graying slope of the hills, and shrugged the duffel from his shoulders. "Where's your tools?" he asked.

The trucker gestured toward the cab. "In there," he said. "Under the sleeper bunk, you'll find my box and the jack."

Beam nodded and lifted himself up into the rig. The cab smelled of mildew. Sprouts of smoke grew from an overburdened ashtray, and there were maps and stray porno magazines strewn over the dash. In the sleeper cab, he found the metal tool box and a huge bottlejack that had been spray-painted silver. He gathered these implements and stepped down from the rig.

The trucker sat on the guardrail rolling a cigarette. He licked the paper, flashed a Zippo, and then smiled through a veil of smoke at Beam as he approached with the tools.

"Let's see what kind of hand you are tire changing," he said.

Beam silently sat the tools beside the burst radial and set to work. He took a four-way wrench from the toolbox and budged the lugs with it, then slid the jack under one of the rig's tandem axles, smelling the black scorched stink of diesel and road tar. When he'd jacked the axle, he sat on his rear and, grasping the tire with his hands, slowly moved it off the spindle, using his toes for leverage. When he had the bad tire off, he unsettled the spare from its carriage under the trailer, and placed it flush over the greasy spindles before torquing the nuts into place with the tire wrench. He lowered the jack and stood, wiping his smudged hands over his jeans.

"Care for a smoke?" the trucker asked.

Beam shook his head. "No," he said. He stepped back and looked at the trailer with its greasy coat of char and road residue. "What are you hauling?" he asked.

The trucker thumped the cherry from the end of his cigarette and then tossed the butt away. "Suits," he answered.

"Suits? What for?"

"All occasions."

"I guess I'd have to say I never wore one," Beam said.

The trucker gawked incredulous. "Say you never did?"

Beam shook his head. "Not that I can recall."

"Now see, we can fix that." The trucker stood up from the guardrail and wobbled off to the rear of the trailer. "Come here," he called, lifting the trailer door.

Beam walked to the back of the rig. Its interior loomed in cavernous dark, but the gray light filtering in revealed the first rows of plastic-wrapped suits hanging like cocoons, their sleeves pressed and freshly cleaned, cufflinks winking asterisks of light.

The trucker climbed into the trailer and disappeared. Beam heard him rummaging through them, the plastic crackling and breathing, and when he reemerged and stepped down onto the gritty shoulder, he was carrying a brown worsted suit folded over his arms.

"This one here looks like it'd fit you," he said. He made to hold the suit against him, but Beam backed away quickly.

"I don't want to wear any suit," he said. "I'm fine in the clothes I already got on."

The trucker dangled the suit from his fingertips. "You don't look fine," he said.

"Well, I don't intend to put on any suit."

The trucker shrugged and tossed the suit back into the trailer. "You'll wear one someday," he said. "Whether you intend to or not."

"No." Beam shook his head slowly. "I don't believe I will."

The trucker shrugged again and then reached up and yanked the trailer door closed and secured the latch.

"It don't matter at the moment," he said. He turned and walked back to the cab. "Come on. We're going."

Beam walked around the trailer to the rig's passenger door and pulled himself inside. He settled the duffel at his feet and rolled the window down and rested his arm on the sill. The rain had stopped, and thin yeasty smears of mist spumed over the treetops and the highway. The trucker fixed himself behind the wheel, cranked the engine over, and the rig quivered to life, the stack pipes croaking diesel smoke. He turned to Beam, his eyes grayed in the dim of the cab as if taking cue and color from the glum weather outside.

"Where is it you're headed?" he asked.

"Wherever," said Beam. "As far as you'll take me."

The trucker nodded once and put the rig in gear. "Now see, that's just fine," he said, pulling out onto the highway.

# VIII

# THURSDAY

It was still early when Derna left in Old Dog. She followed the river road out of the bottoms and drove slowly, leaving the emerald flats of corn until the shade of the hardwoods covered her so that she traveled through a murk stretched cool and thick over the highway. From a thermos, she drank warm sassafras tea and she briefly played the radio until it grew tedious and she flicked it off so that only the clatter of the truck's engine filled the cab.

An old way led her to the place she sought. At first, she thought she wouldn't remember how to get there but then it all came back to her, up from the country of farm-loam into a bulbous knot of hills smelling hot with morning, onward past slumping barns and trailers sulking in sedge grass, limp wire fences torn loose by the winds, then coasting by the sawmill where mounds of dust stood like melted tallow on the sludgy black ground, the men pacing to work as the light fled down about them in a tremulous spray, a few lifting hands to her as she drove past.

At a small gas station, she stopped and bought cigarettes and a ham sandwich on light bread with mustard, which she ate in the truck while sitting in the parking lot, her hands trembling some as she lifted the food to her lips. When she was finished, she brushed the crumbs from her blouse and went on to the place she'd never forgotten.

The house had been repainted a faint blue. It sat above the road amid pin oak trees, and the tossing shadows of the leaves made it appear to wobble like a mirage.

She pulled into the yard and parked beside Loat's Cadillac.

He owned two, a white late sixties model, which was the car sitting in the driveway, and a powder blue one with tailfins. Owning two Cadillacs wasn't a display of wealth on Loat's part, but a manifestation of his superstitious ways, as he wouldn't drive the white Cadillac at night, believing that riding in a white car after dark could invite madness or even death. He was full of such beliefs. He checked the cycles of the moon, thumbed through almanacs for cures and ways to read the weather for sign of things to come or the whereabouts of things passed on from this world.

Derna hadn't minded his penchant for what many considered nonsense because Loat was a man others respected and feared and he seemed at first to be the everything she'd often dreamed of while growing up poor and hungry in the mud hills. But all of that was before. Before she took to drink and became a whore out at Daryl Vanlandingham's bar, before she'd learned what Loat really was.

She exited the pickup. A collection of rusted box springs leaned against the north side of the house, and lengths of mirrored glass had been nailed to the wall in various spots. Derna adjusted her hair in the mirrors as she approached the porch, then rose up the rock stoop and onto the boards, her black plastic shoes worrying tiny eddies of dust around her ankles.

She moved to knock on the screen door, but instead stopped and turned to look at the yard. It had been mowed, and the smell of bruised grass hung damp and sweet on the air. Beyond the yard lay Loat's garden, tended and firm with stalks of corn and caged tomato plants spread down the lengthy furrows, along with several hills of potatoes whose leaves showed the white powder of Sevin dope. There were squash and okra, as well as a trellis of half-runner beans and a row of peas. Loat had strung a dead crow from a cane pole in the center as a deterrent to others of its kind, and the bird dangled by a single foot, its splayed black wings glinting with blue-black iridescence.

Derna remembered standing on this porch while evening

plummeted to earth and she listened to the cars brushing by on the highway beyond, wondering if one would take her away. Of a night sometime, she would stand there until Loat found her and led her by the hand back to the house, his voice far off and subtle as he placed her again on the old mattress ticking in her room, the creak of the springs as they bore her sleepy weight like the sound of a stone sliding perfectly flush against other stones, a thing being guided into its exact slotted place.

"Found your way back didn't you, Dollbaby," she heard Loat say.

She turned to find him standing in the doorway just behind the storm screen, which made his features grainy and blurred. He opened the door for her and she entered. The house flexed dim around her, the only light what seeped in through the curtained windows. Immediately, she smelled the dogs.

"What about your hounds?" she asked.

Loat raked the hair flush over his scalp and smiled as he closed the door behind her. "They ain't here," he said. "Presto's taken them out to run a few rabbits." He moved away from the door and stood back to regard her, looking her up and down as if trying to reckon a price, his dentures set in his bottom lip and his hands stowed in the back pockets of his trousers.

"You look good, Dollbaby," he said. "Considering what all you been through here lately, you look real good."

"I see you painted the house blue," she said.

"Some time ago. I forgot it'd been that long since you been out." He walked deeper into the living room that was empty save for a ragged Lay-Z-Boy recliner and chewed Naugahyde footstool. "Come on in here to the kitchen. We'll sit a spell."

She followed him. A brown boot lace hung from the ceiling fan, and Loat pulled it and light scattered over the chairs and Formica table spread with envelopes, prescription pill bottles, a few gnawed pieces of white bread, drill bits, and a jelly jar full of nails and ink pens. The strippings of a deer rifle lay across one of the table chairs, the barrel slick with fresh bluing, and a wire bore brush blackened from use lay on the floor. Flies droned everywhere.

Loat went to the faucet and ran water in a coffee cup. He brought it to Derna, and she held it with both her hands as if the room was cold and she expected the cup to warm her fingers.

"Drink that," said Loat. "It's good water."

Derna held the cup to her nose and sniffed. "Used to not be," she said. "I can remember when you could hold a match to what came out of that tap and it'd flame there was so much sulfur in the water."

Loat smirked and scratched the small bud of his nose. "Not anymore," he said. "I got some of those asshole magistrates to finally run a city pipe out here." He pointed to the cup in her hands. "That is some of the best water dirty money can buy."

Derna sniffed the cup again, then tipped it to her lips and drank. The water tasted warm and vaguely metallic and she held it in her mouth a long time before she swallowed.

"What'd I say? It drinks good, don't it?" Loat smiled.

"Yes," she said. "It's good."

Loat pointed to an empty seat at the table. "Sit down," he said. He lifted the deer rifle from the chair, placed it on the four-eye stove and then sat down himself.

Derna sat down at the table, stowing the cup of water in her lap. "I heard you're sick," she said.

Loat placed his hands on his knees and leaned toward her, his eyes hooded and cold as craters on the moon.

"People talk," he said.

"Usually not without they got a reason to."

"They don't need a reason other than it gives them something to do with the air other than breathe it."

Derna placed her cup on the table. "You aren't well though, are you?"

"The one thing wrong with me," said Loat, "is that I'm getting old."

Derna leaned back in her chair and stared at Loat. His cheeks had grown sallow and lean, and a raggedy tremor clutched in his chest when he drew air as though his lungs were cluttered with trash.

"My kidneys are bad," Loat finally said. "I can't pass good water and when I do, I'm pissing blood."

Derna pinched her fingers into a beak and poked them into the coffee cup, then dribbled some water over her wrist and worked it in until her skin felt damp. "It don't matter none to me," she said flatly.

"I know it don't. But you didn't come out here to ask questions about my health. You want to know about your boys."

She looked at him. There were things she wished to say but she held her tongue. It felt like glue between her jaws, and what could she say, really? Too many things, she supposed. Curses and prayers. More questions that led down old nowhere paths to old nowhere ends. She'd lived with Loat for close to six years and in all that time she'd never known the man to allow talk to go any way he didn't want it to. It was a strange power he held, and she felt it working on her now.

"Must be real hard on you," he said. "Paul's gone and now that other one Beam has lit out." Loat put his chin against his chest and stared at her, his eyes softening a bit.

"What do you know about Beam?" she asked.

"I know what Clem told me the other night ain't so. I know Beam ain't just off tomcatting. He's straight gone, ain't he?"

Derna clinched her fists in her lap. "Clem says he's just out on a drunk. But he's been gone since Tuesday and he's got that sleeping sickness." She kneaded the dress in her lap, making biscuits like a cat. "Are you looking for him?" she asked.

Loat shook his head. "What would I want with Beam?" He sat back in his chair and stroked his cheeks. "Though it is some curious the way he just up and left so close to Paul winding up drowned in the river."

Derna brought the cup to her lips and felt the cool porcelain as she sipped the last of the water down.

"Why did Clem lie to me the other night?" Loat asked. "Beam's off tomcatting? If that's the case, nobody's seen him. So where's he at?"

She felt him pulling her a way she did not want to go, his voice clinging to her like mud as it sucked her down.

"Did you kill Paul?" she managed to ask.

The question caught Loat off guard and his eyes roiled slightly before steadying.

"You've gone wrong asking that," he said. "Why would I kill Paul? He was mine."

"You've gotten rid of plenty that belonged to you."

Loat clicked his tongue and swallowed. "Same could be said of you, I reckon." He stood and went to a cabinet, where he took down a bottle of Lord Calvert. He poured some into a coffee mug and drank it, then poured himself another shot and turned to her.

"As I recall, you're the one left Paul behind for me to raise," he said.

Derna ticked her fingernail against the cold coffee cup on the table. She felt Loat leading her toward things she didn't want to talk about, not with him, and she lurched a bit in her chair as she fumbled with her own thoughts. Outside, the wind tossed and wrapped itself about the house like a palsied hand hiding a candle flame, and the windows bucked and bowed with each gust.

"That's a nice garden you got outside, Loat," she said. "Why don't you show it to me?"

Loat stared at her for a moment, then threw back the last drink of his whisky. He wheezed as the liquor bit through him. When the burn had passed, he wiped his lips on the back of his hand.

"Come on then," he said, moving toward the door.

Loat picked some ripe squash, placing them in a blue plastic Wal-Mart sack.

"Deer eat most of what I grow," he said, handing the sack to Derna. "I lay for them with my rifle in the mornings sometimes, but I've yet to fell a one."

Derna held the sack of vegetables like a purse. The wind blew the garden's loess against her ankles and she pinched her eyes against the hard sun, feeling the sweat as it leaked down her back. "I wish you'd look for Beam," she said, staring at the woodline as if her lost boy might be hidden somewhere in the shady trees.

Loat stooped and yanked a morning glory vine from the soil and coiled it in his hands. "And why is that?" he asked.

She turned to him. "I've lost one son already, Loat," she said. "I can't bear losing the other."

Loat snorted and snapped the morning glory vine in two. "Finding a pup with running blood ain't my bag, Dollbaby. Especially one that don't mean no more to me than the shit on my heels."

"Then why'd you come by the house last night?"

"I wanted to give you the news about Paul. Sheriff said he'd run by and tell you and I guess he did, but I wanted you to hear it from me, too."

The wind conjured Derna's hair. She tried to smooth it down, but it leapt up beneath her hand and sprawled across her brow and into her eyes so that for a moment the image of Loat standing before her in the garden blurred and wavered.

"What's Clem not telling me, Dollbaby?" he asked impatiently.

She used to tell him everything he wanted to know, sometimes before he even asked. She enjoyed being able to speak freely to a man about her secrets, usually while she lay sweating in the crook of his arm, smelling the humid aroma of whisky that clung to his skin.

But over time, all that changed. It began when Loat took to making her sleep alone on a twin bed in the far back of the house. "I can't sleep good with no one in the bed beside me," was his reason, and she believed him, even after his visits to her little room attained the air of a quick conjugal visit inside a prison. She believed him because he'd taken her away from that failing house in the mud hills where she'd lived with her mother and two sisters, all of them bitter women with needle-sharp tongues, believed him because his body was lean and muscled as it slid into her own with all the calm easy sway and deceptive power of a river.

Then one day, she lifted herself from the bed in the back room, tried the door and found it locked. She stood with her hand on the cold brassy knob and pressed her shoulder into the scuffed unpainted wood, but there was no give to it. Turning to the window, she saw Loat lift a flat board to the bottom of the glass outside and begin nailing it flush against the house. The light slowly leaked from the room as she screamed.

"You're not telling me everything I want to know, Dollbaby," Loat yelled from outside after he'd finished nailing her in. "I've got to let you stay in here a few days until you get your mind right. You're young and sometimes young girls like you need a little breaking down before they know how to deal right with their men."

Now, he took her arm and slowly ran his callused palm through the crook of her elbow. She looked into his eyes, clear and precise as a hawk's.

"Clem sent Beam away," she said quickly. "He won't say it, but I know that's what he did."

Loat went on stroking her arm. "How do you know?"

"He told you a lie about wrecking the ferry. It wasn't him that did it. It was Beam." The words came swiftly and without cease, and she could no more stop them than she could stop the sun from clocking through the sky. "Beam was running the ferry Tuesday night. He run it aground some way and when he come to the house to tell Clem, he looked bad scared and that's the last I've seen of him. They left to go see about it and it was nearly daylight when Clem came in, but Beam wasn't with him."

"Where did Clem say he'd gone?"

"He didn't. He just acted like Beam was in the house and like nothing unusual at all was going on. When I asked, he give me that line about Beam just going off on a drunk. Same line he handed you."

Loat let his hand fall from her arm.

"You must not trust Clem awful much to come out here and tell me such things," he said.

"I don't trust anyone. I'm trying to find my son and you're the only one can help me."

Loat pursed his lips and drew a high wheezy breath through his nostrils. "It's strange how them that go out to multiply got to then try and get back what they loosed in the world, ain't it?"

"You don't have to preach me a sermon, Loat."

"No." He shook his head slowly. "But stranger still is the way it's come to be. You going up and down in the world trying to find your last born child when you didn't want the first born."

"I was just a child myself when I had Paul. You can't hold a child guilty for being foolish."

"I can hold all guilty. Man, woman, and child."

"I was scared, Loat."

"Scared of what?"

Derna looked at the ground. "You," she said quietly.

"I guess you ain't afraid no more? That why you're standing out here in my garden?"

Derna raised her eyes to him. "I can't afford to trust my fear," she said. "I need my son back and I need you to help me find him."

Loat shook his head quickly and then spat. "I don't see that you got much to deal with, Dollbaby. You know I don't do nothing without a price."

Derna ran her thumb along the inside of her dress collar. Her gaze darted to the pale blue house seated beneath the pin oak trees, and then back to Loat's hard beveled face.

"We could go back inside," she said. "It's lots cooler in the house."

Loat grunted a small laugh and then pulled a shabby handkerchief from his back pocket, which he used to wipe his cheeks dry.

"Ain't this something?" he remarked. "First you tell me I'm scary and now you're flashing me them big ole eyes. What's this about, Dollbaby?"

She slid a curl of hair behind her ear. "You done me bad, Loat," she said in a near whisper. "But it weren't all your fault. I know I done you some bad myself. I know you loved me a long time ago and I'm so sorry for the way I hurt you back then."

She took a step closer to him and placed a hand on his arm. "I hurt you bad, didn't I?" she said.

For a moment, something shifted in Loat's eyes and Derna thought she might actually be about to regain a loose control over him. She slid her hand higher up his arm and felt his bicep flex at her touch.

"We should try and do good to each other," she said. "Now that Paul's gone."

That was too much. At the mention of his son's name, the fire rekindled in Loat's eyes. He slid his arm around Derna's waist and she smelled the bitter talc of his dentures and the soured whisky reek from the back of his throat. She tried to pull away, but it was too late as he led her out of the garden and through the yard onto the porch, her shoes echoing off the warped boards and then the closeness of the house enveloped her until she heard only the kitchen faucet dropping its one recurrent note against the metal sink, a sound as undaunted as blood and breath.

# IX

## THURSDAY

Beam had allowed sleep to fool him once again. It had come upon him just after the trucker pulled back onto the Natcher Road, and now he awoke in the rig's cab, the strange man shaking his arm and chittering like a squirrel about dancing and cold beer. Beam opened his eyes and looked out the truck's bug-smeared windshield at a large gravel parking lot framed by fields sown with heat-withered soybeans. A long Quonset hut with a rusted roof sat in the middle of the parking lot. Above the building's oaken double doors hung a hand painted sign that read COLD BEER DANCING JUKEBOX AT DARYLS.

"Get up, Sleepy Head," said the trucker. He shook him forcibly until Beam slapped the man's hand away .

The trucker giggled. "A might touchy this evening, ain't you?" He slouched with his back against the greasy driver's side window. "Time to punch your ticket, bud." He rested his hands on the grooved steering wheel and nodded toward the Quonset hut. "Now see, I'm fixing to go in here and drink them out of business. You're welcome to come along, but you can't stay in my rig."

Beam clawed the sleep from his eyes. "You don't want to go in there," he said.

"No? And why not?"

"I know this bar. You go in there dressed like that, you're liable to wind up drowned in somebody's well."

"My God, that sounds like one helluva goddamn place. What are the women like in there?"

"I tell you one thing," Beam said, "the women in there ain't seen a man wearing a suit since they shut the lid on their daddy's caskets."

"So you're saying I'd be prime real estate for them."

"Oh, sure," said Beam. "They'd plow you like new ground."

The trucker slapped the steering wheel. "Now see, that settles it then. I'm going in." He opened the door and stepped down onto the truck's running board, then turned to look back into the cab at Beam. "You can come along or sit out here in the sun, but you got to get out of my rig."

Beam shook his head and then opened his door and climbed down into the burning white parking lot. He immediately began to sweat and could feel the heat stabbing up through the soles of his boots.

"Adios there, bud," the trucker said, waving a hand.

Beam watched him walk to the hut, and when he opened the double doors, a brief jangle of steel music spilled out before they slammed shut again and only the buzzing hum of the day remained. He hitched the duffel onto his shoulder and thought about what to do.

Even if he hadn't killed the man on the ferry, Beam knew that Daryl's was no place for him to be. Someone might know him, and there was a stout chance the law would come snooping around due to a fight or some other business Beam had no involvement in. Though he had never been inside the bar, Beam knew that the proprietor, Daryl Vandlandingham, a double amputee and pusher of whores and prime stroke grass, was a man who settled his accounts on his own terms, and those terms often involved blood. No, a better move would simply be to move on, to hitch a ride to another town. He had the twenty dollar bill he'd taken from the man on the ferry, plus the fifty his father had given him before he left, and that would last him a spell.

Beam took a few steps toward the highway and then stopped. It suddenly occurred to him that he'd fallen asleep in the rig and that anything might have happened while he dozed. He dropped the duffel onto the ground and squatted down beside it, rifling through the bundled clothing, searching for the Ziploc bag where he'd stowed the money. It was gone.

A thick rage boiled up inside him. He walked through the flailing heat to the bar and hurled the doors open. A blast of cool, fecund air smoothed over his face. When the doors closed at his back, he stood in a pulsing dim until his eyes adjusted and steadied.

The Quonset spanned long and narrow before him like a bowling lane. The floor was marked with a scuffed red varnish that had faded over time so that the wood now held a dull luster. A black painted bar spread the length of one wall. Behind it, bottles stood in their tiered ranks, whiskeys, vodkas, bourbons and gin demijohns spangling from a drape of milky light that spilled from a halogen tube hung above the gilt-framed mirror behind the bar. A few picnic tables papered with newsprint sat to his right, in front of a stage. Amplifiers and microphones lay bundled in a corner like shock fodder. In the center of the stage was a large four-poster bed with a velvet red canopy and fresh crimson linens and mauve pillows piled in thick drifts atop the mattress. A piebald billy goat stood tethered to one of the bed posts, nibbling steadily at the hem of one of the sheets. Neon signs for Falstaff and Falls City and Pabst drooled garish light down the walls. Picture frames displaying large panties and bloomers were tacked here and there like gallery art, and Beam stood wondering if there were really women with body enough to fill such copious drawers.

The trucker was nowhere, and the entire place seemed empty. A whorl of air came from a box fan sitting on the bar and Beam went and stood in the cool draft, letting the sweat dry on his cheeks. He propped a boot on the brass foot-rail and stared the length of the bar to where the hut narrowed to a long hallway of doors. The jukebox played low in the background, Gene Watson singing "Fourteen Carat Mind."

Beam leaned his elbows on the bar. At one end, a gallon pickling jar sat half-full with what looked to be human teeth. A handwritten sign taped to the side of the jar read: ANY TEETH LOST DURING A FIGHT INSIDE THE BAR BECOME THE PROPERTY OF DARYLS. Beam stared at the jar until someone shouted, "There he is!"

When Beam turned, his eyes met those of the old ginseng hunter from the forest who sat at one of the newspapered picnic tables, a beady bottle of Milwaukee's Best and what appeared to be a microwave pizza placed in front of him. His ginseng tote sack lay under the table at his feet.

"Where you been?" he asked, waving Beam over. "We ain't been doing nothing but waiting on you."

Beam crossed the floor to him. The old man smiled broadly, his lips cracking open like dry earth. He nodded for him to sit, but Beam was wary, still searching the shadows of the bar for the trucker, and remained standing.

"Did a trucker wearing a suit just come in here?" he asked.

The old man lifted his beer and took a drink, then set the bottle back down in front of him. "I don't know if he was a trucker or not, but a fellow did come in here dressed slick as a Methodist minister." He bobbed his head toward the hallway. "Went back yonder with one of the girls. Believe he aims to take up residence."

Beam looked toward the hallway. The duffel suddenly felt heavy on his back and he shrugged it off so that it fell to the floor behind him. "He's got my money," he said.

The old man picked an olive from his pizza and tossed it into his mouth. "That don't sound good," he said. "Did you give it to him?"

"No. He stole it from me while I was asleep."

"How much did he peel off you?"

"Seventy dollars."

The ginseng hunter took a bite of pizza, chewed and

swallowed, then brushed his hands together. From his shirt pocket, he pulled a roll of bills banded together with a wire twist-tie. He untied the roll and peeled off three twenties and a ten and slid the money across the table toward Beam.

"There you go," he said. "You're square now, so I'd go on and get out of here and not worry about it none."

Beam looked at the money lying on the table. He hadn't expected this, not from a man he'd spoken to only once. He'd never accepted charity before, even when he needed it during lean times on the ferry, and it seemed insulting that he hadn't the nerve to ask for it now but that the old man had simply offered it.

"Why'd you do that?" he asked.

The old man drank from his beer again and then stared at Beam. "You need it more than me," he said. "Besides, you don't want the kind of trouble looking for money in a place like this will get you."

"I don't need your money," Beam said. "I got my own."

"No." The old man shook his head. "By what you just told me, that feller in them fancy clothes has got your money." He patted the bills with his hand. "You best take these dollars and head on out to wherever it was you were going to when I come across you this morning."

"I ain't leaving here without my own money," Beam said.

The old man placed his hands on the table. "How old are you?" he asked.

"What's that got to do with anything?"

"A lot," he said. "You're young, I can tell. Man your age, he thinks the world will break if he hits it hard enough. He thinks it's something he can best, but that's not the way it works." The old man moved his hands so that they rested with the palms turned up on the smeared newsprint. "The world can't be broken," he said. "The best a man can do is get out of its way and hope it doesn't notice him." He reached out and scooted the money closer to Beam's side of the table. "Take that," he said. "Take that and get your ass out of here before somebody notices you ain't where you're supposed to be."

"Like I said, I got my own money." Beam turned to go back to the hallway of doors where the trucker had disappeared, but the old man shot a clawed brown hand out and grabbed his arm.

"You can't go just yet," he insisted.

Beam jerked at the old man's touch, but his fingers were fastened to his arm. "And why the hell not?" he asked.

"You can't go cause you ain't asked what the goat is for." The old man pointed toward the stage where the goat stood with the bed sheet in its mouth, its white beard twitching while it chewed. "That goat is a devil," he said, releasing Beam's arm. "His name's Samhill Doug, and he's some popular with the girls out here." The old man cocked a single blue eye at Beam. "You understand what I mean by that?" he asked.

Beam looked at the goat with the limp coverlet in its mouth, its cold eyes regarding him with something akin to a sad indifference, as if he were only one more unlucky wayfarer to pass through these grim and ancient halls.

"I ain't worried about any goat," he said, shaking his head. "I'm worried about getting my money back." Beam strode off quickly to the hallway, his boots clomping on the boards as he slipped deeper into the darkness, as if his very body were something the shadows were absconding with.

The first door he came to felt cool to the touch when he pressed his ear against it, but he heard nothing on the other side and went on to the next. A woman spoke beyond the scored oak. Her voice bubbled and spritzed with laughter, and then the trucker coughed and giggled.

When Beam kicked the door, the bolt sheared away from the lockbracing in a mist of wood pulp and sawdust. The woman, who was lying on a rumpled bed, screamed and pulled a sheet over her large breasts that were so white they appeared powdered with confectioner's sugar.

The trucker sat on the edge of the mattress unlacing his boots. When he saw Beam, he stopped and smiled.

"Now see, bud, you can't just come in here like that. It ain't natural," he said. "Anyway, I'm afraid you'll have to take seconds as I'm first in line for the pussy today."

Beam stood in the doorway. "Where's my money?" he asked.

"Money? You got money?"

"I did until you stole if off me while I was sleeping."

Beam stepped deeper into the room and the smell of sudsy water and rank bedding flung itself at him. The whore, who'd backed against the wall still holding the sheet to her chest, snarled at him. "Fuck you!" she said. "You ain't got no right to bust up in my room without paying first."

Beam ignored her and held his empty hand out to the trucker. "Give me my money back."

The trucker's smile tightened. He took off the steel-toed boot he'd been unlacing and sat it in his lap. "You best go on back outside," he said. "I got business to attend to right here and you're holding me up."

Beam let his hand fall to his side. The air inside the room had turned heavy and tainted.

"I got to have my money," he said. "You took it and you got to give it back."

The trucker jerked his head once. "Come on and get it, then," he said.

There was a brief pause, and then Beam rushed at the trucker, who slammed the steel-toed boot against the side of his head, sending him sprawling back into the wall, his arm knocking over a glass lamp, which shattered on the floor. Beam tried to right himself, but the trucker kicked him in the ribs. Beam slumped against the baseboard, curling his knees up into his gut and covering his head with his hands as the trucker began to beat him with the boot.

Then it all suddenly stopped. The trucker stepped away and

flung the boot into a corner, and when Beam uncovered his face, Daryl Vanlandingham was standing in the room, the red stumps of his arms crooked at his sides. Beside him were two other men, in jeans and grimy t-shirts. Each of them held wooden tire-knockers.

"I don't like trouble in this place unless I'm the one to bring it," said Daryl. He wobbled over to Beam and looked down at him. The paunch of his belly curled over the waist of his jeans, and his sweaty bald scalp and bloated green face gave him the appearance of a seasick snowman. He was sucking hard at the stifling air in the room.

"What is all this?" he wheezed.

"I'd call it a friendly misunderstanding," said the trucker.

Daryl turned and took in the sight of the man standing there in his blue sport coat and pressed slacks.

"Why in all holy fuck are you dressed like that?" he asked.

"It's for business purposes," he said, straightening the cuffs of his shirt.

"Business purposes?" Daryl turned to the whore seated on the bed. "Shelly, what happened in here?"

The whore shook her head, and a loose smile curled beneath her nose. "That one," she said, pointing at Beam on the floor, "bust in here wanting money from this one." She tossed her hand in the trucker's direction and then let it fall into her lap. "That's all the know of it I got."

Daryl snorted and peered down at Beam. The trucker's boot had cut him just beneath the ear at his jawline, and blood spilled over his neck and into the collar of his shirt.

"That true?" Daryl asked, nudging him with his shoe. "You bust my door down like Shelly said?"

Beam mumbled and shook his head. He tried to look up at Daryl, but his sight had gone cloudy so that he could make out only the vaguest shapes of things.

"Who are you?" Daryl asked. "You look like somebody I

ought to know." He turned to the men standing in the broken doorway. "Fetch this one out to the bar so we can get a better look at him."

The men lifted Beam by the arms and dragged him out of the room and down the hallway to the front of the Quonset hut where the light was better. They left him seated on the floor with his back propped against the bar. One of the men used his tire-knocker to hoist his chin up.

"You're Beam Sheetmire, ain't you?" Daryl said. "Clem and Derna's boy?"

Beam shook his head, then leaned over and spat a red stream of blood and saliva onto the wood floor.

Daryl and the men looked at one another. The trucker and the whore had come out to the front of the Quonset hut, and they stood leaning on the bar, meek smiles drifting across their lips.

"I know you," Daryl said, nudging Beam with his shoe once again. "I seen you plenty tending to that broke down old ferry your daddy owns." He jerked his chin and one of the men came and unbuttoned his shirt and slid it off his body. Daryl's torso was creamy gray and hairless but for a few black flecks sprouting from his nipples, and the curdy flesh about his abdomen was striped with streaky blue veins.

"You see this?" he asked Beam, bending a pink stump toward him, the cleft flesh slick and glistening in its folds like the body of a blind worm. "Your daddy is the cause of this. I aim to make a few cuts on you to settle that account. Get on the phone and holler up to Loat's," Daryl told one of the men holding a tire knocker. "Tell him we caught us a possum he might like a gander at."

Someone began to stroke a rotary phone. Beam felt the blood filling his mouth again. He spat and closed his eyes. Then someone said, "Step away from that boy" and he opened them again.

In the doorway of the Quonset stood the old ginseng hunter.

At his hip, he held a two barrel over-under shotgun.

"This business don't belong to you, Pete," Daryl said to the old man. "You best clear on out of here unless you feel like scalding your ass in hell tonight."

The old man broke the gun open and loaded a shell into each barrel and then swung it upward so the breech snapped closed. "I got all the hell I need right here," he said. "Now get away from that boy. I'm taking him with me."

Daryl said nothing for a few moments. Then he wagged his large oblong head and fetched a swift kick to Beam's groin, who doubled up in agony against the bar. "You're quite the prize, Beam," Daryl said. "Even old worn out drunks want you."

"Back off, Daryl," said the ginseng hunter. "I'll cut you in half with this gun and not bat an eye."

Slowly, Daryl stepped away from Beam. Behind him, the man on the phone hung the receiver back in its cradle.

"Loat's on his way," he said.

"Heard that didn't you, Pete," said Daryl. "This ain't some heathen land where you can barge in a man's place of business with a shotgun and not pay the price."

Pete moved slowly toward the bar, keeping the gun leveled at Daryl's belly. "I'm taking this boy," he said. "Loat don't figure into what I do." He bent and slung Beam's arm over his shoulder and lifted him up. Beam felt like he was going to pass out, but the old man jabbed a thumb under his ribs and the pain brought him round again so that he managed to get his legs under him.

The two of them backed toward the doors slowly. When they reached the exit, Pete kicked the doors open and dragged Beam into the lewd heat of the parking lot. Beam felt loose gravel under his feet, then the uneven metal of a truck bed beneath him. The truck's mangy engine barked alive and he soon felt the rush of motion swim over him, then the blackness of sleep.

# X

## THURSDAY

Beam awoke to the crackle of a campfire as it snapped at knots of hickory kindling, the surrounding dark loud with crickets and the soughing of trees in the wind.

He lay on his back atop a green tarpaulin. Someone had pillowed his head with a sack full of pine chips, and the blood had been washed from his face with pumice soap that left his cheeks scoured and flecked with clean grit.

Pete, the old ginseng hunter, sat across from him on a fallen elm log tending the fire with a two-pronged skewer. Flames sprouted up through a metal grille atop the flat rocks of the fire pit and licked the sides of a bean tin, but what cooked there was not beans as it smelled vaguely of shoe polish. In the light of the fire, Pete's worn features seemed soft and nearly angelic so that Beam believed he might have passed into a heaven shoddy and incongruous where night and flame had become the colors raised to declare a ramshackle salvation.

Beam turned his head and looked out into the darkness. Beyond the hem of firelight, he made out the shapes of headstones. Crumbling marble and some of Quikrete, the homemade cenotaphs of the poor and unmoneyed. Tussocks of foxtail and yucca grew around the markers, and a dead cedar had fallen over one of the graves so that its stone spilled in a wild broken chaos across the black-grown earth.

"You're in a cemetery," said Pete. "In case you were wondering."

Beam dragged the hair from his eyes. He tried to sit up, but it was too painful, so he lay back again, looking up at the night sky that seemed with its spread of stars like a sherdpiece of charred crockery, cracks of weltering light zagging off through the void, the bone-fingers of comet trails holding up the dark bowl of the fissured heavens. Stars were failing up there. Planets were being felled, shooting off in arcing traceries and burning out in vague plumes that flared and then were gone, but he was here in this world beside a fire in the warm night.

"You aim to bury me out here?" Beam asked.

Pete's shoulders jostled with quiet laughter. "No," he said. "You're stove up, but miles off from being dead just yet." He rested his elbows on his knees and folded his hands together. "Do you hurt?"

Beam rested his hands on his chest. His head ached and a long sluice of pain seemed to run behind his eyeballs, and some of his ribs were possibly broken as each breath made his lungs feel like a pair of old worn out accordions.

"No. I don't hurt," he said. "Not even a little bit."

Pete pushed a log deeper into the fire with his boot. "Go 'head. Tell another one."

The smoke from the bean tin thickened and blew over Beam so that he caught its rank and sour smell.

"What is that you're cooking?" he asked.

"Salve."

"Salve?"

"Yes." Pete crouched closer to the fire and drew a rag from his back pocket. He wrapped it around the tin of beans and lifted it from the grille. Some of the liquid, which was a thick syrupy brown, spilled over the side onto his fingers and he cursed and pushed his thumb into his mouth. "Hot," he said. Then he winced and spat. "But not too tasty."

At his side was a possibles bag that appeared fashioned from calf skin. Pete folded the flap over and took out a ring of aluminum measuring spoons, leaning into the firelight and squinting until he had selected the right one. "Daughter says I need cataract surgery but I say good sense makes up for a double round of walking blindness," he said. "Course, my eyes are so bad anymore I got to put my glasses on to go to sleep."

Finally finding the correct spoon, he took out a small baggie filled with what appeared to be ground red pepper. He measured out a dose and stirred it into the salve, the liquid thickening as it cooled to the consistency and color of paving tar, its smell growing loud and woodsy.

"Soon as this gets cool enough I'll doctor on you," said Pete.

"Right," said Beam. "Tell another one."

Pete looked across the fire at him. "This stuff here is a fix," he said. "You don't got to take it but I'd not advise that. You was beat pretty bad back there at Daryl's and this salve will put you on the mend."

"What's in it?"

Pete lifted a gallon milk jug filled with water and poured some into the tin, causing a thick steam to boil up. "Oh," he said, "few newts and toads. Dick bone from a crooked back coon. A little paint thinner for flavoring."

Beam stared at the old man. He didn't feel much like joking at the moment. The past few days had sent his mind plummeting through an electric maze until his nerves felt like the bitten and frayed ends of wiring in a house too long left vacant. He didn't know that trouble could actually hunt a man, but that seemed to be the case with him, as every move he made only sank him lower and lower in the quicksand of bad news and wrongdoings. He thought suddenly of how the stranger on the ferry had said that the river had no bottom. Now, he wondered if trouble had a bottom, and if he'd ever find it.

The smoke from the fire had dried his mouth out and he reached a hand toward the milk jug. "Can I have some of that water?"

Pete picked the jug up and shook it so that the water sloshed around inside. "This?" he asked.

"Yeah, give me a drink."

"Sure. Anytime you want it, it's right here." Pete set the jug back on the ground and smiled. "Then again, maybe you ain't so healthy that you can get up and get your own drink of water. Maybe you better take this salve after all." He stared at Beam, waiting to see if he might raise himself up from the ground to take the milk jug. When he didn't move, Pete picked up the jug and stepped over to where Beam lay and handed it down to him. Beam uncapped the top and drank the cold water down in long, refreshing pulls.

"They could just take you up yonder, honey," Pete said when Beam had finished and handed the jug back to him. He seated himself on the elm log and placed the jug between his feet.

"Why are we in a graveyard?" Beam asked.

"Was there some other place you needed to be?"

"It ain't what I had in mind, to tell the truth," he said.

Pete chuckled. "I expect you was looking to wake up on satin sheets with the Queen of Sheba?"

Beam didn't say anything. His chest pained him greatly, and the breath dragged through him in thin serried gusts, as if one of his lungs might have collapsed. He managed to get up on his elbows and, arching his back, propped himself against the sack of pine chips that had served as his pillow. Suddenly, he coughed violently and spat a bloody clot onto the ground. His breathing evened, and a sudden lightness filled his chest.

"We're in a graveyard because they won't look for us here," Pete said, taking a pack of non-filtered Berley cigarettes from his shirt pocket. He shook one free, struck a match, and began to smoke. He offered the pack to Beam.

"I don't smoke," Beam said.

Pete nodded and tucked the pack into his pocket again. He stroked the side of his belly, then spat a sprig of tobacco. "You're a Sheetmire?" he asked.

"If you know that," Beam said, "there's no need for me to talk."

"Plenty I don't know." Pete drew on the cigarette. "Like the kind of trouble you're in."

"I don't know exactly what kind of trouble I'm in," Beam said, shutting his eyes.

"Does Clem know?"

Beam opened his eyes. Across from him, the firelight bronzed the old man's features so that they seemed hardened and polished.

"You know my dad?"

"Yes, know your mama, too. Not well enough to speak to, but I could sure enough spot both of them if I was to see them in a crowd somewheres. Do either of them know the kind of trouble you're in?"

"It don't matter what they know. They can't help me."

Pete studied the embers swarming up from the fire into the blackness overhead. "Maybe not," he said. "But Clem is your daddy, right?"

Beam settled himself against the sack of pine chips. He recalled the Sheetmire homecoming, and the rowed kinfolks lining up to fill their plates, each with the sad loose smile of his father, and none bearing neither trace nor sliver of resemblance to himself.

"I don't know who else would be my daddy," he answered.

Pete pinched the fabric of his pants between two fingers and then crossed his legs. "What does Loat want with you?" he asked.

"You know about Loat Duncan?"

"Everybody knows about Loat Duncan," Pete answered. "But not everybody who gets in a fight up a Daryl's forces a phone call to the sonuvabitch. If you've gotten yourself in trouble with Loat, then you've waded out over your head." Pete picked up the metal skewer and stoked the inner coals of the fire until they burned even hotter. "You're in some bad country and it's full of bad men," he continued. "There are folks around here that don't never even see all the trouble that's right under their noses. They sit out in the evenings on their porches listening to the whippoorwills and think that everything is peaceful. Then there's the other kind. The kind the porch sitters don't like to think about. These are the ones that stand up and walk around with the dark all their lives until they are the dark. And who knows, maybe they are the whippoorwill singing way off in the wild places while the homefolks swing on their porches. Maybe that's what they are. The birds and the dogs crying and howling in the nighttime."

Beam didn't know what the old man was trying to tell him; his voice sounded far off and lost in the night. "I got no truck with Loat," he said. He waited for Pete to respond, but the old man remained silent, for once.

Beam lay his head back against the sack of pine chips and watched the stars in the great and silent distance of the night sky. His breathing leveled and steadied until he was on the verge of slipping quietly into the realm of sleep. He felt calm, as if all he'd done was some flimsy dream fetched from the back closets of his mind, easily forgettable and forgiven.

"You like graveyards?" Pete asked.

Beam snorted awake in surprise. "Can't say I ever thought much about them," he said.

"You can tell a lot about a patch of ground by who's buried under it. Who was in the wars, when and where they fought. You can tell if there was a tough winter by how many babies and women were buried one year. All of that's on these stones." Pete waved through the firelight. "The great marble orchard. That's what all it is."

"What are you talking about?"

"History." Pete patted the ground. "Right here under us is history."

Beam looked at the headstones that were visible. He had never thought of any of this before, and he didn't want to think about it now. What he wanted was a soft bed and silence from the old man.

"You like ghost stories?" Pete asked.

"I don't believe in ghosts," Beam answered.

"That's not what I asked. I asked if you like ghost stories."

"No." Beam shook his head. "I don't. That's kid shit. I don't believe in any of it."

Pete stubbed his cigarette out on the ground and pitched the butt into the fire. "I don't believe it neither," he said. "But what I will say is that there's an old house down in the woods here where ain't nobody lived in quite a time and there ain't money enough in the president's wallet to make me sleep in there of a night."

Beam readied himself. He knew another long story was coming.

"There were these two brothers," Pete began. "Grown men. They lived there with their mother. Had a little farm, but they never worked it much that I know of." He spread his hands on his lap and began picking at the dirt under his fingernails. "So it was the three of them. The brothers and the old woman. I don't know where the old man had gone. Maybe he just left. I would have. But they lived there and the brothers never went out chasing girls. Or work neither. They just lived down there in that holler. One was all right, but the other, he was kindly simple and the woman was old. One day she says to her eldest, the one who wasn't simple, she says, 'Jessup'—that was his name—'I think it's time we took care of David.' That was the one that was simple. She says, 'We have got to be rid of David. He eats all the groceries and can't hardly talk plain and he's not bringing any respect to me and you.' Jessup said he reckoned that was right, though I don't know why any of them would care what other folks thought. They never seemed to before. And I don't think they never even saw many folks. But, and now this is something you may not believe though it is what happened, Jessup took David out one night in the woods and got him drunk and tied him to an old dray pony they had. I guess they wanted rid of the pony as well. So he's got David drunk and tied in the saddle and then he knots a rag soaked in kerosene to the pony's tail and lights it and there they go, off through the dark, the horse bucking wild and screaming and poor David screaming too with that flame growing smaller and smaller as it went slithering off through the trees." Pete dipped a spoon into the salve and held his hand over it, to see if it was cool enough. "Jessup didn't have the heart to just knock the poor boy in the head, but he got rid of him just the same he reckoned. But then Jessup went out one day, doing I don't know what. Maybe he had him a still going somewhere, though they take work and I don't think that old boy Jessup was too much of a hand at anything other than getting rid of simple-minded brothers. Anyway, he come back and the old woman was gone, which was some curious, seeing as she never went further than the toilet they'd dug out back. But the house was empty as Christ's tomb. Jessup sat around the house for two days waiting for the old woman to return. Finally, he goes out looking for her, thinking how maybe she'd got drunk and wandered off somewhere and he's gone for the good part of a day and when he comes home it's night and there's a lamp burning in the window and he creeps up and looks inside. And there his mother is. Sitting on the bare floor of the living room with not a stitch of clothes on. Hair full of leaves and streaked with mud like she'd been drug through a creek. When Jessup looked in at her she started screaming, beating herself and waving her arms. And then the horse comes tromping into the living room, blinking its sad eyes. Like it was wondering what the old woman had to scream about. It didn't have but a stub of a tail left and its rump was burned black and it stood there in the house looking at the crazy old woman while she screamed and beat herself."

Pete sat back against the log he'd been resting on. "That's the way Jessup told it when he wandered into town the next morning. He was white as an old fish bone. But all that we found, me and the ones who went out to the place, was that horse in the living room, standing with its head in the fireplace like it was a feed trough. There weren't no old woman and there weren't no David.

And they weren't never found neither. But I've heard a few old fox hunters say they've seen things in these woods. In the black of the moon, they say they see an old naked woman wandering lost through the trees and that they hear a horse screaming awful. They say the hounds won't run in that holler where the house still stands. It's marked ground, you see. And the dogs know it. Me, I don't much believe in hauntings. But I will say that a place can get old just like a body. And a place can die out just like a body. And once a thing dies it starts to rot. And what is rot but a kind of haunting. You think blood don't remain with a spot? You think all the trouble that goes on in certain little places just goes away once it's over?"

Beam thought about the man on the ferry. He saw him sprawled across the floor of the boat with his head smashed, a trickle of blood seeping from his ears. His lean face seemed sculpted out of clay and his eyes were two empty smoking holes.

"What happened to the horse?" he asked.

"What horse?"

"The dray pony. The one with its tail burned off. What happened to it?"

Pete dragged on his cigarette. "Oh, he just plain didn't give a shit after that," he said. "But anyhow, what happened to that horse ain't part of the telling."

"Why'd you tell me that story?" Beam asked.

"I don't rightly know," Pete answered. "Maybe I thought it might make you feel a little better to know there's been a whole score of folks worse off than you."

"It don't make me feel no better."

"No, guess not." Pete covered his hand with the rag and picked up the can of salve and moved to where Beam lay atop the green tarpaulin. "It never does." He stirred the salve with one of the aluminum spoons and then measured out a dose. "Lift up your shirt," he said.

Beam did as he was told.

Pete began ladling the salve over Beam's bruised torso. Beam winced at the heat, but the discomfort quickly faded.

"Keep that shirt up and I'll get some bandages," Pete said. He went to his possibles bag and returned with a roll of gauze and some athletic tape.

"What are you anyway?" Beam asked. "Some kind of country doctor?"

"I ain't no doctor. What I am is just somebody that knows enough to get well without heading to the hospital ever time my nose runs. Used to be that's how most folks were. But not no more. Now everybody runs to the doctor at the first ache or pain. Hell, when I was growing up we never called the doctor unless one of the women was getting ready to calve. And there were times when we even tended to that ourselves. My aunt Gracie midwifed more babies in this county than I can count. But not no more." Finished with the bandaging, Pete pulled Beam's shirt down. "You keep soap and water and salve on those bruises and they'll not swell so bad."

Beam felt the bandages under his shirt. The pain was already drifting away.

"Why'd you help me?" he asked.

Pete laughed. He stood up slowly, rubbing his thighs, and went back to his place beside the fire. He lifted the flap on his bag and brought out a tall green bottle nestled in a cooling glove of woven henequen. He gnawed the cork off and drank. The bottle giggled as the liquor washed into him. When he was done, he stoppered the cork back in with the heel of his palm and dragged his knuckles over his lips.

"What else was there to do beside help?"

"I don't know. Walk away. That's what most people would have done." Beam shook his head. "I know it's what I would have done."

Pete set the bottle between his legs. "The thought never even occurred to me to walk away. Those fellers back there at Daryl's would have killed you."

"They might do it anyway."

"That's surely true. But not yet. Because you're right there in front of me, drawing air." Pete passed the bottle to Beam, who held it briefly before yanking the cork out and taking a large swig. The liquor was full of fire and it burned down through him, a bald clean fire that settled in his gut and tended to the warmth already growing inside him.

"You sound proud," Beam said.

"Take a look at me," Pete said. "I'm dirty and old with hardly a tooth in my head. What else has a man like me got to be proud of other than helping somebody?"

Beam took another big swig. "I wouldn't help nobody," he said, coughing.

Pete took the bottle from Beam and corked it. "That's no way to be," he said.

Beam drew a long breath and let it out slowly. The image of the man he'd killed floated before him again, his mouth caught in the rictus of death, his eyes agape in the low burning lights of the ferry.

"Do you think you can change the way you are?" he asked.

Pete cleared his throat and then spat into the fire. "I'd say that's pretty much got to be the one choice God gives a man," he answered. "You looking to change yourself?"

"I don't know. I think I'd rather change a few things I've done."

"Now there's a druthers I've not heard before." Pete leaned his head back and yawned.

Beam looked across the fire at the old man. His eyes were closed. Light glinted off the wet hairs growing from his nostrils and his chest moved with each slow breath. After a time, he began to snore quietly.

Beam rested his back against the hard sack and folded his hands over his belly. He wished he hadn't taken the liquor. He was not used to drink and now he felt it dragging him toward sleep. He fought to stay awake, but soon his eyes closed and he heard only silence.

In the hollow of the night, Pete woke to the sound of screaming. Beam was having a nightmare, a blurred watery vision where he was being pulled underwater by clawing white hands, dozens of them, pulling him on down.

Pete shook him. "Wake up. It's not real. It's a dream," he said.

Beam shuddered awake, trembling.

"I'll build the fire back. Don't worry." Pete turned to the smoldering kindling and began stoking it up with a hickory stick, startling brief flares from the embers while Beam continued to quiver like a child beset by the feral terrors of night.

Pete held a match to a crude tender of oak leaves and cedar straw. "I'll build it back again," he said. "Don't worry. I'll build it back again."

# XI

## FRIDAY

The morning lay worn and frayed on the Gasping River. Sickly anemic light floated down from a sky of clouds, and everything was silent except for the slosh of the current against the shore and the sound of sucking mud and driftwood clashing in the shoals.

Clem had winched the ferry boat ashore and lifted it with a pair of engine hoists so that its rent and broken hull was exposed. He'd already spot-welded the gouges in the bottom and was finishing up by padding tar over the remaining hairline fractures. A small transistor at his side yawned out the early news of the world and then played some kind of country music. Clem worked and tried not to think.

When he was done, he washed the tar from his skin with gasoline from a red plastic jug, cleaned his hands and face in a bucket of suds, and then rinsed himself in the river. He was toweling off with a torn piece of yellow shirtsleeve when the cruiser came down the boat ramp and parked under the locust trees. Clem eyed the vehicle, feeling a pinch in his belly. He fetched the box of Arm 'N Hammer from the spot in the grass where he'd stowed it and gave himself a healthy tablespoon, choking down the chalky white powder until the roil and splash of his stomach had ceased.

Elvis stepped out of the cruiser, short and thin in his khaki uniform. An empty leather holster on his hip shone brightly.

"Forgot your gun," Clem called out, poking the spoon back in the box of baking soda as the sheriff approached.

"I don't need it."

"Glad you think so highly of me." Clem sat the baking soda back in the grass and returned to the hull of the ferry boat. He began scraping a putty knife against a patching of J.B. Weld, peeling the gunk off the aluminum and then slinging it from the end of the blade onto the ground.

"Any news?" he asked the sheriff.

"Not really. None that concerns you, anyhow."

"That's my favorite kind."

Elvis leaned against the ferry. He studied its hull, noting the fresh welds and the tar streaked over its keel. "Looks like you met with an accident," he said.

Clem went on with the knife. "Throttle stuck on me the other night. Run her into the landing."

Elvis whistled through his teeth. "It's dangerous work out here on the Gasping, ain't it?" He noticed that Clem's hands trembled some as he worked to patch the boat.

Clem gave the sheriff a brief glance, then continued peeling the patches from the hull.

"Stopped by your house before I came down here," said Elvis. "Derna's not home. How's she doing?"

"As well as can be expected. She was gone a few hours yesterday. I don't know where she went. Driving around I guess." Clem picked up a square of hard grit sandpaper and began smoothing the repairs flush against the bottom.

"Probably good for her to get out of the house."

"I suppose."

Done with his work, Clem laid the putty knife on the ground and walked off the landing into the vetch and pig weeds growing up from the mud. On a dead ironwood branch, he'd tied a stringer of Falls City in the river to cool. He pulled the cans up and they jangled together like chimes as he tore one free and then he let the remaining beers bob down into the water again.

"Care to let me have one of those?" Elvis asked.

Clem looked at him for a moment, then fetched another can

out of the river. He walked out of the weeds to the landing where the sheriff stood and passed the beer to him.

"Didn't know you drank on the job?"

"I'm not on the job." Elvis threw his arm out and checked his watch. "Not until thirty minutes ago." He opened the beer and drank. "I'm clocking in late today. Which means whatever passes between us is off the record."

"I'll take that into consideration."

Elvis nodded and looked across the water toward the far shore where bitterns scratched at the sandy soil in search of grubs, their buffed tawny wings ruffling in the breeze.

"How are you holding up, Clem?"

Clem slugged at his beer. "Helluva thing to ask," he answered.

Elvis propped his arms over the top of the ferry and looked at Clem. His eyes were strained and bore the hollowed look of lost sleep, the whites a bit jaundiced and cloudy.

"Reason I come out here," the sheriff said, "was to tell you a few things I thought you should be aware of." Elvis took a few more sips of beer, then set the can on top of the ferry. "Main one being that Paul had help getting out." He watched Clem closely for any sign of a reaction, but he only lifted the sandpaper from the ground and began scraping the hull and keel again.

"As you know," Elvis continued, "he was a trusty down there at Eddyville. They had him on yard duty picking up candy wrappers and sweeping cigarette butts and that's when he cut the wires. Had to cut through three sets before he reached the outside and not a soul claims to have seen him do it. That strike you as odd?"

"I don't know."

"It strikes me as odd. Where'd Paul get the bolt cutters? And nobody claims to have seen him? Those guards at Eddyville are trigger-friendly. They set up there in those towers all day just waiting for somebody to try and escape, but not a one of them saw a thing?"

Clem stroked the sandpaper over the hull over and over

again, the grit making a lean rasping sound against the metal.

Elvis propped his shoe on one of the engine hoists and straightened the crease in his pants. "He had to have been helped," he said. "There's no way he could have gotten out of there so clear and easy unless somebody paid off those guards. And then he comes down here and gets knocked in the head and put in the river. Now that's a pretty blatant mystery, don't you think?"

Clem stopped scraping the sandpaper over the hull. "Blatant?" he asked.

"Sorry. I use too many words. My sister bought me some of these tapes that's supposed to increase your vocabulary. Guess she thinks it'll keep my mind occupied. The word for today is 'blatant.' It means apparent, or obvious."

Clem pushed his tongue into the side of his mouth. "If it's obvious, how can it be a mystery?" he asked.

Elvis stared at Clem for a moment, then smiled. "I can see your point," he said.

"That's why I made it. It's blatant."

Elvis broadened his smile, but Clem remained stoic and immobile. "If you're looking for whoever sprung Paul out of Eddyville," he said, "I'd start with Loat Duncan."

"I've already thought about Loat. I'm still thinking about him. But I wanted to come down here and get your take on it. Why would Loat go through the trouble of bribing those tower guards just for Paul's sake? Way I understand, the two of them weren't ever on very good terms."

Clem spat onto the landing. "I don't try and figure out why Loat does anything," he said. "Whatever he does, he does it out of some store of reasons that wouldn't never cross the minds of most folks."

Elvis picked up the can, took another swig of beer, and poured the rest onto the landing, the yellow foam flowing down the slanted pavement into the river. He dropped the empty can on the ground, flattened it with one of his bright black shoes, then kicked it into the mud beside the ferry ramp.

"What about Beam?" he asked.

Clem crumpled the sandpaper in his fist. "He ain't here right now."

"Where's he gone off to?"

"Couldn't tell you." Clem shook his head. "Beam is nineteen and full of bull piss. You know how they are at that age. They just want to go every chance they get."

Elvis knew most young men were of the type Clem had described, restless and hungry for the night and the going and the wandering, searching out the fumes of girls and the smoky craze of wild life, but Beam had never struck him as this kind.

"Well, maybe he'll be back around here shortly. I'd appreciate you calling me when he shows up."

Clem took a long sip of his beer and stared at the sheriff. "What for?" he asked.

"I'd just like to talk to him. Paul's body was found just a few miles downstream from here. I thought maybe Beam might've seen something strange one of these nights he was running the ferry."

"I'll call you if he turns up."

Without another word, Elvis turned and walked back to the cruiser. Once seated behind the wheel, he picked his black revolver off the passenger seat and shucked it into the holster on his hip. He then took his hat off and laid it on the car's center console. Cranking the engine, he drove up the landing ramp and passed out of the bottoms, the river winking brightly in his rearview mirror until the dust rose behind him to veil it away.

Elvis parked in front of the courthouse. He sat in his cruiser for a time, wondering if the ladies at the front desk would be able to smell the beer on his breath. Then he wondered at Clem drinking so early in the day. The man had looked worried. And then there was the ferry, which he claimed to have run aground because of a stuck throttle. Maybe that was the truth, but Elvis had his doubts.

He searched through his glove box for a roll of Certs or a stick of Doublemint, but there was none, so he exited the cruiser and walked up the granite steps of the courthouse, breathing into a cupped hand. Walking with his head down, Elvis didn't see the man dressed in the navy blue suit astraddle the defunct artillery gun on the courthouse lawn.

"Hot morning, ain't it?" the man said. He dismounted the gun and walked across the grass, then up the steps.

"It is a hot one," Elvis responded, looking the man over. His long yellow hair hung over his shoulders in loose damp strands, and the blazer he wore was smudged and dirty. Elvis caught a whiff of him; he smelled foul, as though he had been sleeping out of doors of late. "Can I help you?"

The man put his hands into his pockets and crossed his feet. "I need a spell of talk with you," he said, smiling.

"Well, that might can be arranged. Come on in here and make an appointment with one of the secretaries." Elvis moved to ascend the steps into the courthouse, but stopped when he realized the man wasn't following him. "You coming inside?"

"Now see, I just don't make appointments," the man answered. His smile broadened and he swayed a bit lazily on his feet.

"I do," said Elvis. "That's the only way you get a spell of talk with me."

The man shook his head. "What I have to say needs no appointing. I have information on a certain person of interest. A young man who's gone missing. Goes by the name Beam Sheetmire."

A wind ghosted out of the alleyway across the street and ruffled the lapels of the man's suit and charmed the hair up about his head.

"I didn't know Beam was missing," Elvis said.

"He is." The man nodded. "Missing and lost."

Elvis ran a thumb along his belt. "Then I guess you'd better come inside," he said.

"I guess I better had."

Elvis straightened a few files on his desk and placed a rusted muskrat trap he used for a paperweight on top of them. Then he turned on an oscillating table fan, which fluttered pendular and sadly disaffirming, throwing a warm draft through the room that smelled of underarm and evergreen air freshener.

The man in the suit took a chair in front of the desk. Elvis remained standing, leaning against a filing cabinet. The man claimed his name was Browning, but Elvis figured this a lie. He'd learned long ago that most things people told him in this office were lies.

"Now see, Beam was over at Daryl's bar yesterday afternoon," the man began. "I know because I gave him a ride there. Picked him up on the side of the Natcher Road. He changed the tire on my rig, so I give him a ride. I thought we were being real chummy, but once we got to Daryl's, I had to beat him with my boot."

"Why did you do that?"

"He come at me." The man slung the hair from his face and grinned. "Claimed I'd took some money from him, but that weren't the case. He sure thought it was the case, though. That's why he come at me and why I had to beat him with my boot. I guess I would've killed him if Daryl hadn't stopped me. Once he got a good look at Beam he claimed he knew him and that this other fellow, man named Loat Duncan, knew him, too. And I guess they were all some mad at Beam for one reason or another and likely would have killed him themselves if this old coot with a shotgun hadn't come in."

"And what did this old man with the shotgun do?"

The man's head rolled between his shoulders as if he were fighting off a fit of laughter. "Why, he plucked that Beam child off the floor and led him away into the world."

Elvis stroked the edge of the filing cabinet. Despite the fan, a steady heat had risen in the office, and he felt the sweat dribbling down his ribs and into his pants. "And you didn't know this man with the shotgun?" he asked.

The man shook his head. "Now see, I'm strange to this country and only passing through. Don't know anyone. But I heard Daryl call him Pete Daugherty. All I can say beyond that is he was some peculiar."

"How so?"

"Well, it's some strange for a man that age to come and rescue a boy he doesn't know." The man leaned forward and stared up at the sheriff from beneath his eyebrows. "Don't you think?"

Elvis took a handkerchief from his pocket. "What is odd is a man coming to me, a man I've never set eyes on before and who is wearing a suit telling me these things," he said. "That's what I think is peculiar." He opened the filing cabinet and took out a small spritzer bottle of water and sprayed his handkerchief and then daubed it over his hands and the back of his neck.

"That's just what I know," the man said. "Take it for what it is worth to you."

Elvis sat the spritzer bottle back in the cabinet and then leaned against the corner of his desk. "Why are you telling me this?" he asked. "There's no reward."

A sheepish grin of joy crossed the man's face. "Say, Sheriff. A citizen has to be concerned, don't he? If you got folks walking around not caring about the law, well, you don't really have citizens, do you?"

"You care about the law?"

"I do."

"I don't believe you, Mr. *Browning*. I think there's some other reason you're here telling these things to me right now and I don't think it has anything to do with the law."

The man swiveled in his chair, which made a rusty squeak beneath him. His eyes went narrow. "Maybe not your law," he said.

"How's that?"

"You might find it hard to believe, but there's an order out of your reach. You don't figure in with it. Stand next to that law and you'd be as small as a speck of dirt under my fingernail."

"What are you talking about?"

"I'm talking about the way you can maintain what you've got here." The man waved his hand through the air. "Your little office. Your desk. Your cap pistol. You can keep all that and trickle on down to retirement and be all right. But you have to stand out of the way of the bigger rule."

Elvis leaned over his desk. "I don't understand anything you're telling me right now," he said. "Now, what you told me about Beam might be true. At least some of it. But I don't like you. I think you should know that. I don't like the things you say and I don't like the way you're sitting in my chair. I don't like the way you smell and I don't like the fact that you're wearing a suit. It makes me nervous and I don't never like to be nervous."

"Well, what are you going to do about it, sheriff?" the man asked.

Elvis opened a desk drawer and took out a form and slapped it down. He began penning something down on the paper. "I'm going to arrest you."

"Oh?" the man said, expectantly. "And what are you going to charge me with?"

"Misuse of public property." Elvis pointed out the window with his pen. "That gun you were sitting on out there is a World War I monument, not a park bench. I'll charge you with vagrancy too unless you can provide a valid address." Elvis bent his head down and continued filling out the form. "What do you think about that?"

Only the squeak of the chair answered.

Elvis lifted his eyes. The man had disappeared.

Elvis dropped his pen and drew his revolver and ran to the doorway, but the hall was only glistening tile. He rushed down the empty corridor, past the shocked covey of secretaries at the front desk and out the door and onto the courthouse lawn, looking everywhere for the man who called himself Browning, but he was gone. As if he never had been. A few cigarette butts and Styrofoam cups blew over the pavement. That was all.

# XII

## FRIDAY

Clem sat at the kitchen table paring bits of tar from beneath his fingernails with a hawkbill knife. He didn't stop when Derna walked through the back door, her shoes sighing crisply over the unswept linoleum, her form shifting through the window light to flick an ashy scatter of shadow over him as she pulled a chair out for herself and sat down. She placed her purse on the table top and folded her hands in her lap, and yet he still continued working the knife under his fingernails, drawing the blade beneath them carefully and then rubbing it clean on his Wranglers.

"I want to know why you sent Beam off the way you did," she said, suddenly.

Clem's knife went on, his eyes steady on his work. "And I want to know where it is you been going in my truck these past couple days," he said.

The cords of Derna's throat tightened and she swallowed. "I've been looking for him," she said.

Clem finished with the knife and raked a few dried crumbs of tar from the table into the floor. He looked at Derna. "Ain't had no luck, have you?"

"Where is he?"

"I don't know."

"Yes you do."

"No. I don't. I only sent him off. I didn't give him no directions other than to get away from here."

Derna placed her hands on the table, pressing her fingertips into the bright Formica until her knuckles whitened. "Why would you do such a thing?"

Clem leaned toward her. "Out on the river," he said. "He killed Paul. He didn't know who he was, but he did it and that's why I sent him off."

Derna felt the room flow away from her as if she'd suddenly dropped through a trap in the floor.

"Paul tried to take the till and Beam hit him with a wrench and killed him," said Clem. "So I give him a change of clothes and showed him the highway. It was the best thing I knew to do. It didn't matter if it was self-defense because Loat will still be looking to kill him."

Derna shook her head. "You're lying," she said.

"No, Derna. I ain't."

"No. There's no reason why Paul would be at the ferry."

Clem sighed and drew a hand over the tabletop. "I don't know why it come to happen. I don't know why or how anything ever came to happen in life. But I'm telling you the truth. Paul showed up to the ferry and Beam killed him."

Derna stood up and walked over to the kitchen sink. She looked out the window at the locust trees along the river as they trembled in the wind, the muddy water below them raked and riffled by the breeze.

"He didn't know who he was," said Clem. "Beam didn't know it was Paul he'd killed and I didn't tell him. I think the whole thing was just a bad accident. I don't know if that helps or not, but that's the way it happened."

"You shouldn't have sent Beam away," Derna said.

"I wanted to help him. It's the one thing I could do that might."

"If you'd wanted to help him, you should have sent him away years ago."

"You don't need to say that, Derna."

"No, but I do say it and you shouldn't be surprised." She turned quickly from the window, a black streak of hair leaping across her forehead so she appeared as a consecrated penitent. "My oldest is dead and you tell me you've sent my youngest off for killing him. You think I'm just going to sit back and keep all the blame for myself? I can't do that. I won't do that."

Clem's eyes tightened. "You're riding me," he snarled, whipping a hand through the air.

"I want you to go find him," she implored.

"Beam's not even mine. Mine ain't never drawed breath one in this world. But you want me to go out and stick my neck on the chopping block for him. Ain't that pretty?"

Derna stared sharply at Clem, who sat hunched over the table, taking long heavy gusts of breath.

"Shit," he finally said after a few moments, raking his chair back suddenly from the table. "Go out and find him? That's what you want me to do?"

Derna nodded.

"If Loat don't kill him, they'll put him in prison," said Clem.

"Not forever. Not if it's like you really say. Not if it was all just a bad accident. He'll get out if that's true."

Clem said nothing, gazing off into the white haze of the room. He felt diminished, his form reduced to the mere jack-scrabble of denim and hearsay, a rumor of a man who had loved a woman with all the sad implacable wrong of his heart, who had loved her even though she had been a whore and had borne the children of other men.

When he put his eyes on her again, she saw his great vault of sorrow, and knew he would do what she asked.

"Go out and find him, Clem," she said. "He's your boy as much as he is mine. He never belonged to nobody but me and you."

Clem stood up quickly, the chair clattering to the floor behind him, and went over to Derna. She put her arms around his neck and felt the stumble of his heart through the faded work shirt he wore, and smelled the dirt and mud and sweat on him. It seemed as if his very scent, his aroma of harshness and hard living, was what she had clung to all these years rather than the man.

"I shouldn't have sent him off like I done," he said, his voice nearly a shudder.

"No." She stroked the back of his neck. "But you can go get him now. You can go get him and make it all right."

He bent and rested his head against her cheek. "We should have told him," he said. "We should have told him he had a brother."

Derna took Clem by the arm and led him to the table where she sat him down carefully, the tremble of his fingers in her own like the quiver of a startled bird. She went to cabinet and took down a bottle of Wayfaring Stranger and poured him three fingers in a coffee cup. He drank it down and his cheeks reddened as if he'd been a long time lost in the cold.

Derna stood by his Clem's side and thought of her children, Beam and Paul, the one she had clung to, and the other that she had surrendered out of fear. She remembered Paul being wrinkled and knobby as an old sweet potato when she took him to her breast, and now he was gone and she felt his loss squirming in the crook of her arm, nuzzling her flesh until it seemed like the very clutch and flutter of her own heart.

He'd been only two years old when she left Loat. "You can leave if you want," Loat had told her. "But you're not taking this boy." He sat in the glazed wooden dark of his house, holding Paul in his lap, the boy suckling a piece of horehound candy and watching Derna where she stood quiet in the lit frame of the door. She held her traveling bag and the day blew cool against her legs that were bare below her skirt hem.

"I can't go without him," she said.

Loat shook his head. He drew a knife out of his pocket, unclasped it with his teeth and laid the blue iron blade against Paul's cheek.

"How about I cut one of his eyes out," he said. "Would you

still want him then?"

Derna stood silent.

"Or maybe his tongue." Loat yanked the child's mouth open and held the knife against his lips until he began crying, brown dribbles of horehound candy slipping down his chin. "He couldn't talk to bother you then. Maybe you'd like him better that way." His great joy would've been to slice the boy up into tiny pieces and feed him to the catfish in the river. She saw that now, remembering that day from so long ago. And she'd left. Maybe more to save herself than the boy. Or to at least spare herself the sight of what Loat would turn the boy into. She couldn't say for certain.

Clem turned the coffee cup in his hands. "I'll go find Beam," he said, standing slowly. "I guess that's what all is left for me to do."

He took the truck keys from their hook beside the door and jostled them like a pair of throwing dice. His eyes were wild now, and Derna stood backed against the counter again, looking off absently into nowhere, her bare feet scratching against the linoleum.

"You don't have to worry," said Clem, opening the door. "I'll go get him back again."

And then he left.

Derna heard Old Dog moan to life out in the yard, the tires scooting through the gravel as Clem reached the river road and then the noise shrank away to a low whine and then nothing and she was alone in the hot kitchen.

After a spell, she turned to the window that showed the lawn and the landing running down to the slow brown river that looked thick and almost like rubber in the heat of the day. Beyond it, the flats spread out to a rise of black hills flung against the sky like blood, and some deep part of her knew that they were old hills there, older than all the small struggling life that lived in them, or had ever lived in them, the land itself ancient beyond all measure and remote beyond all reckoning.

# XIII

## FRIDAY

Beam hadn't realized how hungry he was until he began to eat a
can of Vienna sausages that Pete gave him. He quickly finished
all of the salty links, chasing them down with lukewarm water
from the milk jug. When he was done, he poured some of the
water over his head, scrubbing away at his matted hair, peeling
the dried flecks of blood and buzzard sick from his scalp.

Pete sat against the elm log eating slowly at his own can
of sausages. When he was finished, he tipped the can back and
drank the vinegar and wiped his chin, then sat the can carefully
in the grass beside the one Beam had thrown away.

The day was grimy hot. Yellow jackets hovered and trembled
beside the empty sausage tins. The sunlight hummed. Off in the
graveyard, grasshoppers and snake doctors fluttered. Blackbirds
scattered over the sky like tossed soil. Pete and Beam sat sweating
beside the fire that had deadened during the night, a thin blade of
smoke rising lazy and scant from the charred wood.

Beam drank from the milk jug again, poured the last of the
water over his hands and ground them together, then dried them
against his jeans. His head felt better now and he was certain that
none of his ribs were broken.

"I need to be getting on," he said.

"Where to?" Pete asked.

"I don't know." Beam gave a little shrug. "I just need to go."

Pete chuckled and shook his head. "Not a cent to your name
and there's a good number in this land that want to do you harm
and you aim to leave?"

Beam lifted himself off the tarpaulin and stretched his back and legs, feeling the blood rush back to place. Stiffness settled on him like a yoke, but he knew he could walk it out.

"You better not go," Pete said. He tilted his head back and shut his eyes against the sun falling through the cedars.

"What else I got to do?" Beam asked. "Sit around a graveyard and wait for them to come bury me?" He began to pace around the campsite, stamping restless through the grass. He was glad Pete had helped him—he'd likely be dead if he hadn't—but he also felt a bit riled that he was now beholden to the old man. For most of his short life, he'd worked at keeping his ties loose. Once a man began to gather obligations, things became cluttered, and he wound up staring at the walls of a prison built by his own hand.

"Well, go on, then." Pete answered. "I ain't your mother and I'm not gonna try and stop you."

Beam looked down at Pete, his gray whiskered throat damp with sweat, his cheeks reddening with sun. Then he looked at the graveyard. A narrow lane of shallow pea gravel, its berm choked with smartweed and sorrel, curved off through the stones.

"Highway out that way?"

"It is." Pete waved a hand at the weedy road leading away from the graves.

"Well, I'm gone."

"There's your way," Pete said.

Beam nodded and began walking, kicking up tiny puffs of dust. He hadn't gone twenty yards when he heard the chuggle of an engine crawling up the road.

"Somebody's coming," he said.

Pete struggled up, dusting his lap free of sausage crumbs. "Sounds like they are."

"We got to hide! They're coming right now," Beam exclaimed. But there was nowhere to run—the country surrounding him offered no quarter and he could only squirm by the dead campfire, waiting for the car to come up the lane.

It was a long primered LTD, its muffler fussing, the gravel knocking against its fenderwells. The car's vinyl roof was peeling and the windshield was smeared with bird shit and bugs. Behind the wheel sat a woman. She drove the car up the lane and parked beside Pete's truck. When she stepped out, Beam saw that she was older, but still firm in her flesh, her clean white thighs descending from the cutoff denims she wore, her faded blonde hair tied behind her neck in a sharp neat ponytail. She wore sunglasses and sneakers. A cigarette burned between her long pale fingers.

She stopped a few feet from the campsite, took a last draw from her cigarette, and flung it into the weeds. Her lips were unpainted and thin.

"I saw it plain this morning that it was up to me to find you," she said to Pete. "Don't you ever think to pick up a telephone?"

Pete spat into the dirt and toed the spot with his boot. "Why waste a quarter? I knew you'd figure it out."

"Not before I had a healthy dose of worrying." She rocked her head toward Beam. "Who is this you've taken up with?"

"That's Beam Sheetmire," Pete said.

"The one runs the ferry on the Gasping?"

"That'd be him."

The woman looked at Beam. "You sure ought to be sorry then," she said to him.

"Why's that?"

"Anybody would have to be sorry to run around with the likes of this old man. He's liable to make you just as sorry as you want to get."

"Don't listen to her," Pete said, smiling at Beam.

"What kind of trouble have y'all found that you've got to lay out here in this boneyard?" the woman asked.

Pete scrubbed his jaw whiskers. "Got in a little scrape over at Daryl's. Things got a might hairy so I thought it best to hide away for a time."

"Christ Jesus." The woman shook her head.

"Beam," Pete said. "This is my daughter, Ella."

"Hell, don't tell him my name," the woman said. "I don't want him to know me."

"He's all right." Pete waved a hand at Beam. "Other than being young without hardly no brains squirming in his head, he's pretty good. Takes a beating right well."

Pete and Ella laughed together.

Beam looked at the car. The keys were still in the ignition, and he thought of jumping in and driving away from this place with its slouching graves and slick heat, beating a path to other towns where no one knew him well enough to laugh at the things he'd done.

"Drove by your house this morning," Ella said.

Pete bent and picked a piece of gravel from the ground and juggled it between his brown palms. "How'd it look?"

"Same as ever. Likely to fall in with the first hard wind. Anyway, it's still there, if that's what you're asking."

Pete took his cap off and smoothed the damp loose strands of hair back over his scalp.

"I figured them to burn me out."

"Really? You must of put on a real show then if you've pissed Daryl off that much." Ella crossed her arms over her breasts. "What do you want to do?"

Pete sniffed the air, which smelled of gasoline and warm vinyl. "Best get on back to the homeplace, I'd say. Maybe they don't want this boy bad enough to come looking for me. Least we can go there for a night. Resupply. Head out in the morning if we got to." He turned and began packing up his possibles, the cans and jugs clattering together. He slung the pack over his shoulder, scraped the campfire with a cedar limb, raking the embers cold, and then started walking toward his truck.

"You sure you want to go back home?" Ella asked. "Might not be a good idea."

"Just follow me on down," Pete said over his shoulder. "What can they do to us?"

"Oh, I don't know." Ella shrugged. "Shoot us and throw us down a mineshaft, maybe. Cut us into little pieces and feed us to a bunch of hogs. Burn us alive. You want me to go on?"

Pete gawked at her. "How the hell you think of this stuff?"

"I watch the news."

When he reached his truck, Pete opened the door, slung his pack in and sat down. "Well, I don't look for it to be too awful bad," he said out the window. "Besides, Loat thinks I'm touched so he'll leave me alone."

"What about Beam, here?" she asked. "Is he coming with us?"

Pete shook his head. "Naw, he ain't coming," he said. "Claims he's fed up with this country. Wants to hit the road and take off for Hey-Hirah."

Ella shook her head. "Well, if that's the case I say leave him to it." She walked back to her car and settled herself behind the wheel.

Beam watched all of this with a kind of frozen amazement. Were they really going to leave him here, in this ragged spot where the trees loomed sepulchral and cryptic, where the dark came slithering out at night and where light was hard to come by during the day?

"Hold it," he shouted. "Y'all ain't just going to leave me here, are you?"

Pete slapped the truck's steering wheel. "Hell, Beam, I thought you were putting out for sea, way you talked."

Beam gnawed at his finger. "No," he said. "I don't want that."

"Leave him here," said Ella. "Maybe if he sulks out here with the buzzards for awhile, he'll learn how to act."

Pete looked out at Beam, standing beside the mute campfire. He cranked his truck and the engine prowled beneath the hood. He waved a hand.

"I ain't gonna whistle for you like a dog," he said. "If you're riding, get in."

Beam hurried to the truck, glancing at Ella idling in her LTD. The look she gave him was fierce and ironhot.

Once the truck reached the highway, the world became walled off by thin elms and poplar trees. Beam rode in quiet, waiting to come to the next place he would have to leave.

# XIV

# FRIDAY

In the late of the afternoon, Loat fished himself from a strange bed and sat on the mattress staring at his feet, white as streaks of paint on the walnut floorboards. The whisky he'd drunk the night before boiled up into his throat raw and scorching, and he swallowed it down again. Beside him, the girl rolled onto her stomach. Her snoring quickened sharp and brittle, and a pair of flies crawled through the peroxide blonde tangles of her hair sprawled across the pillows. Lifting the sheet, Loat stared at the teeth marks he'd left on her buttocks, red and threaded like the seams of a baseball, and he shook his head and laughed quietly.

But when he thought of Derna, the laughter died out of him. He recollected her browned wavy flesh, the slight pout of her belly, her eyes staring over his shoulder as he bent between her thighs, and something about the hiss of her breath drying the sweat on his skin while he rode her down into the sour mattress made his heart tremble wickery and frail. She'd brought several ghosts with her when she'd visited his house, and now they stood at his back in a crowd.

Breathing deep, Loat caught the stink of the room, like the inside of a dry cistern, rusty and tarnished. He coughed into his hand and strode naked across the room to the dresser against the wall where a fifth of Lord Calvert sat. He took a long drink and shook the burn away. Beside the bed was a small porcelain wash bowl full of water, which he dipped his cock into, the first cold shock making him shiver before he let the piss go. The water glowed golden before him, a drop of blood clinging to the brim of the basin. Suddenly, a sharp pain cut through the small of his back, and he had to steady himself against the dresser until it passed.

Shaking himself dry, Loat found his pants and shirt on the floor and dressed himself slowly in the drear light of the room. His Remington .45 lay on the dresser. He flipped the cylinder open, checked the cartridges glinting in their chambers, then snapped the cylinder home and stuffed the gun into the elastic of his Hanes, the barrel cold against his groin.

His boots slouched by the door. He struggled into them without sitting or retying, stamping his legs deep into the soft mealy leather, rocking a wild shadow out onto the wall greased with sunlight leaking through the curtained window. His straw hat hung on a bedpost. Lifting it up, he stroked the brim clockwise, a morning ritual taught to him by a dimly remembered uncle as a way to ward off thoughts of death. His fingers whispered over the straw and he circled the brim twelve times, a half-day's revolution, massaging out the grim dreams that might assail him.

He settled the hat over his head carefully, watching the tilt of it in the dresser mirror. He'd long been a studier of signs, a watcher of skies. All his family seemed touched by such gifts. His father, a man dark and thin as a riding crop, had been the one to tell him the way of careful eyes. When he was a boy, Loat had stood on a ridge of black trees in a dawn broken gray and cold as the old man had pointed out the tremble of ants, the quiver of pine needles, the catch of a note in a warbler's throat, and announced that it was all the melody of the future, that what was to be could be foretold and even changed if one knew how to cipher the song. "These are the ancient tones," he said. "You learn them like you know your own name." And Loat had, through years of the old man bursting into his room in the night, drunk and angry, roughing him from sleep and yanking him into the kitchen to read a scattering of eggshells, to prod and dig through a cup of wormy earth, to tongue the pith of a turnip and say what the taste meant.

His father lost his eyes for ciphering in later years, or so he said. The woman gone—where to? who could say?—and his life a flume washing him into the gullet of death, one day he needed Loat to study a tapeworm the dog had vomited up, to say what its writhings were—rain? flood? ruin?—to make the day yet born to stand shivery and wobble-kneed before him. "What's it say? Read it, boy!" The old man shouted, pushing Loat's nose toward the slick, bisected worm as it twisted and suppurated on the walnut tabletop. "What's to come? What's the worm say?" Loat tried to read the sway and shiver of it, but his eyes were bleary from sleep and his father was shouting and he couldn't say for certain what anything meant at such a dead hour.

"I don't know," he finally stammered. "I can't read it."

The old man let him up. He stood back and his eyes jerked with nervy light. "Then you'll eat it," he said, taking the pieces of worm from the table and clamping Loat by the hair and yanking his head back to force his mouth open.

Loat clutched his belly and thought of the worm. He wondered if it yet spiraled in his innards. Times came and he felt he could see to the very end, actually reach out and graze the downy cheek of the future. But those were days of rarity. Mostly, he wondered at how he'd lost his ciphering eye just as his father had, and if blindness was not a congenital failing of his blood.

He took the bottle of Calvert from the dresser. It dangled from his hand like a dead fowl, the liquor sloshing inside. When he opened the door, his best hound was there, the one he alone tended to. It lifted its head from its paws and in the crystalline dark of the hall its eyes glowed like ironlode.

"Enoch," he said. The dog stood, wagging its tail nub. "Let's walk."

The two of then went down the hall. Loat kept close to the

wall, letting his free hand drag over the peeling oilpaper while the dog trotted behind like a vague canine ghost, ashy and gray in the shadows, until they emerged into the light of the bar. Suddenly, everywhere was the clink of glasses, the chisel of talk, the light through the windows withering down over the floor into the long jots of dust and gravel that had been tracked in from the parking lot. The jukebox played something nervous and stricken.

Loat sat down at the bar with his bottle. The tender stood at the other end using a butter knife to prize gold fillings out of the teeth from the jar, scooping out handfuls of them and scattering them on the bar panel. When he looked up and saw Loat, he took a shot glass down from a shelf and brought it to him, then went back to his paring.

Loat poured himself a shot of Calvert and sipped, petting the dog beside him, running his hand under its collar while the whisky flamed beneath his ribs. In the mirror, he studied the patrons. Mostly folks he knew, scabrous farmers and coal miners milling about like forms hacked out of shadows. An outcropping of the vagabonded and derelict.

He tapped his glass against the bar and the tender came down to him.

"Got something for Enoch?" Loat asked.

The tender, a large man with a face fat and yellow as wax, nodded. He lifted up a metal gallon bucket of pickled eggs and sat it on the bar. Loat took two out, flung the brine off, and fed them to the dog, the greenish yolks crumbling onto the floor. The tender smiled and sat the bucket back behind the bar and returned to working the teeth.

Loat turned to regard the crowd. Daryl, clearly drunk, sat on the bed on stage with the goat, its head resting in his lap. The suit-wearing trucker sat in a chair against the wall drinking a bottle of Falstaff. Tilting his head to catch a view of the cage of rafters above, the previous night came back to Loat, crawling up like a black spider from a sink drain. After Derna had left him, he'd received the call about Beam being here at the bar, but when he'd arrived the boy was gone. He spent most of the night looking for him. First to Pete Daugherty's shack, but the place stood blank and lightless, the windows showing only the old man's clutter, racks of magazines slouching on the floor and rungs of peppers hanging from the ceiling joists to dry. Then it was into Drakesboro, barreling full horse, coasting motel parking lots looking for Pete's truck, but they had found nothing. Asking questions at the movie house, the restaurant and diesel station out on the parkway, but all the waitresses and vendors seemed beleaguered with ignorance, their jaws slack as they yanked popcorn from their hair or lit cigarettes under the dull marquee lights. Presto had gone back with the dogs to wait in the woods behind Pete's shack, and that's where he was now, but Loat knew it was a gamble that the old man would return anytime soon. He could lie out in the high weeds for weeks, living off creek water and grub worms, and as long as Beam stayed with him, he could do the same. Then just as suddenly, the two might be spotted in town drinking milkshakes at The Dairy Queen. It was that inconsistency, that inability to predict the old man's next move, that made him so hard to track. Loat didn't know if it was cunning or simple luck, but Pete had a way of shifting and shaping himself to fit any crack in the earth, sliding in quietly as water. The man was a wood witch, a healer. Loat had always kept his distance because of this, but when the sickness struck, he went to Pete for a fix because he was known to trade in such, but the healing didn't take and now Loat fumed with hatred toward the old man and his quack medicine. And, to top it off, he'd commandeered Beam, pushing himself into business not his own. Whatever magic Pete might possess, Loat would make him use it.

He turned back to his whisky. In the mirror, he watched Daryl cross the floor to the bar and come up beside him.

"How'd Freda treat you?" he asked, swinging himself down onto a stool. The tender sat a bottle of Jax in front of him with a straw.

"She's got an old blowed out pussy." Loat shook his head slowly and sipped his Calvert. "But I guess I can't complain about what comes free."

Daryl smiled. "There are other girls not quite so broke in. You know you're the one picked Freda."

"I'm aware."

"But then, maybe your mind is somewheres else." Daryl leaned into his straw. "Maybe you're thinking about somebody else."

Loat dipped a finger into his whisky and sucked it dry. "I don't think about women," he said.

"You don't?"

"I never understood men that thought too much about them. Women are like freight trains. Every ten minutes another one comes down the line." He raised his glass and clinked it against Daryl's beer. "Freight trains," he said, throwing the rest of the shot back.

"What have the doctors told to you?" Daryl asked.

Loat turned the shot glass upside down and rested his hand on it. "A year," he said. "That's how long I go without something gets done. It's in the early stages so I can still fuck. I just can't hardly piss and my blood is getting bad. They wanted to put me on that dialysis, but I told them to kiss my ass."

Daryl suckled his beer. "It had to have been Beam that killed him," he said after a spell. "After what Derna told you about Beam being the one to wreck the ferry and Paul winding up drowned like that, there's no way it could've have been anybody but Beam."

Loat folded his hands and propped his chin on his knuckles. "I know that."

"But you can't figure out why, can you?"

"I'm not trying to figure on the why of it. What I care about is finding him. He's put me to death, killing Paul. I aim to do the same for him." Loat turned on his stool and looked out across the floor. A few couples were dancing, the women smearing their makeup on their men's shirtsleeves while the music brayed. Against the far wall, the trucker in the suit leaned in his chair. A beer bottle poked from his breast pocket. His hair drooped oiled and sloppy into his eyes. "That trucker there is making himself at home, ain't he?"

Daryl watched the mirror. "Claims he wants to dress you," he said.

"Dress me?"

"In a suit. Thinks he's some kind of tailor. Got a load of fancy clothes in his rig. Says you're the kind of man that needs sharpening with slacks and a blazer."

Loat poured another shot and drank it down quickly. "Only man I'll ever let dress me is the undertaker."

"I've told him as much."

Loat placed the empty shot glass on top of the bottle of Lord Calvert. Then he stood and stretched himself, the blear of the whisky making the room tilt and sway.

"Know what else he claims?"

Loat balanced himself with a hand on the bar.

"He claims," said Daryl, "that if we find a kidney, he can do the surgery. Calls himself a night doctor."

"Is that right?"

"Says he learned it in the service." He turned and looked at the trucker leaning in his chair, the bottle of Falstaff sprouting from his breast pocket like a boutonnière. "If he can do it, that'd save us trying to squeeze one of these county doctors. I know you don't trust doctors no way."

"What makes you think I'd trust some truck driver wearing a suit?"

"It's your general disposition."

"Is that so?"

Daryl licked his teeth. "You've not heard this feller talk on life and the wide straying ways of it. He's a silver tongue."

"That don't mean he's worth a damn as a sawbones."

"No. But he's your kind. Believe me."

Loat spread his hands out on the bar. "I'd have to see some evidence that he knows what the hell he's doing before I let him cut on me." He patted the wood, his nails scratching the varnish. "I don't think he can do that."

Daryl shrugged. "You get your back to the wall, you might be about ready to try anything."

"I ain't even thinking on getting a kidney now."

"On account of Paul getting killed?"

"It has to come from blood," Loat said. "When Paul turned up dead I knew that was it. It don't matter now what kind of dirt I've got on any of these county doctors because Paul was it, he was bringing it to me, carrying my life with him. No way in hell I'm going to the county clinic to get on one of those fucking waitlists like every other cocksucker that's dying and get some piece off a somebody I don't even know. Hell, they might even give me a nigger kidney."

Daryl giggled, his squat form jouncing on the bar stool. "It's got to come from blood? What the fuck does that mean?"

"It's what I believe."

"What you believe?"

Loat nodded. "Blood is the only thing you can count on." He straightened his hat in the bar mirror. "There ain't nothing else. Not where I'm coming from. It's blood or it's nothing. Money, women, land—none of that don't add up to anything close to righting a man or giving him what he needs."

"You sound like you been reading the Bible too much," Daryl said.

"What's the Bible? It's a book some crazy fool wrote because he was scared to death of dying. Of not being no more. What I'm talking about is older than the Bible. What I'm talking about will still be around when the Bible has been forgot and throwed away."

Loat took his hands from the bar and scraped them over his

cheeks, feeling the bones under his thinned flesh. Already, the sickness had pared him down, winding its blind path through his body, chiseling his days away. For most of his life, he'd simply accepted death as an eventual given, but now that its certainty stared him flush in the eye, he found himself checking the mirror more often, as if to gauge how much ground he was losing.

"What do you think Clem cares about any of this?" Daryl asked.

Loat looked away from the mirror. "Who knows," he said. "Clem's the one sent Beam off once he'd killed Paul, so you'd think he's got a spot in his heart for the little sonuvabitch. Almost have to after raising him like his own. Course, he could've been just looking out for his own ass. Why you ask?"

"No reason," Daryl grunted. "Just curious some."

Loat leaned in close and put his hand hard on the back of Daryl's neck. "You think on something else," he said softly. "I don't want nobody worrying about Clem. I know you been wanting to even the score since he rolled those bad dice out at the mines, but he don't matter right now. You think on getting Beam." He released Daryl's neck.

"You always keeping Clem safe," Daryl said, turning his head slightly to flex away the pain from Loat's grip had left. "Why is that?"

"I like to keep all my tools handy."

"I believe Clem is one that's worn out his use."

"Could be," Loat said. He turned and looked at the crowd in the mirror behind him, his eyes settling on the trucker, who sat propped against the wall in his chair, his greasy hair slung over his head. "I'll be damned if that sumbitch trucker don't look like Jerry Lee Lewis."

Daryl half turned on his stool and looked across the bar at the stranger in the tailored suit. The man's face was gaunt and famished, the lean cheeks and damp curls of his hair making him seem like a fop fallen on hard times. But his eyes seemed to burn as if something hellish cooked inside them, and a faint sneer rode his lips.

"By God, he does look like Jerry Lee, don't he," said Daryl, laughing.

"The Killer," said Loat, shaking his head. He laughed, then pushed himself away from the bar. "I need some air after hearing that Jerry Lee Lewis wants to be my tailor." He turned and strode outside, where the sun flared and raked over the white gravel lot.

He was standing beneath the door eaves in what shade they gave when Clem came walking up in the strong heat.

"I didn't look for you to come out this way," Loat said.

"I guess it ain't like me."

"Not usually. What finally brought you round?"

"I'm looking for Beam," Clem said. Loat noticed that his hands were trembling at his sides, and his eyes were squinty and bloodshot.

"Beam's not here," Loat answered. "Though you probably want me to take you inside and show you every room just so you know I'm telling the truth. I understand that, so I won't take it as an insult. You thinking I'm a liar, I mean." Loat picked absently at a thread on his pants. "But I don't believe you want to go in there."

"And why's that?"

Loat jerked his head at the double doors. "Daryl will have you laid out like a side of beef if you set foot inside."

"I don't give a shit. I come here to find Beam." Clem made to open the doors, but Loat stepped in front of him.

"I'm telling you something right now. If you go inside, there won't be enough left of you to spread on a piece of light bread. Go on back to Derna. She needs you more'n Beam does." Loat put his hand on Clem's shoulder and squeezed it softly. "Go home, Clem. You can't do no good out here."

Clem looked down at Loat's fingers lying on his shoulder, the flesh browned and scabbed, the nails yellowed and cracked as old teeth.

"I want to know something," he said, raising his eyes to meet Loat's. "I want to know why you gave me those bad dice to roll with Daryl out at the mines. I want to know why you're always protecting me."

Loat took his hand from Clem's shoulder, then flexed his jaw and spat. "I could ask why both you and Daryl were always so eager to do what I said."

"You'd have killed us if we did otherwise."

"That's likely so."

"Why give me those bad dice, then? Why even have us roll at all? Why do it that way when you could've just told Daryl to monkey up that power pole?"

The wind shuffled bits of trash over the parking lot, a few paper cups and beer bottles tinkling against the gravel.

"Then it'd be me he'd be looking to kill," Loat said. "Not you."

Clem's eyes squirmed like a pair of slugs doused with salt. "How do you know I ain't told Daryl about those dice? How you know I ain't told him everything?"

"You spook too easy, Clem. That's how I know. I could say boo right now and you'd scamper back to Derna." He placed his hand on Clem's shoulder again. "I don't have to worry about you breathing a word to Daryl because if that was going to happen it already would have by now. All that you're going to do is turn around and go home."

Clem stepped back, and Loat's hand fell from his shoulder. His eyes jumped a little, a cold light flaring in them, and his breath shortened as if he were on the verge of vomiting. "You're looking for Beam," he said.

"So are you," said Loat. "Which means what you told me the other night about Beam just being off tomcatting was a lie."

Clem slid his hand to his pocket, hooking a finger in his belt. Behind the Quonset hut doors, the noise of the bar scuffled, making a dull quiver like distant thunder.

"What do you want with Beam?" Clem asked. "He's never done anything to you."

Loat spat into the dust. "If he ain't done nothing to me, then there's nothing for him to worry about," he said. "Only, you and I both know that's not the way it is, is it? There wouldn't be a need for Beam to hide if he hadn't done something. Maybe what he's done is the worst thing he could do. That'd sure give a man reason to run for cover."

Clem's eyes widened. He took another step back from Loat, his boots scratching in the gravel lot. He seemed to be waiting, drawing the moment out, as if he thought it might come to an end other than the way he'd expected.

"Go home, Clem," Loat said. "There's nothing left for you here."

A warm breeze startled the grass in the ditches and turned up the white underneathes of the tree leaves. In the spread of fields across the road, dust coiled and spun in evanescent volutes and the air held a loud smell of rain.

Clem fixed his eyes on the ground and seemed almost about to leave when he suddenly shoved past Loat and opened the Quonset hut's two oaken doors and disappeared inside, the bar noise cutting sudden through the day like brash weather.

Loat stood there for a few seconds, then turned and went inside to the trouble that was beginning.

# XV

# FRIDAY

They followed the drive, a lane of washed out river rock, the ruts clotted with mud and gashes of ochre glaur, and then crossed a crude bridge where a brook needled away beneath sumac and elder trees. The house sat small beneath maples and pawpaws and a smell of damp and rotted wood lingered in the air. A rusted burnbarrel smoked grayly beside the porch, which was cluttered with several kinds of footwear: tromping boots and loafers of cracked leather, even a few pairs of women's slippers, all piled against the hickory railings. Squirrel hides dangled from nails driven into the porch's support posts. Beyond the house was a spread of outbuildings, all succumbing to varying degrees of ruin, and past their mired sprawl was the garden where corn and beans and volunteer cane grew in long green currents.

Pete parked the truck on a bare patch of dirt in the yard, and Ella pulled in beside him. "This is where I get my mail," he announced. He got out of the truck and walked to the porch. A curtain rod barred the way up the steps. A homemade sign dangling from its rings read, in black shoe polish, GONE INTO TOWN. Pete lifted the sign up and sat it carefully aside. "Come on in here and we'll see if we can't find us a cool drink of water," he said.

When they entered the musky house, Ella planted herself on a calico sofa beside the front door. She took an ashtray blown from green Coke glass off the television, sat it in her lap, and lit a cigarette. Beam remained beside the door. Down the hallway, he could see a woodstove and ricks of oak lined against a wall. Above this were nailhung hacksaws and come-alongs and singletrees. Through another door he spotted a wrinkled calendar for the year 1974 depending from a wire. It was all like some exhibit at a rustic museum

"Find a seat," Ella said, pointing to a dinette chair beside the television.

"I need to find a sink and wash up first," said Beam. "Do y'all have a bathroom?"

"First door on your left," said Ella.

Beam walked down the hallway, which spanned dim and unlighted. Framed and ancient photographs hung on the walls. A ringer washing machine crouched at the far end like a giant albino toad, its white metal streaked with rust. When he found the bathroom door, Beam yanked the pull-chain and the bare bulb drizzled a feeble urine-colored light over him. Cracked blue tiles lined the walls above the pale green tub, and the linoleum floor was peeling up. Brown water stains coated the unpapered sheetrock about the vanity, and the sink sat in a chinking of grout and spackle. A slice of glazed mirror hung above it.

Water that smelled vaguely of sulfur gushed and spat when he turned the tap. Beam took his shirt off and lathered himself with a bar of homemade soap from a dish on the vanity, scrubbing away the stink. He doused his hair and scrubbed his neck down and soaped his underarms and finally rinsed his mouth, the water burning his throat slightly.

When he returned to the living room, Pete and Ella were sitting together on the sofa, a trio of beers before them on the coffee table.

"These are lukewarm," Pete said, handing Beam a can. "My fridge don't get real cool this time of year. But they'll drink, I guess." He took up his own can and slurped some down.

Ella picked up a beer and took a sip. She crossed her legs and water dripped from the bottom of the can onto her knee. She stared at Beam with a look he couldn't place.

"What about those beans?" she asked. "I don't smell anything cooking."

"Right on," Pete said. He got up and retreated to the kitchen, Soon, the scuffle of pans and faucet water came clanging down the hallway. "I'll be for fixing them," he called out.

"No hurry," Ella yelled back. "We're only starving to death out here." She stared sharply at Beam, who quickly turned away from her blistering look to gaze at the clutter surrounding him: dingy framed photos and mounded clothing, a weatherbred trunk with split rope handles, three red buttons fallen like a blood spoor in the shag, curious oddments shorn and fragmentary in their corners.

"Why ain't you in school?" Ella asked.

"I'm too old," Beam answered, sitting down in the dinette chair beside the television.

"So you graduated then?"

Beam tipped his beer and drank a bit. "A year ago."

Ella leaned back into the sofa and recrossed her legs, dangling a sandal off her toe and rocking her foot slowly. "I've heard some things about that ferry you and your folks run. Don't know if any of it's true, but most of what I hear ain't too good." She took a long drink of beer. "Is any of it right?"

"Depends on what you've been told, I guess."

Ella ran a finger around the rim of her beer can. "I think maybe I had you pegged wrong," she said. "You looked just like some punk kid trying to get past a hangover when I drove up into the graveyard this morning. Now you're starting to look, I don't know…different."

"How's that?"

"I'm not sure."

She had a look of strangeness to her now, as if she'd suddenly happened upon something she'd previously overlooked. Beam let his eyes wander to the window behind her. He wasn't used to being looked at by women. At The Doe Eyed Lady, he occasionally flirted with a few of the waitresses and sometimes made his way to the backseat of a car in the parking lot for a quick grab and stab of fucking, but most of his sexual past was a forgettable assortment of the usual fare of bubblegum girls.

"What will you do?" Ella asked.

"Do?"

"With yourself."

"I don't know. Maybe I can go home after a while. Maybe they'll let me do that." He downed the rest of his beer.

"Who's they?"

"The folks after me."

Ella pursed her lips. "If they let you go home, then what? Are you just going to ride it out on the ferry like before?"

"I don't see why not."

Ella pulled a cigarette from a pack and lit it. The smoke bowered thick and white and then trailed off into the other rooms of the house. "I want to know what kind of trouble you and Dad got into over at Daryl's. You need to tell me because he won't."

"It was just trouble," Beam said.

"No." Ella shook her head slowly. "It wasn't just trouble. Not if he had to hide you up there in that cemetery. He only goes there if things get bad."

Beam tightened his jaw. He didn't want to speak, and didn't know if he could.

"Tell me," Ella implored, pinching the cigarette out in the ashtray.

"This fella took my money," Beam said. "I tried to get it back and he beat me pretty bad. Your dad saved me."

Ella shook her head again. A strand of hair clung to the sweat on her brow. Like a fracture in porcelain. "There's more," she said. "I know there is. Why aren't you telling me all of it? It can't be that bad."

"It can."

"Listen," Ella said. "Whatever you've done or had done to

you, it ain't nothing so bad that you got to act proud around me."
She moved to the edge of the sofa. Beam thought she was going
to touch him then and he stiffened, but her hand never came.
"I'm old enough and have seen enough where nothing don't
shock me no more. So you go on and tell it. That's my daddy in
there. He won't tell me because I'm his little girl and I'm all he's
got so he thinks he's got to keep me safe. But I need to know
what he's gotten himself wound up in. I've got to make sure that
I'm keeping him safe."

Beam leaned back in the dinette chair. The aluminum legs
creaked beneath him. It seemed odd to think of a woman keeping
anyone safe. He'd never considered such a thing possible. But
then he thought of his mother, going through her duties without
a word, and he wondered if all of that was a way of sheltering
everything she loved.

"I did something awful," Beam said. "You ever done anything
awful?"

"I have."

"Well, I bet you never done nothing near as bad as what I
did." Beam wiped absently at his lap, though it seemed like the
dirt was fastened there and he couldn't clear it away.

Ella's eyes lay blue and cool upon him. "A woman can get in
as much trouble as any man. Maybe more. We can get in more
trouble because we're not allowed to be in trouble. So when it
finds us, it's worse."

"What's all this talk I'm hearing about trouble?" Pete called
out as he entered the room bearing a pot with cotton holders. He
sat the pot on the coffee table and lifted the lid, letting the steamy
smell of hog jowl and beans boil out. "Can't be no trouble when
you got beans like that," he said, waving one of the holders over
the pot. He went back to the kitchen and returned with bowls,
spoons, more beer, and a sack of Wonderbread. He ladled out the
beans, thick in their sauce, and the three of them set to eating.

It was some time before any of them had the energy to

speak again. They seemed to have come to the end of a large and ponderous labor, and sat there in a numb and jolly silence. Beam was the first one to speak. He'd been studying a ring of small slender bones hanging on the wall above the television and his curiosity brought him slowly out of the fog of eating.

"What are those?" he asked, pointing at the bones.

"Those," Pete grunted, rising to pull the ring from its keeper nail, "are coon dicks."

"Pardon?"

Pete shook the bones and handed them to Beam. "Coon dicks," he said. "Coon has a bone in his peter. They're good for luck."

Beam ran his fingers through the bones as if drawing his hand over a lacey fringe. They had a faint tinge of brown age, and bits of hide clung to them.

"Take you one off there." Pete reached and jostled the ring. "You might need it."

"No," said Beam. "I don't think I do." But he continued to hold the bones in his hand, and after a moment, he unhinged the hasp holding the ring together and unstrung one, slipping it into the pocket of his jeans.

"Maybe it'll bring you a spell of fortune," Pete said, as he hung the ring back on the wall. "As you can see, they've made me a rich man." He fell into a fit of beery giggles, and Beam and Ella joined him.

As the sun tilted down into the house, it seemed possible that trouble had become something hidden so deep in the far away woods that it could never reach them again.

They spent the rest of the night talking and drinking. Long tales told in the quiet house, stories fetched down from the rafters like aged heirloom quilts. Beam weaved in his chair, a cairn of beer cans building under his feet. He was full of words, his jaw oiled by alcohol. He spoke boldly of things that held little consequence, which made bright slivers of light rise in Ella's eyes.

Very late, Pete rose, yawning. "I believe it's time for me to bed down." He wobbled in his boots when he stood up. "Beam, you can just lay out on the couch here. Take that old throw off the back if you get cold." Ella and Beam watched him slowly leave the room. For a spell, they heard him bumbling in the back of the house, and then there was the creak of box springs, the settling of blankets, and they were alone. Moths bumped against the ceiling. Somewhere off in the dark, frogs boomed and creek water rushed over stones in a low ferny place.

"Why don't you turn out the light," Ella said.

Beam looked at her. Her eyes had turned low like lantern wicks.

He stood and yanked the string hanging from the ceiling, remaining still as his eyes adjusted to the darkness. After a time, he could make out the shape of Ella on the couch. Her thighs appeared smooth as jade in the loose moonlight falling through the window.

"Why did you want me to do that?" he asked.

"Because it's nice sometimes," she said. "Do you want to come sit down here by me?"

Beam nodded. Then he remembered the light was out. "Yes," he said. "I do."

The couch felt airless beneath him. He smelled Ella, her sweat and a hint of citrus perfume.

"I was married once," she said. "He wasn't a bad man, but we never got along much." Ella moved closer to Beam; her breath fell warmly on his neck. "It didn't last long. It wasn't supposed to, so I don't miss him. It might have gone on for a long while, but I didn't let it. He caught me, just this one time, with another man. I don't know why I did that. But it happened and he caught me and that ended it."

Beam let his head rest on the back of the couch and waited for her to speak again, but there was only the moonlight and the frogs and the creek going off somewhere in the night. He thought of the girls he'd been with before, always a rush of messed clothing in the back of a car or in some bedroom where things spilled out quickly and then were done, rank places reeking of soured carpet and cigarettes. He knew this was different somehow, and the thought of how different it was made his blood pulse stormy and thick.

"Sometimes, I get to worrying about it," Ella continued. "Whether or not he's forgiven me."

Beam picked at the ravelings of thread poking out of the sofa. "Sure," he mumbled. He didn't know what to say. He'd never known what to say to a woman.

What success he'd had with them was due either to the false confidence of alcohol, or to the fact he caught them in a moment when they were as desperate and hungry as he was. It wasn't that any ever chose him. Ella was different though. The soft warmth in her eyes told him that she did choose him, not with bravado or arrogance, but with the slow careful ease of one who has waited a long time to make this choice.

"Lay back," she whispered.

Beam took his head off the back of the sofa.

"What?"

"Lay back," she repeated.

Slowly, he slid himself down on the couch. He was drunk from all the beer and the room wound out around him in blue shaking shades. When he felt her roll against him, he nearly coughed.

"Easy," she breathed, as if trying to calm a spooked horse. Then her hands were on him. They swam under his shirt, over the washboard of his stomach, her nails pinching the hair on his chest, rattling the bandages on his wounds.

"What's this?" she asked, thumbing the gauze.

"Your dad doctored on me."

She patted the bandages, and then undid his jeans, the brass fasteners clinking. When her hands touched him again, he jerked at the coolness of her palm. She crept between his thighs and ran her tongue over him and he groaned dully, feeling her teeth. She was stroking him now, a kind of ghostly shape rearing in the slats of moon.

"Is this all right?" she asked.

"Yes," he said.

She took her shorts off and he smelled her sex, a bright aroma of salt and sweat. When she straddled him, he lifted his hips to her as she slid down slowly to fit the wet grip of herself to him. She pushed him down with her palms, and their breathing, hushed and steady, quickened together as Ella's hair sprawled over her damp cheeks. Beam felt his thighs shiver. His body spread electric to its very ends until Ella seized up and moaned and fell heaving onto his chest, her hair wadded thickly in his mouth, the patter of her heart loud against his ribs.

He lay there with her, tracing her spine, until here were only dreams and then night and nothing else.

Her cold, dry hand shook him out of sleep, her voice in his ear whispering, "Get up."

Through the blinds, the moonlight seeped in thick and frigid.

Outside, a man called steadily, the sound sinking long and drowsy through the night.

Beam sat up. "What is that?" he asked.

Ella pushed herself off the sofa. She dressed quickly, shucking her shorts and blouse on, then parted the blinds. "Somebody's out there," she said.

Beam dressed himself, bumbling into his boots, and when he looked out the window he saw the long span of a Cadillac sitting in the yard, a mess of dogs standing in front of the car next to a man who held a rifle perched on his hip. "Sheetmire," he called. "You come on out here so I don't have to come in and get you. Be easier on everybody that way." The man's voice sounded like gravel spitting against the wood siding of the house.

"Who is it?" asked Ella.

Beam backed away from the window, startling the beer cans piled on the floor. "I don't know," he said. The sudden sound of a rifle being loaded spooked him. He turned and Pete stood in the doorway feeding cartridges into a battered Springfield.

"That's Presto Geary," he said. "Loat's right hand."

Beam and Ella crawfished their way to the far corner of the room, where they stood motionless. Pete finished loading the rifle and wiped the barrel with his shirtsleeve, then crossed the floor to the blinds and pinched them down with his thumb. "It's just him and the dogs far as I can tell," he said. His breath made a small blossom of fog on the pane. He let the blinds settle back. "There could be others hid out behind us somewhere though."

Ella drew the hair away from her eyes. "What are we going to do?" she asked.

"You need to sit down, first thing," Pete said.

Before she had a chance to, a shot fired and the front window shattered, the glass falling over the back of the sofa, the blinds clattering as a gush of wind blew in. All three of them dove to the floor.

"Hey, Pete," Presto called from outside. "Better let me have that boy in there. He ain't worth getting killed over."

Pete clicked the safety off his rifle. "Sure thing, Presto," he hollered back. "Hold your fire. He's coming out." Pete scooted on his haunches to the door and put his hand on the knob. Looking over his shoulder at Ella and Beam, he said, "Y'all lay down flat." Then he yanked the door open and fired three quick shots in succession, the rifle's muzzle barking white fire. Two of the Dobermans yelped and fell curled and writhing in the dirt, while the last shot shattered one of the Cadillac's headlights and then went singing off into the dark. Pete slammed the door and rolled deep inside the room, propping his back against the sofa. Presto then opened up, a series of shots slapping the house, bursting the windows and splintering the door.

When the gunfire ended, Pete drew himself into a crouch against the sofa and reloaded the Springfield and laid it over his knees.

"Everybody good?" he asked.

"Yes," said Ella.

"Beam?" Pete asked.

"Yeah?"

"You ever been in a gunfight before?"

"No, sir."

Pete shook his head. "Damn. I was hoping somebody here would know just how the hell this kinda thing was supposed to turn out." He ran his hand over the rifle. "I guess we'll just have to learn by doing."

Quiet settled among them briefly as they listened to the trees clawing the roof. "What are we going to do?" Ella finally asked.

Pete continued to stroke the stock of his rifle. "If we can hold on until daylight maybe he'll give and leave. He's parked in the moonlight so I might could peg him if I got to."

"We need to call somebody," Ella said.

"And who might that be?"

"The sheriff."

Pete grunted. "Of course. Crawl over to the phone there and see if the line ain't been cut. But I can tell you now, Presto has already done thought that."

"Maybe he forgot."

"Go on then, try the phone."

Ella stared at her father seated against the edge of the sofa. Then she rose up and ran to the phone and pulled it from its cradle, but only empty air whirred in her ear. She fingered the rotary, but no tone came.

"It's dead," she whispered.

"I know," said Pete. "Now get down and don't get up again."

She lay down beside Beam again, her face in the carpet, her

arms wrapped over her head, her shoulders shivering as she began to cry. Beam reached out and touched her, but she jerked away and he drew his hand back as if it had been kissed by fire.

From outside, they heard the sound of Presto slashing their tires.

Beam drew himself up into a crouch and eased his back against the wall. The hiss of the leaking tires snaked long and thin, and his sweat draped over him coldly. The blinds rattling in the broken front window tinkled eerily. Ella was beside him on the floor, and Pete was crouched beneath the sofa with his Springfield, and none of this was their fault. They'd only tried to help him. He had asked for none of it, yet they had both given freely of themselves. He wondered what it was that made folks behave in such a way.

"Let me go on out there," he said. "He'll take me and the two of you won't have to be in this anymore."

"We're in it already," said Pete, shaking his head.

"You don't have to be. I can walk out that door and it'll all be over for you."

"It don't work like that, Beam. This ain't the kind of thing a man can be over and done with."

Beam looked down at Ella. She had turned on her side, and her eyes bit at him through the moonlight. "Let him go," she said coldly. "It's the only way we'll ever get out of this."

"You want to let him go?" asked Pete.

"He wants to," she said. "We might as well let him."

Beam felt something twist inside him at the sound of her voice and at the sound of what she had said. He thought of all the movies he'd seen at the two-screen cinema in Drakesboro where the departing hero was wept over by a bosomy maiden who couldn't bear the heartbreak of losing him. Beam knew he wasn't any hero and he knew this wasn't any movie, but it pained him to hear Ella's bluntness.

"You sure you want to go, Beam?" Pete asked. "You don't have to."

"I think I need to," he answered.

Pete studied him for a moment, then slowly crawled to a chest of drawers sitting beside the television. He opened the bottom drawer and took out a tarnished pistol, its silver plated barrel stained with powder burns.

"This is a Walther .380," he said. "Do you know how to use it?"

Beam nodded.

"It's got six cartridges in the clip." Pete pushed the release and held the clip in his palm, then snicked it back flush into the gun. "Take it."

Beam took the gun. He felt a brief glow of warmth, but then he saw Ella, and the way she stared at him from her spot on the floor, and the warmth drifted away. She wanted him to go.

"Can you do this, Beam?" Pete asked. The old man peered at him through the shadows, and Beam was about to say yes, he could do it, when one of the hounds crashed through the broken front window. Pete only had time to half turn before the dog disentangled itself from the blinds and leapt at him. It ripped its fangs over his throat so the blood gushed sudden and all at once and the Springfield clattered useless at his feet as Pete staggered and then fell to the floor with the dog on top of him snarling and heaving, the quick ratchets of its teeth clicking against his neck bones.

Beam tried to slide a round into the chamber of the Walther, but it was an old weapon and hard to prime, its barrel crusted with burned cordite. Ella screamed at him to shoot the dog, but his fingers were sweaty and he fumbled and dropped the pistol and then picked it up and managed to slide a round into the chamber and he fired twice and the shots sent the dog sprawling against the door where it seized and then died in the endlessness of its own blood.

Pete lay motionless on his back. He wore a collar of gore, and his eyes pooled like milk in his head. He gave a small whine of breath, and then he was gone. Ella fell over him, her face smeared with his blood as great sobs pulsed out of her.

Presto Geary opened the front door and entered the house. He held a Winchester 30-06 rifle at his hip, its wide bore pointed at Beam. He was a large man, and he stooped a bit because of his height as he came through the door. The two remaining Dobermans squirmed and whined behind him.

"Let it go," Presto said, motioning with the rifle to the pistol Beam held. "Let it go and me and you can walk out of here and nobody else has to get hurt."

Beam wedged himself as far back against a wall as he could, the Walther warm and steaming in his hand. Only half of Presto's face was visible to him; his lips were glazed and flattened beneath his nose, and his eye winked and sputtered continuously in a nervous tick like the gutter and bob of a match.

"I don't know you," said Beam.

"That's okay," answered Presto. "I'll click on a light so you can see me better and we can get acquainted." He hit a switch beside the door, revealing himself. He was wearing a slim black Stetson with the brimwings pinned up at either side so that the hat seemed like a crow roosted on his head. The rest of his dress was sleek and crisp; pressed button-down chambray shirt and stone-washed denim jeans, and the toes of his boots were polished bright as mirrors.

"Now that you know how I look, you best come with me." Presto smiled thinly and motioned toward the doorway.

Ella rose up from the floor, her fingers damp with her father's blood. "He's not going with you," she said.

Presto pointed the rifle at her. "You're a feisty one, I can tell. I may just have to fuck some of the bitch out of you."

Ella jerked her chin at him. "You don't get off this place, I'll kill you."

A small wet laugh squirted out of Presto. "I never killed a woman before," he giggled.

"You ain't nothing," Ella muttered. Her voice quavered a bit, but her eyes remained steady and fastened on Presto. "You ain't nothing at all."

Presto laughed again. "Baby doll," he said, "I am something. I'm the something you been having nightmares about since you was pissing in your Underroos. Now you best back away from me unless you want a hole in your chest."

Ella slowly backed away from Presto.

"Atta girl," he said. Presto stepped further into the house, turning the rifle on Beam. "Lay that pistol down," he commanded.

Beam crouched down and laid the gun on the carpet.

"That's good. Now step towards me. And do it slow."

Beam took a single step. Suddenly, Ella leapt forward, grabbed the barrel of the rifle and jerked it upward. The weapon discharged with a great thunder, blowing a hole in the ceiling and calling down a drizzle of plaster. Presto laughed again and tried to throw Ella off his shoulder, but she clasped to him tightly and bit down into his cheek and didn't let go, not even when the Dobermans bounded into the room and sank their fangs into her legs and they all clattered to the floor in a massed tangle. The rifle discharged a second time, the bullet tearing through Presto's shoulder as a spray of blood fanned against the wall. Beam, who'd stood shocked and frozen, picked the Walther pistol from the floor and started running, past the dogs and Presto and Ella sprawled on the floor and out across the soft grass of the yard and beyond the maples and pawpaws and past the Cadillac, the breath aboil in his chest as he rushed over the knotty ground, and he did not look back as he ran without direction through the dark as if he meant to chase stars down from the sky, running until he slammed into a fence and fell back winded and startled on the warm earth, his belly cut from the barbwire. Behind him, the rifle fired again, and he pulled himself from the ground and jumped the fence and ran until he came to the edge of a black forest where the trees took him and he tripped and fell again, rolling down into a draw through a ticking of damp dead leaves and kindling.

At the bottom of the draw, a creek scurried by. He waited, his breath heaving. Far off, he heard the dogs coming. Without a thought, he ran into the creek, splashing downstream through the shallows, the water damping his legs so that he moved slowly as if in a dream. When he climbed up a sandy bank, dragging himself out of the creek by the roots of trees, his fingernails were broken and bloody. He ran alongside the creek for a spell, past beaver flumes and muskrat tunnels until out of the darkness a large beech tree loomed. The branches were low. He went to climb them and when he did, he found he still carried the pistol. There in his hand like a miracle, its heft cold and dead. He stowed it in the waist of his jeans and went up, ascending the branches with the leaves clattering like rolled bones until he found the fork. There, he pushed himself against the crotch of branches and took the pistol out, holding it close over his heart, letting the blood simmer down inside him. He listened, but couldn't hear the dogs any longer. Somewhere, he thought he heard rain blowing, but the world around him was dry and empty. Old fencing shivered. The snap of a broken twig. The wind having its way, fondling the earth. That was all there was, and he lay quiet as his breath began to ease, and he strained to listen to the night and to all that lived inside it.

After Beam fled, the dogs released their grip on Ella. They paced onto the porch and stared into the night, but they didn't follow Beam, their loyalties seemingly torn between pursuit and remaining nearby their wounded keeper.

Presto rolled onto his back and pulled himself up into a sitting position. He held a hand over his shoulder as the blood dripped loose as silk between his splayed fingers. Somehow, he was still wearing his hat.

Ella lay on her stomach, her legs bleeding. She rose up

raggedly, pulling herself to the couch. On the floor, her father was dead, his eyes fixed open. And then there was the rifle—it rested on the floor between her and Presto. They both stared at it as the breath caught up to them in spacey gusts.

"Well, now," Presto groaned, propping himself up against the wall. "Just what are we gonna do about this, little girl?" He waved a hand at the dogs. "Fetch 'em up," he hissed, and the dogs sprang off the porch and bounded into the darkness, howling until their noise faded away.

He turned and looked at Ella on the couch. "You go easy," he said. He winced and tightened the grip on his shoulder. "I could've whistled those dogs on you, but I didn't. I sent them after our boy Beam and you ought to thank me for that."

Ella remained quiet. Through the open front door, the porch lay bare and clean in the moonlight, the shadow of tree branches falling over the boards.

"Here's what's gonna happen," Presto grunted. "I'm gonna reach for that rifle and you're gonna set right there and not think about nothing. You're gonna do that because you're a good girl that don't want nothing worse to happen tonight. That's the way it has to be, okay? You hearing me?"

Ella looked at him. He was pale and sweating and the breath bluttered inside his chest.

"Okay," she answered.

"I knew you were a good girl."

Presto pushed himself up into a slow standing. His eyes rolled in his head for a moment, and when his gaze steadied, a startled recognition passed over his face, as if he was seeing for the first time what he'd spent all his life looking for.

"Girl?" he whispered.

Ella grabbed the rifle, shucked a shell into the chamber and swung the muzzle around. When she pulled the trigger, there came a bald thrust of light and sound that threw Presto against the wall, his blood spattering the sheetrock, and then he slumped to the floor, his eyes staring dead and empty.

The rifle clattered at Ella's feet.

She didn't wait. She fished a ring of keys from Presto's pocket, grabbed her purse off the floor, and ran through the open door and down the porch steps, limping on her dog-bitten legs. She got into the Cadillac, and when she turned the engine over, the rumbling was thick and strong. She turned the car in the yard and peeled out up the driveway. In a haze, she found a circuitry of back roads, her mind spasming with fear and blood loss, and in her rushing horror she took a curve too quick and the car fishtailed in the loose gravel. It left the road in a soundless leap, and it seemed, in that yawning stalled moment before the crash of lights and the boom and shear of metal, that the night had suddenly hushed as it opened up to hold her.

# XVI

## SATURDAY

In the dry morning, Elvis arrived at Pete Daugherty's place, accompanied by a deputy named Filback. Two Doberman hounds lay dead in the dust of the yard, their carcasses covered with a swarm of blowflies. Pete's truck was parked in the shade of a stand of pawpaw trees, as was Ella's LTD. The tires of both vehicles slouched flat and airless on their rims. The front door of the house swung idly on its hinges.

"This don't look good at all," said Filback. He was young and portly, his hair still wet beneath his hat, razor burn on his throat. The father of three squall-prone children he often brought to departmental functions, he spoke with the kind of vexing tones only those settled in marriage use, quick and sure of everything already obvious.

He went to open his door, but Elvis halted him. "Let's wait a second," he said. Elvis stared at the house as the morning light fell against the tin roof. "What you got to learn is not to rush into anything." He took his hat off the console and fixed it on his head, taking care that the brim was straight, checking himself in the rearview mirror. "Always take time to put your hat on. That gives you a second to figure out what you need to do—in this case, call an ambulance for the ones that are laying there and arrest the ones that done it."

Filback snickered. "You want me to call an ambulance for those dogs?"

"No. But likely there's a least one somebody in that house who's not in walking condition." Elvis slid his gun out of its holster, checked the loads, and fixed the weapon back on his hip. "Take the shotgun and go around back," he said. "After you've radioed for an ambulance."

Once the paramedics had been called, the two peace officers got out of the cruiser. Filback shucked shells into the breech of his Benelli, but Elvis kept his pistol holstered as he moved slowly through the yard under the hanging pawpaw and maple branches. When he came up onto the porch, he paused, listening as Filback moved around back through the joe-pye and jimson weeds.

The front door drifted closed, and then open. There was no clean way to do this. That much he'd learned. Whatever lay inside a house, it was just going to have to be dealt with. There was no way to stop any of it now. This was going to happen. Just as it always had. No matter how long you took to put your hat on, eventually you had to go through a door and meet whatever waited on the other side for you.

Elvis squinted through the cracked door at the innards of the house. Sunlight glared off the blank television screen. A pile of beer cans were scattered about the carpet. A front window had been shattered.

"Pete," he called. Then again, louder, "Pete, this is Elvis. You all right?" No one answered. A cold draft leeched from the house and licked his hands. Around back, Filback tromped through the high weeds, peering into windows and making nothing but noise and trouble.

Elvis drew his revolver and went inside. Another Doberman lay dead on the carpet against the far wall, its tongue lolled out swollen and pale from between its jaws. Pete was slouched against a close wall, his eyes dead and open, his hands sprawled empty and bloody in his lap. He had the look of someone who'd recently been swindled. Beside him, Presto Geary lay swathed in blood, and Elvis noted a small entry wound in his chest and a fist-sized exit wound in his back.

Slowly, Elvis made his way through the house, down the dim

hall with its warped paneling, through the kitchen stinking of unwashed dishes and fried bologna and beans, to the back rooms, which held only a bed and ricks of junk—sewing machines and come-alongs and all the old man's tinkerings.

When he returned to the front room, Filback was standing in the doorway, the shotgun hanging loose at his side.

"Put the safety on, Filback," Elvis told him.

The deputy jerked at the sound of Elvis's voice. He looked at the gun he held and then clicked it dead.

"Nobody home," said Elvis. He holstered his pistol and sat down on the sofa, looking at the two dead men on the floor. Flies crawled through their hair and eyelashes and into the open maw of Pete's throat, their buzzing loud and awful in the hot closeness of the house.

"This party didn't turn out too well, did it?" said Filback.

Elvis looked up at Filback, who wore a limp grin. A single snaggly tooth hung over his bottom lip so he looked like a gawker come to the carnival to witness strange evil and give crude commentary.

"Sit down, Filback. Mind you don't step in the blood."

The deputy looked about the room and then made for the chair sitting beside the television. It creaked with his weight. He stowed the shotgun between his legs and the damp hair hanging from under his hat made him resemble a widow waiting in a bus terminal, as if he were a bereft woman bound somewhere. "I wouldn't have thought Pete to go out this way," he said.

Elvis leaned forward and scanned the bloody carpet covered with shell casings, the pile of beer cans beside Filback's feet, and the rifle on the floor. He reached down and picked up one of the empty brass shells, pinching it between his fingers. "Believe this is a pistol round here," he said. He jiggled the casing in his hand and nodded toward Presto's body. "But he wasn't shot with any pistol round. That rifle did the job." He pointed to the long-barrel Winchester 30-06 on the floor, then nodded toward the Doberman. "That's one of Loat's dogs," he said. "And that's Presto Geary lying there, though his ride ain't nowhere around."

Filback tweezed his nostrils with a pair of pinched fingers. "Maybe he walked here," he said.

Elvis squinted at him. "Listen, Filback," he said, "I didn't bring any play-pretties for you to toy with. I don't have any rubber bands or balls of yarn, but maybe you can sit there quiet and not shoot yourself or me and be all right. You think you can do that?"

Filback let his tongue worm through his cheek. He leaned back in the chair, stowing the shotgun against his thigh. "Hell," he said. "You asked me to come out here."

"I sure did," Elvis answered. "And I'm already feeling guilty about that."

The deputy twisted on the hams of his thighs, the chair squirming beneath him. "You're something, know that Elvis?"

"Just remember who signs your paychecks," Elvis said bruskly.

"Election coming up in the fall," Filback replied, smiling. "Might be different handwriting on my checks come January."

Elvis glared at Fillback, then got up from the sofa. He swatted at the pleat in his khakis, stepped carefully around the congealed pools of blood on the floor, and walked to the front door. With one arm braced against the frame, he looked outside on the bright dusty yard and the two dead hounds and the wide fields of billow hay scooting away like whitecaps toward the shade of the treeline.

"I'm going out here to look through the yard, Filback," he said. "Can you sit in here and not get spooked?"

"Hell, I ain't afraid. I've seen worse than this."

Elvis shook his head. He stepped out onto the porch and then down the steps, striding through the pale dirt toward the dogs, whose dead bodies had begun to swell. Flies and yellow jackets lit and drooped over the blood spilled thickly on the ground. One dog had been shot through the throat, its neck blown out in a tear of red meat, while the other had taken it in the chest. Elvis crouched beside their corpses. In the dust, he counted little runs of bird tracks, and a set of boot prints moving off toward the porch. He picked up something that glistened from a clump of cheat grass and held it before his eye, the light prisming down over his hand. It was shard of glass from a headlight. When he checked the headlamps on the LTD and Pete's truck, he noted that all four were intact. Another puzzle.

Chewing his bottom lip, he moved back toward the dogs. From here, two sets of dog prints seemed to head south toward the pasture. He followed the tracks slowly, through the yard to where the grass began to thicken and then down the lip of the lawn to where the fencing was strung. He put his hands on the top strand of barbs. The wire trembled under his fingers. By the look of the grass something had run through the field.

A bunting bird lit on the wire some yards down, its indigo plumage like a daub dropped by a joy-mad painter. It sang a note and then shot off, falling and then rising on a gust. The wire shook beneath Elvis's fingers.

He had been reared by his grandmother in a large farmhouse that had sat at the back of a creek bottom hemmed by chestnut oaks. At night, the cool autumn dark settled down brittle and thin like a piece of cold beaten tin, and he would sit with her, she in a rocker, he on the stoop playing with a toy wagon he'd made, rolling its spool wheels over the boards.

"Elvis, your head ain't right," she would croak. "They yanked you out with forceps and now you got that crease in your scalp, but it's nothing to worry with." The sledrunners of her rocker snicked on the porch. "Though I suspect some will worry anyway." She leaned and spat a crimson streak of tobacco juice into a Folgers can. "Let them go ahead and worry. Me and you are okay and just fine out here. Know why?"

"No," said Elvis.

"Because," she leaned up in her rocker, "we know what birds

mean." Far off, a screech owl screamed in the oak trees. "Hear that? An owl in this moon means good fortune. Mark it. You can tell a lot of things by birds. Take the coloring of a thrush. He'll be russet if the winter is going to be mild. A deeper red if it'll turn heavy snow." She leaned and spat again. Her phlegm fell into the coffee tin like an offered coin, a thing tithed out, and she wiped her lips with the heel of her palm. "Now, that means we're all right. So long as we know what birds mean, can't nothing wrong happen because we can know the wrong that's coming. Or the good. And it is mostly good, Elvis. Remember that."

Touching the fence, he thought maybe he'd forgotten how to remember the good. Certainly, he'd forgotten what a bunting meant, if it divined ill or fortune, and he saw no pattern in the parted grasses of the hayfield.

But he did remember his grandmother telling him that his head wasn't right. Others had said the same thing, and maybe that was so. All the years unmarried, they came back to him as he watched the grass toss and bow. Not just unmarried, but no women to speak of. His house smelled of the rankness of ascetic bachelorhood, of mildew and underwear and shave cream and there were never flowers because he didn't want a woman, because he didn't know how to want a woman. The times he attended revivals or church socials, he made a point to stand away from them, bundled like cloth in their dressy bunches, their glossy lips smacking out quick chirpy sounds. Women were things to be ciphered out, figured on. Men were simpler. They did and were done in, whereas women lingered, pummeled into grist by the slow grinding of years until they were like powder cast before the wind.

He thought of Ella Daugherty. Another woman out in the world and left to its mercy.

He turned and walked away from the hayfield, back into the yard where the dogs lay. The wind raised the pawpaw limbs and the shadows drizzled and swam over the house.

"Come out here, Filback," he called.

A clutzy rattle of beer cans came from inside the house and then the deputy stood in the doorway, the shotgun cradled in his arms.

"I'm going to look for Ella," Elvis said.

The color washed out of Filback's cheeks. "You are? What the hell am I supposed to do?"

"Stay here and wait for the ambulance," Elvis said. "You know how to fill out paperwork. And don't get scared, Filback. There ain't no such thing as ghosts." Elvis opened the door to the cruiser and sat down behind the wheel, the car's shocks rocking under him. He took his hat off and placed it neatly on the passenger seat. Then he cranked the key and the engine groaned over. He turned in the yard and dust rose about him and fled behind as he watched the house and yard disappear in his rearview until he hit the main of the highway and only had to look at what was coming at him instead of worrying about what lay behind.

Ella's single-wide sat vacant and lone, the driveway empty. The garden pinwheels in the crabby yard spun in the breeze, flashing kaleidoscopic blues and reds and greens brightly in the sunlight. Laundry hanging on the clothesline snapped and rolled.

Elvis knocked heavily on the door, the storm screen creaking at his back, but no one answered. He called her name. Once, twice, three times. Again, nothing.

He left for Daryl's.

The day flexed hot and ragged as Elvis got out of the cruiser. He remained in the parking lot for a time, studying the collection of junk trucks and failing vehicles, marking the patronage within by the various makes and models squatting in the gravel. At one end of the lot, a rigless trailer stood on its chickenleg mounts, white paint peeling from the aluminum.

When he walked through the doors of the Quonset hut, the

bar talk turned off. Beery eyes reached through the tangled fog to study him. Light spat off the tiered bottles behind the bar and the jukebox played soft and breathy, the squeak of a greasy fiddle sawing out of the speakers. Elvis strode forth through the abruptly broken quiet, his boots loud on the wooden floor, his own form seeming to recede away from himself as he ebbed deeper into this cauldroning dark.

He put his hands on the bar. The wood beneath his fingers felt scored and rough. The tender, a pale and fat scowler, came over to inspect him.

"Where's Loat?" Elvis asked.

The tender shook his head. "Not here."

"Let me talk to Daryl then."

The tender eyed him, his tongue pushed into his cheek. Then he turned and tromped off to the rear of the Quonset.

Elvis waited. He kept his back to the dance floor, studying the drunks in the mirror hanging behind the bar, their bent and stalled bodies wrapped in the cigarette smoke like the web-trapped prey of spiders.

When Daryl emerged from the back, he wore khaki trousers and a camo vest over his hairy belly. He moved like a buoy in the bar's drafty currents.

"Loat's not here," he said, propping the pink stump of an arm on the bar.

"I know," said Elvis.

"What you want then?"

"You know Beam Sheetmire?"

"Clem's boy? Yeah, I know who he is."

Elvis drummed his fingers against the bar. Behind him, the talk and dancing ignited again, the noise firing back to life, though it was now cautious and uneasy.

"What's he done?" Daryl asked.

Elvis shrugged. "Nothing," he said. "That I know of."

Daryl wiped his chin against his shoulder, a strange and

birdish motion. "If he ain't done nothing and you ain't looking for him, then why are you asking?"

Elvis ignored the question. "Whose trailer is that parked outside?" he asked.

"That's mine," Daryl answered. "Got a good deal on it. Plan on using it for storage."

"Storage, huh?"

Daryl's chalky dry lips broke into a smile. "Business is so good, I'm running out of room."

Elvis propped his elbows on the bar and folded his hands before him, stroking his chin with his thumbs. He tried to see an angle, some profit Daryl might be gleaning from the entire mess, but there seemed little sense to it. He wondered what help he was giving anyone by being in such a place as this.

"You and Loat used to pal around with Clem," he said.

Daryl's head bobbed. "We did at one time. Then Clem started to turn a little churchy. I don't think he ever got real holy, but I know he quit drinking for awhile. Then he wound up with Derna and we never saw him hardly much at all after that."

"What happened with you and him and Loat out at those mines?"

Daryl's eyes went thin. "You know that story already," he said coldly.

"Way I heard it, there's bad blood between you and Clem on account of it. So you tell me why that is."

Daryl squirmed on his stool. He leaned forward, his breath rattling in his nostrils. "There ain't no bad blood," he said. "Not no more."

"Why is that?"

"You get old enough, time squares most of your debts."

"That don't sound like you at all."

"I don't believe you know me well enough to say what is and what ain't like me. Clem wasn't never going to make amends. He's yellow as soap and twice as soft. So I decided I had bigger things to worry over."

Elvis put his hands on the bar again. "What'd he do out there at the mines?" he asked.

Daryl snorted. "Oh, he just saw to it that it was me got the short end of the stick out there. Let's leave it at that."

Elvis wiped absently at the bar top. "Is there bad blood between Loat and Clem?"

Daryl leaned hard against the bar. "If you mean on account of Derna, I'd say there's some. But I can guarantee you it ain't something Loat worries over too much. He's done had that pussy. And there ain't a dollar to be made with it now no how, so you know he ain't walking the floor over Derna. Whether or not it chaps Clem's ass that Loat used to fuck his wife, I can't say."

Elvis stroked the bar. The wood felt frayed and burned. "Loat ever talk about Paul?"

"Not much. He'd say something every now and then, wondering what Paul was gonna do once he got out." His head bobbed and he smiled wetly. "But, the river's done took care of that."

"Somebody and the river."

Daryl's smile faded. Then, quickly, the grin returned and he took to chuckling. "What's all this about, Elvis? You come in here all swagger and swinging dick asking about Beam Sheetmire like he's been lost in the high weeds."

Elvis watched the dancers in the mirror, their bodies dragging through the smoke. The laughter in the room thickened. "Had a feller come visit me at the courthouse the other day," he said. "He was dressed like he'd been to a wedding. In a suit, I mean." Elvis cocked his head, watching Daryl. "The feller told me Beam had been up here. Said he got beat pretty bad. Said he was the one to beat him."

Daryl licked the flesh beneath his nose. "I don't know nothing about that," he said. "Who was this feller?"

Elvis shrugged. "Just a feller," he said. "Anyhow, you ain't seen Beam Sheetmire up here in your bar? That what you're telling me? That it's just been the regular crowd of drunks?"

"That's what I'm telling you."

"And I guess you ain't seen nobody wearing a suit neither?"

"I believe I'd remember that."

"I'd think you would too, but I suspect," Elvis said, rising off his stool, "that you've told me nothing but lies today."

"Helluva thing to say to a businessman," Daryl said.

Elvis straightened his gun belt and hammered Daryl with his stare. "I'm just gonna go ahead and tell you I think you're an outright sonuvabitch," he said. "But that ain't the worst part." Elvis stepped back from the bar. "The worst part is trying to picture how a sonuvabitch like you wipes his ass and takes a piss. By the way you smell, I guess you don't have much luck doing either."

Daryl laughed. "Come on back to the trough then, Elvis. You can shake my dick dry for me."

"I'll get a warrant," Elvis said. "This place will be closed in a day. I know these girls you got out here ain't just waitresses and bar maids."

Daryl chuckled again. "Go on. See if you can get a judge to grant you that warrant. I'd love to hear the story about how Old Black Robes laughed you out of the courtroom and then took your badge. What happened to the last sheriff wanted to serve a warrant on me. You remember that, I know. Best recall how I got too much dirt on folks around here to ever get shut down."

Elvis patted the bar lightly, then turned and looked at the room. In the middle of the dance floor was a large black stain. He strode over and squatted beside it, the dancers giving him the strange eye as they shuffled around him. He bent down and touched the stain, the wood smooth and glossed. "You don't keep your floors too clean out here do you, Daryl?" he yelled.

"Hard to mop up everything that gets spilled," Daryl answered. "There's usually always some leavings left over."

Elvis stood up and slid his shoe over the stain. He looked

over at Daryl on his perch before the bar, seated like some derelict king in a counting house whose currency was blood, a man who bartered only with death itself.

He spat on the floor and left.

# XVII

## SATURDAY

They heard the flash over the scanner bolted to the dash of the trucker's rig. Two bodies had been found at Pete Daughtery's house over on Belltown Road. The radio snored out the details: three dogs shot as well, all parties as yet unidentified. One deputy and Sheriff Dunne were on scene. Coroner and paramedics en route.

Loat and the trucker were soon en route themselves.

Coasting the back roads, Loat rode shotgun in the trucker's Peterbilt, dotting the fields and woods with his stares. Two days ago, he'd left Presto at Pete Daughtery's place with instructions to wait in the briars. Now he'd heard the news over the scanner. In his lap, he kept a Smith and Wesson .40-cal, stroking the grip-embossed handle and listening to the rig's steel-belt tires yawn over the bald pavement.

His plan remained cloudy. In fact, he had no plan at all and didn't know how he hoped to explain to the sheriff his sudden arrival at Pete Daugherty's place. He'd always gone where he pleased, but now he thought that perhaps larger forces had conscripted him and his course long ago, perhaps before his birth. This idea struck him as stupendous and awful, and he quickly threw his mind away from it.

His hound Enoch slept in the floorboards at his feet, its hide twitching as it dreamed through the squawk and bleat of the police scanner. It surprised Loat that the dog could sleep through such. The dreams of dogs must be sturdy. Were he a better man, he would build sturdy dreams for himself. Instead, he was riding over empty roads with this strange trucker and he was dying and there was neither time nor space with which to dream.

"Pretty country," said the trucker as they drove past fields devoid of timber. This land had been strip-mined and later reclaimed with dozers and track hoes that pushed the ruptured earth together again, but the soil had been cursed by its trespassers and was now only Judas dirt where sedge and wire grass spiraled up amidst sapling cedars sown to beat the wind back. It looked like a strange occurrence of prairie where no prairie should be. Certain spots still remained scarred with open strip-pits, and the surface coal flashed bluely in the sun, the ground itself ashy and coated with shale rock so that it appeared gray and shattered like the very geography of dereliction.

"You think so?" Loat asked. He leaned forward and turned the scanner's volume down.

"Looks about like a dirty old wash pan that's been beat to pieces and then glued back together," the trucker answered.

"Well, about all the good it's doing is holding the world in place. Won't nothing grow on it. I'd say it wouldn't even be worth grazing cattle on."

"No?"

Loat shook his head. "Soil has leeched out. So you can't sow clover or fescue on it. Plus, it ain't even sturdy enough to put houses on." He waved a hand at the window. "It's spent ground."

"I bet I could make a living off it," the trucker said. "Now see, what you got to do with a spot like this, one that's had every kind of wrong and sin done against it, you got to purify it. Way you do that is you go out and appease all the ghosts that's wandering round out here. You tell them, 'Go on, shade! Go on out to eternity! Your work here is over and through!' You need to tell them because they ain't been told before. Once you do that, this'll be as fine a place to lay a farm down as you could want."

Loat looked down at the gun in his lap. He wondered when he would have to kill the trucker. The man was mouthy, and Loat knew a time would come when he'd have to stop his tongue and then bury him behind Daryl's, the way the trucker had buried Clem. Something about the man said that he would have to be dealt with. Maybe it was because he was a stranger who had stowed himself away in the affairs of a place he knew nothing about, as if he thought he could find passage among the vexed and angry men he'd happened upon, as if their afflicted vengeance could bear him somewhere else. But who would want to go wherever such as these were bound?

"Anybody ever told you that you're a peculiar bastard?" Loat asked.

The trucker smiled. "Now see, that's an old fortune you're telling. Being peculiar is just being born at the wrong time." He took a curve too fast and the tires groaned before he straightened their course.

Loat scratched the barrel of the pistol with his thumbnail. The bluing greased his finger. "Why are you here?" he asked.

"Here?"

"Yeah. Why in the hell are you riding around with me looking for Beam? That don't square at all."

"What else should I be doing?"

"Hell, I don't know. Hauling your suits. Getting drunk. Getting laid. Anything but driving around in a place you ain't from looking for somebody you don't know."

The trucker pressed his hands into the steering wheel. The ring of keys dangling from the ignition jiggled and chimed. "Now see, it's just like I said about those specters. Some folks ain't been told the news. Well, I'm here to tell them and I also am here to collect on all outstanding debts, with interest," he said. "I am here for a due balance. That one Beam insulted me when he called me a thief. I don't steal anything. I just collect on what I'm owed."

"That don't make one fucking iota of sense," Loat grunted. "The reason you're sticking your neck out is because some punk kid insulted you?"

"Now see, here's a story," the trucker began. "A friend I know used to haul frozen chickens in a refrigerated rig. He stopped in at a Louisville gas station one night off of I-65. All he wanted was coffee and an hour to rest and to smoke. So he sat down in a booth with his cigarettes and his JFG. He's there about fifteen minutes when this fellow with a camp hatchet walks in and my friend is the first poor bastard this man sees. He walks over and swings that hatchet, but my friend is quick, you see, and he raises his arm and the blade gets buried to the bone. Blood everywhere on the white table and tile floor. But my friend is quick again. He pulls the hatchet out of his arm and plants it between this other fellow's eyes. Splits him right down to the nose. Opens his head like an oyster."

"I don't get it," said Loat.

"Which part?"

"Any of it. Why'd that feller hit your friend with the hatchet in the first place?"

The trucker shook his head. "Now see, there just wasn't any reason for it, was there? My friend had never seen this man before in his life. He just came in with his eyes white as boiled eggs and hit him with the hatchet. That's all there is to it."

Loat thumbed the grooved edge of the pistol's barrel. "I've heard stories like this before. None of them point to anything."

"Here's the point to this one. We could try and give a reason why that man came into the gas station with a hatchet. Maybe he was drunk. Maybe his wife had just left him. Or maybe he was on a cocaine blitz. We could say he never was quite right and had a history of antisocial behavior. The newspapers told it like that. Now see, we could say the same. We could say that because it would seem to make things fit to a pattern. But we'd be neglecting the proper truth."

"And what kind of truth is that?" Loat asked.

"The only kind of truth there ever has been. I'm talking about the fact that the heart is a mystery."

"I don't think there's too much mystery in a crazy fellow hitting your friend with a hatchet."

"Now see, the reason you say that is because you think the story don't matter because you know it and have heard a thousand more just like it." The trucker shook his head in a sad, almost defeated way. "But knowing something doesn't mean it isn't a mystery. Take fish, for instance."

"Fish?"

"Yes. Catfish, say. It's easy to believe you know catfish. Where they spawn and how deep to fish for them at certain times of year. But even the best angler can go out and put stink bait on his hook and throw out in a hole he knows is full of cats, a hole where he's caught them many times before even, and still come home hungry. Why is that? The man still knows catfish. But what he can't never know is their coming and going, to and fro, up and down in the waters. If a man was to know that, to know everything he could about a catfish, why, I just think it would break his heart and take the life right out of him." The trucker's head bobbed in silent affirmation. "A man needs to believe there's some kind of miracle at work in the world."

Loat looked out the window at the passing land brushed with morning. The trucker's voice had a brash country snarl inside it, even when he spoke calmly, as if he were perpetually on the verge of murder, and the blonde hair smeared over his skull made him appear whipped and ridden by some devil from the back-of-beyond of hell.

"Doughballs," Loat mumbled to himself.

"What?"

"Doughballs. Maybe that fisherman you was talking about should've used doughballs instead of stink bait. Maybe he wouldn't have gone home hungry then."

The trucker slapped the steering wheel. "That's all right, Loat," he laughed. "Now see, you're all right. You know when somebody is full of bullshit." The trucker shook his head. "Doughballs," he repeated with a chuckle.

They drove on. Passing through a stand of oaks, the light cowered, but then they came beyond the clutch of hardwoods and the stripped land sprawled lewd before them again, the sun a hazy red welt behind a smoothing of clouds that coated the sky like salve. The road turned to gravel, the pebbles knocking against the tire wells.

On the down slope of a hill were two large streaks in the gravel where a car had braked violently, and at the bottom of the hill a clutter of trash had been spilled in the middle of the way. The trucker slowed as the trash became apparent: the scatterings of a purse, compacts and lipstick vials, a mauve wallet, loose change, tissues.

"It looks like some lady lost her goods," said the trucker.

A pair of tire marks curved off to the right of the road, leading to divots in the gravel shoulder. Blue paint was crusted onto some of the riprap piled there and on the elm saplings spoking up from the cheat grass, which lay matted and beaten.

"It looks like there's where she left the road," Loat said. "We better inspect this." He woke Enoch and the dog and the two men descended from the truck. Loat picked up the wallet, undid the clasp and studied the contents. A few dollars. Credit cards. Driver's license. "Ella Daugherty," he said. He passed the wallet to the trucker, who examined the laminated photo. A woman that required some looking.

"You know her?"

"Sure," said Loat. "Pete Daugherty's daughter." He moved toward the edge of the roadway to where the tire marks fled through the cheat grass. Enoch trotted beside him. For a moment, Loat stood looking into the ravine, making note of the way the saplings bent, a few smeared with blue paint. Finally, he made his slow descent.

The Cadillac rested upside down at the bottom, its wheels in the air, the black of its undercarriage showing dull and greased, a crack in the chassis apparent and jaggedly vivid. Loat came down the slope slowly, watching his steps. The dog skulked behind him. Wind rattled the husks of milkweed around them.

When Loat reached the car, he crouched and through the rear windshield discovered Ella sprawled over the backseat, a crease of blood glaring from her forehead. Her eyes were closed, but her chest rose and fell.

"This looks a treasure," said the trucker.

Loat jerked at his voice. He hadn't heard him come down the slope, but now the man squatted beside him, the tails of his blazer leaping in the breeze.

"Help me get her out," Loat said.

They wrenched the driver door open and ladled Ella onto the ground. She seemed to pour into their arms and then drip through their fingers, a liquid weight. The blood on her was dry. As they lifted her up out of the ravine, her light hair straying and catching on sawbriars, she made a few groans of pain and her eyes darted open and then closed again like polyps. The Doberman panted and circled about, so maddened by the scent of blood that Loat had to kick him away.

Returning to the rig, they stowed her in the bunk, resting her on some crusty blankets. For a spell, they watched her, their quiet equal to hers, as if she were a glowing fire they would sleep beside. Finally, they resettled themselves. The trucker cranked the engine over, and they drove away.

"Go on back to Daryl's," Loat instructed.

"You don't want to go on to Pete's?"

"No. I think I can figure what happened." Loat looked out the window at the woods rushing by. "Beam's still out there somewhere."

At the next crossroads, the trucker did a turnabout in the middle of road, and they roared back the way they had come.

The rode in silence for awhile. After a few miles, the trucker spoke. "What do you think happened out there at Pete's?" he asked. "And what about your man Presto?"

Loat shucked the clip from his pistol, drew the slide back to free the round that was in the chamber, then polished the barrel with the sleeve of his shirt. "Fuck Presto," he said. "Man can't take care of my Cadillac, he can't expect me to waste no worry over him."

# XVIII

## SATURDAY

The leaves rattled a whispery snicker as Beam crawled down from the branches and stood on the soft moss like a creature numinous and newly descended to earth. He'd slept sometime during the night, a kind of rigid aimless doze, and his ribs ached from sprawling in the beech limbs.

For a moment, he thought of climbing back into the beech, wondering if the balm of sudden sleep might again befall him. He looked up into the tree. The silver of its bark gleamed in the sun, and its leaves curled like strange feathers in the breeze. He placed his hand on the trunk, which was covered in carvings, vague dendroglyphs, moss-grown runes and dates, the work of blades long rusted to brittleness. He ran his fingers through their grooves. Here was testament to the old troubles—love and loss and the abatement of wealth, the toil come to naught. Rain had drawn canals in the limbs of the tree, water tracing the wood and working its way down the old courses to fade the record cut into the bark.

The wind came up and swatted the last of sleep from his eyes. Beam checked the cartridges in his pistol. He slid the clip out and blew dirt from the housing and then reloaded the gun before stowing it back in the waist of his jeans. The cold barrel gave him a chill.

Before him, the woods lay level and clean, with only scant undergrowth, greenbriars and hogweeds sprouting along the root-runs of trees, a few wind-falls rotting into the black soil. Everything seemed tended and swept, as if some unseen keeper, some impish tenant warden, had broomed away all the debris, all brush, all the wild clutter, and left behind a fine smooth green flowing out and leading, somehow, to peace.

Beam bent to retie his boots and saw the blood crusted along the laces and tongues of his Laramies. Remembering the night and the guns and the dogs, he knew there would be no peace. Pete was dead, maybe Ella as well, and the hounds were still after him and he could run all he wanted, but it wouldn't matter. Picking up a handful of dead leaves, he scraped the toes of his boots, but the stain had set in the leather and nothing could take it away.

He sat on the ground, closed his eyes, and saw Ella and the dogs tangled together on top of Presto Geary, the blood slicking across the floor. The thought that he'd abandoned her gripped him and he felt a sink in his gut. He had left at the moment she needed him most. It didn't matter that she had wanted him to give himself up. Her own fear had worked her down that path, and he could forgive her for it. He could forgive her everything. But he could not forgive himself, and it had always been so. Even the slightest infraction from the way back times of his childhood stood branded in hot lettering on his conscience, whether it was shirking his duties on the ferry or being too quick to use his fists over a poolroom squabble at The Doe Eyed Lady. He heard all his many sins being read aloud to him again.

He raked his boots through the leaves and then got up and began walking. He did not know where he was going, he only knew he couldn't be still. He moved under the low branches and out through the shade of the forest with its deep covering of moss while the full boughs rocked above him in the wind. He did not know where he was going, but he hoped there would be water there. His tongue clung to the roof of his mouth. He had no plan now other than to get water.

After a time, he came to a low spot in the woods where a copper spring trickled out of a rock face, a dull spitting of penny-colored water that piddled over ferns and stones and then disappeared into a sink in the ground. He stood staring at the spring, knowing he couldn't drink it, and his thirst grew large inside him. He went on.

Eventually, he came to a car, a blue and elderly Buick Skylark strangled in sawbriers, rust leeching over the paint, the chrome of the wheels spangling white in the sun. A dead hickory snag had fallen across the trunk and crushed the back end, yet the windows and windshields stood intact. Beam looked around him, but there was not even a trace of road anywhere. This was a car where no car should be.

He looked inside. The faded upholstery foamed yellow stuffing and sprouted rusty springs, and the backseat was diamonded with broken glass. The driveshaft lay in the floorboards. The radio swung pendulous on nervy wires. Birdshit spackled the dashboard, and moss covered the steering column and the door panels. Beam kicked the briers clear and yanked the driver side door open, the hinges squawking, and a smell like the air from a cellar swam over him, a dank aroma of rubber and rotten carpet and mouse droppings. Still, it was a place to sit down. He dragged himself inside and shut the door.

He craned his neck and looked at himself in the rearview. Deep hoops of shadow hung beneath his eyes, and his skin had turned a sick and curdy yellow. His lips were cracked from thirst. On the floorboard was a puddle of rainwater, as a gash in the roof of the car had allowed storms and the passing weather to wander in. Beam struggled down and lapped at the puddle, slapping the lukewarm water over his face. It smelled awful. It tasted worse, a faint hint of carpet and a tinge of metal and paint, but the thirst was large in him and he drank until the puddle was diminished.

He sat back upright in the seat. The heat of the car pulsed around him. He rested his hands on the wheel and watched the sunlight fall casual and scant through the upper canopy of trees into the walnut saplings and briers below. The gun itched his back. He took it out of his jeans and laid it on the seat beside him. Then he leaned his head back and tried to think of nothing.

He might have slept. He didn't know, and that uncertainty made him initially confuse the two Dobermans for a nightmare. They came trotting through the trees, muzzles lowered to the ground. He watched them through the windshield and thought *this is nothing real, this is only dream stuff.* But then the dogs growled and one leapt onto the hood of the Buick, and when its claws clanked on the metal, he knew he was not dreaming.

In his startled fear, Beam grabbed the Walther pistol and pumped two shots through the windshield. The glass cracked but held. The dog jumped back, then came again, growling and snarling as it began to dig at the damaged glass. The other dog trotted in circles around the car, an anxious angry whine rising from its gut until it too sprang up onto the hood of the car. Both dogs pushed their heads through the gash in the metal roof so that their drool fell onto Beam's face and arms in hot steamy blots. He shouted curses at the animals and kicked at the roof with his boots. The metal boomed, but the dogs continued to howl and bark as Beam squirmed lower in the seat.

It was then that he became aware of the wasps. They had built a nest under the front seat, and they erupted in a black and yellow swarm around him. One stung him just below his left eye. He screamed as his eye immediately began to swell shut. Another pricked him on the cheek, another on his hand so that he dropped the gun and it discharged with a heavy cough, leaving a gaping hole in the floor. The wasps were now thick in the car, bumping against the roof and windows, stinging Beam repeatedly so that he fell to the floor. In a great spasm of rage, he managed to pull himself up and yank the nest from under the seat. His hand instantly became black with wasps and the pain that darted up his arm was unlike any he'd known before. Somehow, he rolled the passenger window down a few inches and flung the nest outside and then crawled into the rear seat, his vision blurred from the wasp venom, his head a woozy quiver. He lay down flat on his back. Far off, the dogs continued to wail, but the sound faded as Beam closed his eyes and the dark swallowed him up.

Night had fallen when he awoke. Crickets puzzled over their old concerns in the dark, and moonlight fell in a scattered pattern through the trees. The wasps were gone, but the places on his body where they'd stung him throbbed and ached. The swelling of his left eye had receded, but his vision remained blurry.

Beam climbed into the front seat. Through the cracked windshield, he could see the dogs were lying on the hood, their muzzles resting on their forepaws. When he settled himself, one opened its eyes and lifted its head to watch him as if he were a fish swimming behind aquarium glass.

One shell remained in the pistol. Beam drew the slide back, the brass of the single cartridge flashing in the moonlight. He eased the slide true again and cocked the gun. Then he cranked the driver's side down a few inches. "C'mon, you sonuvabitch," Beam called to the dog. "I'm right here."

The dog stood and clambered down the front of the car. The other dog quickly followed. Their paws scuffled through the leaves. Beam waited. His breath pummeled against his ribs. He could not see the dogs, and a brief hope flared inside him that they had gone away. Then they were there again, shapes turning mystical and formless in the moonlight, heads bent to the ground, creatures that now seemed iridescent as a flexing lunar radiance emanated from their bodies.

Beam cranked the window down all the way and one of the dogs rushed forward, butting its head into the car so that he could smell the creature's foul breath. The dog struggled to get in, raving wildly as globs of drool fell from its muzzle.

Beam brought the Walther up. "Right here," he whispered, and pulled the trigger. The Doberman's lower jaw tore away, its warm blood dousing his legs. The dog fell from the car and crawled through the leaves, a wearied moan slithering up from its belly. The other dog trotted out of the shadows. It paused before the first hound, which coughed and then died. The surviving dog dipped its nose to sniff at the blood, then raised it eyes to stare at Beam in the car.

Beam rolled the window up again and slouched against the passenger door. His chest rocked with breath, and once it had steadied, he slowly unlaced his boots. He tied the long stout rope laces together, knotting them with a clove hitch, and then attached one end to the handle of the driver's side door. He then cranked the passenger window down a few inches and ran the free end of the laces through the opening so that it draped down the outside of the door. Slowly, he opened the passenger side door. The hinges held it agape. Through the driver side window, he saw the Doberman cock its head. Beam moved to the driver side door, and when he opened it, the dog tensed, its forelegs stiffening.

Beam then scooted back toward the passenger door. The dog took a step forward. A long thread of drool dripped from its muzzle.

"I'm here," Beam said, calmly.

When the Doberman bolted forward, Beam crawfished out the passenger side door and slammed it shut as the dog came bounding up into the Buick, moaning and wild, scraping its claws against the dingy window like a creature mad with hunger. Beam then yanked the laces so that the driver's door closed, trapping the dog inside.

The animal went berserk. Foaming and apoplectic, roaring and growling, it leapt first at the front windshield and then tore over the backseat to push its muzzle and paws through the gashed roof. The car rocked and creaked on its rusted chassis.

For a time, Beam stood and watched. Eventually, the dog began to moan at him steadily, a rage drop-forged and flaming in its eyes.

Beam leaned against one of the car's fenders, and saw the other dog, dead in the leaves with its head half gone. Beam's lap was damp with the animal's blood, which he brushed at absently. Then he threw the gun onto the ground and staggered away into the trees, the moonlight dropping over his shoulders like a shawl.

He was still walking when the moon left and the first rays of daylight began pricking through the clouds and trees. A cold dawn's beginning as he journeyed toward someplace obscure, his mind quaking at all he had done, and the wonder of what he might yet do.

# XIX

## SATURDAY

He visited her at night. Alone on the frail porch, the trees casting pickets of moonlight across her feet, she doddered in the old unpainted rocker as he came up into the yard silent and vague as smoke. His boots whispered a hiss in the grass and his belt buckle glinted and then the dog appeared and she knew it was him and not some tatterdemalion dream come wandering out of her whiskeyed half-sleep.

"Hello to the porch," he said. His voice sounded like tin warping in the heat.

"Come on up here, Loat," she answered.

He stayed the dog in the yard and then ascended the steps, his smell of stale musk rising to her. She tipped the coffee mug of whisky back one more time, the dregs burning her throat, and then sat the mug beneath the rocker and looked up at him through the half-gloom, his shadow falling over her like the night robes of a deranged monk so that she was enveloped in the blackness he carried through the world.

"If you come to get a piece you're too late. There ain't none left to give."

"I didn't come for a fuck," said Loat.

"Then you won't be disappointed."

Loat leaned against the porch's veranda, the wood creaking under his weight. "I come to tell you about Clem," he said.

Her eyes steadied on him. "I didn't believe you'd come do that," she said.

"Well, that's the reason I'm here."

She bobbed in the rocker, the runners cracking against the smooth porch boards. "Since you said that, you don't have to say any more of it. I can figure the rest."

A spell of quiet fell between them. Loat breathed huskily in the dark, while Derna swayed in the rotting chair as a dry wind smoothed the hair over her brow like an undertaker arranging the last grayed locks of a corpse.

"I guess it give you some pleasure, doing that to Clem," she finally said.

"I didn't do it."

"You didn't?"

"It was Daryl who had it done."

Derna looked at Loat. His eyes were like a pair of glassy black stones lodged in his face. She could read nothing in them.

"I doubt you tried to stop it," she said.

"If I'd been there I would have."

"That sounds a lie."

"It ain't, though."

"So, you come out here to tell me the way you wished it had turned out?"

Loat ran his hand over the rail of the veranda. "I wanted you to know, just in case you didn't, that Clem was good to you. A sight better than I ever could've been."

"It don't take much to do better than you, Loat."

"I can't argue with that." He turned and braced himself against the railing so that his back was to her and the moon came cowling over his shoulders to drop sleek and damp on the porch behind him. Out in the yard, the Doberman sat on its haunches. When Derna shifted in the chair, the animal snorted and groaned.

"You aim to have that dog eat me?" she asked.

"No, Derna. He's done been fed today."

"What about you? You been fed lately?"

He turned and looked at her, a crooked wicker grimalkin

with her eyes scorched and burning.

"I've not seen hide nor hair of Beam," he said.

"Say you ain't?"

"No. Have you heard from him?"

Derna shook her head slowly. "I looked. Couldn't place a sign of him. Are you saying you want to give up on looking?"

"No. I only wanted to come by and give you some peace about Clem. That's the main reason I'm here."

Derna laughed, harsh and croupy. "I never had no peace from any man. Not Clem. Not you. Not my boys." She steadied in the rocker. "You always were vain. It's no surprise you think you could give me peace."

"I don't guess it were ever mine to give," he answered. "I can't say I ever knowed much peace my ownself."

"Well, that's the first thing I've heard you say tonight I'd put any stock in."

Loat sat down on the top step of the porch. He whistled and the Doberman trotted over to him. He smoothed the dog's ears back over its skull, the dog whining at his touch. Derna saw the absolute devotion the animal held for him, a thing she'd never known nor ever wished to give to anyone, not even herself. She didn't know if the world had killed such a desire, or if she'd simply been born without it, but the more she thought about it, the less it seemed to matter. All she owned was her life now, a small pittance of years left to draw out beside a slow river. All she'd once wanted and hoped for—a man and children—was gone. There was nothing else.

"You still plan on finding Beam, then?" she asked.

"I do," said Loat. He released the dog and its eyes flashed cold and bright.

"And why is that?"

"It's what you asked me to do."

"Maybe that's why, but I don't believe so," she said. "I think maybe you've come to know how it is with you and Beam."

Loat looked at her. "What are you talking about?"

Derna wadded her skirt between her fingers. Her lips fumbled together dryly, and then she swallowed. "You got to remember how I was already showing when I left you and Paul," she said.

"Showing?"

Derna drew a hand across her belly. "In a family way."

Loat snorted. "I'm hearing a tale too thick to stir," he said.

"And you got to remember how I'd been sick a month before I took off. How I wouldn't see hardly no callers out at Daryl's? You remember that, I know."

"Best I recall you never were too eager to keep company out at Daryl's."

"That's true. I didn't like that work none. Never did like laying down and earning my keep with what the Lord put between my legs, but you got to think how what I'm saying right now is the truth and how maybe we could both of us stand to do something right for once."

"Hell, Derna. It could be any one of the studs that used to come to Daryl's that put Beam in your belly."

"You know that's not so. In your heart, you know. I was your favorite girl back then. You'd hardly let any other man come near me."

Loat turned away from her and looked out at the trees and the darkness. "I'm an old man now, Derna. Old and sick, and now you tell me the boy I've been hunting is mine. Don't that shit the bed?"

"I'm old too, Loat," Derna said. "I'm an old woman and I ain't fifty yet. So I'd like to get buried with one of my own still walking the earth."

Loat tongued the corner of his mouth. "Did Clem know about this?"

Derna shook her head. "He thought Beam belonged to some fly-by-night that stopped in at Daryl's," she said. "He never knew he was yours."

"What about Beam? What's he know?"

"Nothing."

"Nothing?"

Derna shook her head again. "He always believed Clem was his daddy."

Loat wiped his mouth and grunted. "And now, after all these years, you tell me that Beam is mine. All on account of Paul winding up drowned. Ain't this some shit?"

"Don't it make a difference at all? You knowing Beam is yours?"

Loat reached down and patted the dog's withers. "I can't say for sure," he said. "Helluva thing to lay on me here in my rickety years."

Her eyes tightened. "Don't say another word about me laying this on you, Loat," she said. "I've been bearing it since I felt the first kick in my belly."

Loat chuckled. "I expect that's so." He took his hand from the Doberman and wiped at his trousers, his expression squashed and cramped as if some great pain teethed at his soul. Which perhaps it did. "And you want me to keep going out and listening and looking and that'll be some step toward doing a right thing? For once in my life?"

Derna picked at her dress collar. "I don't know what else to do," she said.

Arching his back, Loat groaned and then spat. "You know he killed Paul?"

"Yes, I know that."

"And you don't think that colors it some? The way I see him? Paul was the only boy I ever knew to say was mine until right now."

Derna spelled her rocking. She remained silent a long while. Then she rose from the chair and walked across the porch to Loat. The Doberman growled as she came near and Loat turned and stood to meet her and she put a hand on his arm, and felt his blood flowing along under her fingers, moving through its old courses, its allotted places. Loat didn't shy at her touch. She knew he wouldn't. He was calm, sturdy. In his eyes, the fierceness brightened.

"If you're saying you aim to do Beam wrong on account of Paul then I need to kill you right now," she said.

Loat whistled softly. "That's a job many a hard man ain't been able to lay a hand to. What makes you think a dried out whore like you could do it?"

Derna slid a hand into her dress pocket and pulled out Clem's .32 snubnose. She pushed the barrel into Loat's belly. His breathing leveled.

"You make a fine old bitch of a widow," he said.

Derna cocked the gun's hammer back. "You find Beam and you don't harm him. You bring him back here."

He stared at her a moment, pouring his eyes into hers. "Hell, Derna," he laughed. "I won't hurt Beam. He's mine. Him and Paul. I throwed both colts and I don't hurt what's mine."

Derna eased the hammer down. She tucked the gun back into her dress and then floated back to her chair and sat down and began rocking again. "If any hurt comes to him and I hear you were the one to bring it I'll hunt for you and I'll kill you," she said.

"You ain't got to worry none," he said. He descended the steps and walked out of the yard. The dog trotted after him, and they crossed through the moonlight and then the dark of the trees took them.

Derna stilled her rocking to listen. She thought she heard their footsteps, but the only noise was the wind teething on the walnut and locust boughs, a soft drizzling whisper. She was alone, as perhaps she'd always been. She took the gun from her dress and let it rest on her lap. The night was long, and she wanted to be ready for whatever it brought.

# XX

## SUNDAY

Daryl sat in a back room of the Quonset hut behind a long battered desk so old and brown it looked like an ancient Negro washwoman bowing prostrate before him. Two whores dressed in pastel negligees stood at his side filling small sandwich bags with prime leaf marijuana and then placing them in milk crates. A cigar burned in an ashtray on the desk. Occasionally, Daryl cleared his throat and one of the women lifted the cigar to his lips so he could puff on it with a low drowsy leisure.

Sitting there in his plush chair as the smoke snaked through the air, he was nearly asleep when the trucker entered the room.

"Afternoon, Daryl," the trucker said, seating himself in one of the metal folding chairs in front of the desk.

Daryl opened his eyes slowly. He swallowed some phlegm, then jerked his chin toward the doorway. "You girls go on outside," he said to the whores.

The women flowed out of the room in a flurry of perfume and lace. The trucker watched them go and then turned back to Daryl. "Now see, there's just not many men so lucky as to be kept by a clutch of such beauties," he said.

Daryl waved a pink stump through the air. "Cut the bullshit. I want to ask you about some things the sheriff told me when he visited the other day."

The trucker leaned forward, placing his hands on the desk, his pale fingers like strange anemic flora taking root in the black grain of the wood. His eyes were a pale, chilled blue. "Now see, it just don't matter to me," he said. "I can talk all day and tell all kinds of things."

"What I want told is the truth."

"I can sure enough try that."

Daryl squirmed in his chair, the plush vinyl squeaking beneath him. "The sheriff claimed you paid a visit to him," he began. "Said you told him all about the ruckus you had with Beam up here. Is that true?"

"Every word of it." The trucker's lips bent into a smile.

"Give me one good reason why I shouldn't have you put in a hole in the ground then?" Daryl propped his stumps on top of the desk.

The trucker's smile faded to a look cold and savage. Slowly, he reached in his blazer pocket and then drew his fist out, holding it aloft above the desk, and when he opened his fingers a pair of dice clattered down on the wooden top. They were carved from ivory and as yellow and worn as old teeth. "What's the number I just rolled?" he asked

Daryl squinted at him. "I don't have time for any of your shit. I want to know why you went to the sheriff."

The trucker pointed to the dice. "Just tell me what number I rolled."

Daryl leaned forward to study the dice. "Nine," he said.

The trucker scooped up the dice and spilled them across the desk once more.

"And now?"

"It's nine again."

"A third time then." The trucker dropped the dice, one after the other.

"It's still nine," said Daryl.

The trucker reached down and took up the dice and held them in the flat of his palm. They glistened in the sash of window light cutting into the room; their yellow was suddenly gone as if washed away, and they might have been a pair of eyes prized from the head of a ruffian hustler, so white and wet did they now appear. "Now see," he said, "these are loaded dice."

Daryl slouched back in his chair. "I can't say I give a damp shit," he said.

The trucker closed his fist over the dice and rattled them together. "You might, if I tell you where I found them."

"Be for telling me," Daryl asked.

The trucker placed the dice carefully on the desktop. "These were in Clem's pocket," he said.

"Is that right?"

"I found them when I was dragging him out back to the ditch. Right before I put one in his brain." He folded his hands together. "I'd say they're the same pair he threw with you out at the mines many a long night ago."

"Maybe so. It don't make no difference to me either way."

"It should."

"Why's that?"

The trucker produced from his vest pocket a small magnifying glass. He stood and held the glass over the dice, his face so pale he appeared like some manic lapidary ghosted from the outer realms to barter jewels as might dot the crown of a profligate fool, a man brought here by the forces of fate to inspect the fulhams in a gaming room where all stood to win nothing but a loss utter and total.

"Check the initials on these," he said.

Daryl pushed himself forward and peered through the lens. Etched into each die, in a tiny near illegible script, were the letters LD.

"What Clem told me before I took him out back," said the trucker, "is that Loat gave him those dice. That they were the same ones he tossed with you out at the mines. That Loat made sure it turned out the way it did."

"A man who is about to die will say anything," Daryl said. "Plus, you could have plucked those dice off anyone and then scratched those letters on there. I got no reason at all to trust you."

The trucker placed the magnifying glass in his pocket and straightened the lapels of his blazer. "Do you believe that in your heart?" he asked.

"My heart? You talking pretty now, ain't you? I don't ask a thing of my heart. Only children and women are fool enough to go with their heart."

"I won't try and convince you, then," said the trucker.

"And why's that?"

"It's beneath me."

"Beneath you?"

"I won't waste time stringing a fence around the truth so you can see how it's shaped."

Daryl eyed the trucker. He sat sleek and firm, his hair raked over his scalp, his breaths small and easy as if he were sipping idly at the air. "It don't make sense," he said.

"What's that?"

"Loat putting his initials on those. That's a dumb thing to do."

"Now see, there's some men made that way," the trucker said. "They got to put their mark on everything they touch. They got to let the world know what belongs to it and what belongs to them. Now see, Loat's marked you just like he marked these dice."

"What are you talking about?"

The trucker picked up the dice and spilled them forth over the desk again. "Cast these bones out and so he made of you a man only mostly there," he said. He picked up a single die and held it pinched between his fingers. "You got his mark just like these dice. Now see, it's not enough for Loat to have things and have them do what he wants. He's got to put his sign on it. Got to play that old whore whose name is legend and whose strength is legion."

"I don't have one clue what you're talking about," said Daryl, shaking his head.

The trucker placed his hands down flat on the desk. "Now

see, you build a legend around a man with what he owns and what he's done and he'll look as big as God himself from the outside. And Loat ain't no fool. He knows the game well enough to fix it."

"You saying he owns me?"

"Don't he?"

Daryl fell silent. He thought of all the years playing tote-along to Loat, running his drugs and giving him a cut from what he made on the whores, Loat snickering in his dreams so it seemed that Daryl often woke to the sound of the man's laughter. And then his mind pushed even further, to the night at the mines when he'd crouched in the blue moonlight to throw dice with Clem, Loat standing beside them like a sleek totem, his eyes burning down at the circle of dust where the dice lay scattered. "That's it," said Loat. "Clem rolls nine. You got to climb it, Daryl." After that, the rush of light and heat, the fire and the fall, the black pull of the air, the smell of electricity, of singed hair and the soft padding of grass that caught him.

"I don't see why he'd want to save Clem like that," Daryl said, almost whispering now. "Why he'd have him throw those loaded dice so it'd be me to maybe get killed and not Clem."

The trucker slid the dice off the desk into his palm and pocketed them. "The why of it don't matter so much as you knowing it's the truth," he said.

Daryl blinked as if noticing the man seated before him for the first time. "Why are you telling me any of this?" he said. "And why did you go to the sheriff and tell him about Beam?"

The trucker shifted in his chair. "I want a price," he said. "You can understand that, I'm sure. Being a businessman, you have to shop around."

"Did you think there'd be some kind of reward out?"

"I didn't think that."

"Then why go to Elvis?"

"I didn't say the price had to be money."

Daryl raised a pink stump to his chin and scratched his whiskers. "If it ain't in money, then how would it get paid?"

The trucker looked around the room, as if perusing it for appraisal, eyeing the scattered wealth of televisions, liquor, the promise of women that might be worth his services. "I'll not refuse a dollar," he said. "But I might like to have it paid in other ways."

"I still don't know what you're talking about. Prices and payments. What the fuck is it you're selling, anyway?"

The trucker cocked his head back and drew a long breath that made it sound as if the air about him were sizzling. "Now see," he said, "I got this trade. It's the thing I was born to, so I got to go out and work it. Man don't work at the trade he's born to, he's lower than dirt in my opinion. When I stopped in your bar the other day and seen the doings that went on here I knew I'd come to the right place to work." He leaned forward and placed his hands on the desktop again. "You give me a fair price and I'll bring Loat to you."

"That your trade? Murder for hire?"

"That's part of it. I'm a damn fine hand at piano, too. Play that boogie-woogie. That doo-wop. That rock 'n roll. Got some Mozart and Beethoven up my sleeve, too. Classical shit, you know."

"I ain't in the market for a piano player," Daryl said. "And if I wanted Loat gone, I could've done it myself years ago."

"Now see, I just don't think that's the truth. He's the big fish in this pond. But I can tell you ain't no small fry yourself. Pond's too small for two big fish. One got to go belly up. But you ain't had the sauce to catch that big fish all these years so I think you need a man got the bait."

Daryl stroked the desktop with one of his stumps. "Let me get this straight," he said. "You just happen by my bar after giving Beam Sheetmire a ride up here. Okay, maybe that just happened. But now you're telling me you'll kill Loat for a price? And all this after going to the sheriff?" Daryl shook his head. "That don't hold water."

"Going to the sheriff was just me shopping around," said the trucker. "I had to gauge all the angles and make the best play. Now see, it's like a piece of music. You can play it just like the sheet says and that's what most do. But they's a kind like me that wants to push the song and make it really talk. Make their own arrangement. Going to the sheriff was just me playing a scale and seeing how the notes all fit together."

Daryl sat silent for a spell, his eyes leveled on the trucker as if he could see something ancient and undiluted in him, like the misty banks of the first morning's broken shore where the waters lapped at the warming mud, and it might have been the print of God's own finger there.

"All I want," the trucker said, breaking the silence, "is to bring you Loat. You leave Beam to me to deal with as I see fit."

"What do you want with Beam?"

"He called me a thief."

"And that's enough to make you want him dead?"

"I can't abide it."

"And you can't get Beam unless Loat is out of the way. You saw that clear off, didn't you?"

"I see lots of things."

"How much would it cost to do this?" Daryl asked.

"Forty," said the trucker.

"Forty?" Daryl coughed. "That's steep trade."

"Now see, I don't mean forty large," he said. "I just mean forty."

"Just forty?"

"That's right. All I need is a little walking around money. Enough to buy a sandwich and put some diesel in my rig. You can even consider me doing that Clem feller a cash back advance on services soon to be rendered."

"This all sounds like a pile of hot horse turds," Daryl said.

"You may think so," the trucker said, "but I don't like to be called a thief. I don't like to be called nothing I ain't. Don't mind a bit if a man calls me all kinds of dreadful things, so long as they're accurate. Why, a man might say, 'He's low down scum. He's killed men and he's whored and gambled and he fucked my grandmother. He's an egg-sucking dog and I hope he dies.' Now see, none of that don't bother me because ever bit of it's true."

"Whose grandmother did you fuck?" Daryl asked.

"Can't remember." The trucker lifted a hand and slung the greasy net of his hair over his head. "I used to try and fuck 'em all every chance I got. Now see, I can't keep track of the ones I fucked and the ones I was aiming to fuck but never got around to. It's a bad and worrisome state to be in."

Daryl stared at the man seated in front of his desk, his eyes a cruel and frozen blue. He'd never seen such a creature in his life. Suddenly, his chest began to quiver as a jolt of cold ran the length of his spine. It felt as if someone were stabbing the soles of his feet with chilled ice picks. He'd only felt this way once before, and that was the night out at the mines when Loat commanded him to climb the power pole with the pair of bolt cutters.

"I can do for Loat same as I did for Clem," said the trucker.

Daryl tapped his feet against the floor. The sharp pains continued to run up his calves, and the ends of his stumps began to itch so that he scratched them against the edge of the desk. What the trucker said was true. Loat had always treated him like a lapdog, tossing him a few scraps here and there, but never letting him gnaw his own steak. And then there were the dice. He heard them clattering down over and over in his mind, and their echo gave him all the reason he needed.

"There's a roll of dollars in the top drawer of this desk," he said.

The trucker rose from his chair and came around the desk. He opened the top drawer and took out the roll of money and peeled off two twenties and then re-banded the roll and replaced it in the desk and shut the drawer. He folded the money into the breast pocket of his blazer and looked down at Daryl. "That Loat got a grandmother?" he asked.

Daryl shook his head. "She's been dead a long time."

"Well, I still might fuck her anyway," he said. Then he winked at Daryl and left the room.

# XXI

## SUNDAY

She was eating her lunch aboard the ferry when the cruiser slipped under the locust trees and parked on the landing. As the sheriff walked up, she continued to stir her fork through the bowl of tuna salad and she kept her head down and did not look up when his black shoes boomed on the metal hull.

"Afternoon, Derna," he said.

She chewed and swallowed. "Elvis," she answered.

"Clem not working today?"

Derna laid the fork in the bowl and placed it beneath the lawn chair she was sitting in. "Clem's gone," she said.

"Oh? Where to?"

"I don't know."

"You don't know?"

She shook her head once. "He left out Friday afternoon. Said he was going for groceries but he never come back."

Elvis rested his hands on his hips. "He took the truck?"

"He took Old Dog." She nodded. "I don't look for him to be back."

Elvis moved closer to her and squatted beside the lawn chair, catching the sour scent of her body mixed with the warm muggy stench of the river.

"Why don't you think he'll be back?"

Derna narrowed her eyes at him. "I think some folks have seen to it that he can't never come back," she said.

Elvis stood up. "What time did he leave Friday?"

Derna shrugged and looked out at the river where the shoals

flexed against the hull of the ferry. "Two or three, I guess. But it don't matter. You won't never find him. Be wasting your time if you was to even start looking. Same goes for that boy Beam of mine." She threw a hand out, wiping it through the damp air. "Both of them gone."

"You didn't tell me Beam had left."

"Clem sent him off," she said.

"Why did he do that?"

"I don't know."

Elvis rolled his tongue inside his mouth nervously and then gripped the boat rails, his hands braced and spread before him as if to stall the waters, or at least slow them to the sidereal coming and going of the world itself as it clocked imperceptible through the void and its glassy black hourlessness. "You said some folks had seen to it that Clem wouldn't come home. Who did you mean?" he asked.

"You know who I mean. Don't make me say it."

"Do you think saying a name to me is going to bring you more trouble than you've already had?"

"You don't know him like I do. He can read sign. He can track what's gone and know what's to come."

"Next you'll be telling me he can fly, too."

Derna hardened her eyes and glared at Elvis. "I'd not mock what you don't understand," she said. "He was born in the dark of the moon with a caul over his head. You can't know what that means other than he isn't the kind of man that can be touched by the law. Not your law, anyway. Maybe not even God's law." She pulled at the edge of her collar and a smile crawled up one side of her face. "You think I'm crazy, don't you?" she said.

Elvis looked at her. With her eyes as fixed and solid as knobs of cold white bone, Derna did look a bit crazy, though he'd never tell her such a thing. He thought back through the years to when he'd first become sheriff and had learned of Derna, and the rumors of her whoring days, and he realized he'd never been anything but worried for this woman, who seemed to stare in constant aghast surprise at the world, as if she could not believe how far it had come away from what she had hoped it would be. "I think," he said, "you're a woman who's had more than her share of hardship and that it's no wonder the things it's causing you to say. But what I really care about knowing is why all of this is happening. There's two men missing and one drowned in the river. You need to tell me what you know, Derna."

She fretted with the collar of her blouse some more and then sighed. "Most men," she began, "they love something, they see that it gets satisfied. They want to keep it and tend it so that it grows and gets healthy. Loat's not that way. He takes love and swallows it down until there's not a bit of it left in the world. You understand that and maybe you can know what it is you are up against."

"You and him were in love?"

Derna nodded. "A bad kind of it." She stood creakily and moved beside Elvis at the boat rails. Her fingers tapped the steel, her eyes studying the river as if it were a book, a worn keep of verses that even now were being writ with the ceaseless churn of the waters. "I left off whoring because I loved him. So I could only be with him. Then I found I had to leave him because what stood between us was the kind of love that would be a ruin to the both of us." She turned and looked at the sheriff. "That's when I took up with Clem. Clem could give me peace, but not love, so Loat didn't mind me being with him. At first, I thought that meant Loat loved me so much he only wanted me happy. But I know that's not how it is now. He wanted Clem to have me because he could keep me close that way. He could say anything and Clem would do it." She blew a long breath out and raked her hand along the rail. "And it's that Daryl that has been laying for Clem for now on twenty years. Ever since what happened out at the mines."

"I was out at Daryl's just yesterday," said Elvis. "There wasn't a sign of Clem or his truck."

"And there won't never be. Clem is somewhere at the bottom of a strip-pit and that's where his truck is as well, I imagine."

Elvis straightened himself. "You think Daryl caught him out somewhere?"

"No. I think he went to Daryl's looking for Beam. I think he had to go out there. It kept eating at him, the way he'd been all his life, in the keep of Loat. I think he finally got tired of it and he had to go out there. He never was a hard man, but the world kept asking him to be. I suppose I did some of the asking myself."

"I'll get a warrant and search Daryl's bar."

Derna slammed an open hand against the boat rail and a long tone shivered down the metal. "You're not listening," she said. "There's nothing left of Clem. He's gone. You can peek under every rug and curtain out at Daryl's and that's not going to change. I am telling you this because you came to me. And you looked like you wanted to know. Well, I'm saying it. You can't best these men. So don't try."

Elvis raked a shoe over the hull of the ferry. "Clem sent Beam off and then went looking for him? That what you're telling me?"

Derna crossed her arms and stared at him. "I guess you think that don't make sense."

"No, I can't say that it does."

Darts of shadow bled across the brown shoalwater beside the ferry and then coalesced into a single blot as a school of shad fled from a largemouth bass. Derna watched the chop and sling of the river while it broke on the white riprap along the bank. "Get old," she said. "Get old and then you'll see it. The way it is for most folks, they spend a good bit of their life trying to get back what they give away. They believe giving it away will save them because to have it makes them afraid. But then it's gone and they're the ones that made it leave and that eats at them until they go out to get it back again. Clem wasn't any different." She dropped her hands over the rails and watched the shad tremble and shift beneath the surface of the river. "*I* ain't any different," she said.

"Does this have anything to do with Paul getting killed?"

Derna twisted her eyes away from him. "It's no harder thing in the world for a mother to say, I don't reckon. And I just don't believe I've got it in me to say it."

Elvis took his hat off and stroked the brim. "I don't believe you need to say anything," he said. "There's room enough in the not saying for me to figure what you mean."

A car braked on the far landing and honked its horn once. Derna slid her hands along the rails. "I thank you for the visit," she said, "but I got to work now. I'm what all is left to do it."

Elvis placed his hat back on his head. "I'm going to help, Derna," he said. "I don't know if you believe that or not, but it's what I'm going to do."

Derna smiled at him as she tucked a few strands of hair behind her ears. "You'd do well to wake up so you can see the ditch you're headed for," she said flatly. She moved off to start the tug. The motor gurgled up, a yellow froth churgling from the trolling prop.

Elvis stepped off the deck onto the landing and watched as the ferry drifted into the river, the brown current furrowed and wimpling against its hull as the hawsers strained through their pulleys. He watched for awhile as the rudder cut its faint brief grooves in the river, and then he walked back to the cruiser and drove to the courthouse in town.

# XXII

## MONDAY

In the afternoon, a quaky crowd of whores and miners gathered behind the Quonset hut. They sipped whisky from jelly jars, the men hugging closely to their women, many of whom were dressed in satin negligees. Loat stood among the crowd patting the head of the goat Samhill Doug. The day before, he had paid Daryl seventy-five dollars for the animal. He had then attached a dog collar and leash to the animal and led it out into the gravel lot behind the bar, where he left him overnight, without food or water. The fasting had sharpened the goat's eyes to a hard and steely meanness and his hackles bristled with anger.

The trucker, prim and slick in his suit, his hair gleaming under the day's cloudy light, bounced over. He tickled Samhill under the chin, which drew a neigh.

"I want you to show us just how good of a surgeon you are," Loat said. "It's what you claim, so I want to see some evidence."

"You want me to take this goat's kidney out?" the trucker asked in response.

"I'll need it done myself," Loat said, whispering to keep from being overheard by the onlookers. "But before I let somebody that dresses like you put me under the knife, I got see whether or not you can do it."

"I can sure enough do it," the trucker said. "Cutting a goat is no different than cutting a man. It ain't nothin' but a simple division of the flesh."

"Well then," Loat said, "let's be for having it divided." He walked over to a lounge chair someone had brought out and sat down and folded his hands behind his head. "Go to it," he commanded.

The trucker lifted himself on his boot toes and bobbed in the gravel. The crowd stirred jokey. The whores chirped and gushed, scooting their bare feet over the ground and stirring the dust in their ceaseless talking.

"First thing we need to do," began the trucker, "is to put a little sleep on this goat. Sing him a lullaby, you know." He bent down and took a jar of bonded whisky and a vial of brown glass from the pocket of his trousers. He opened the vial and poured a faint yellow solution into the whisky, stirring the concoction with a finger long and pale as a skewer.

"What's that you're putting in the Old Crow?" Loat asked.

The trucker capped the vial and returned it to the bag. "Laudanum," he said. He then straddled the goat. Samhill bucked, but the trucker put his knees into the animal's ribs and lowered him to the ground. He pushed two fingers into the goat's nostrils, lifted its snout, and poured the entire jar of whisky down his gullet. The goat swallowed and gagged and shook its head, flapping its ears as it stood and staggered.

"We'll wait a time," the trucker said. "Give the whisky space. Let it abide in him."

The interval between sobriety and drunkenness was perhaps a quarter hour. The trucker paced the lot during this time, his lips pulled into a dreamy smirk until eventually the goat lay down and rested its head on its forepaws.

"Is he ready?" Daryl asked. He had taken a seat beside Loat in a nylon lawn chair, his cheeks glossy with sweat.

"He's nearly there," answered the trucker.

"I hope to hell he is." Daryl looked over toward a wall of clouds rising in the west. "Looks like rain to me."

The trucker turned and glanced at the coming weather. Then he knelt beside the goat, lifting and releasing its head, which slapped the ground loosely. "I believe he's ready."

Rolling Samhill onto his belly, the trucker slung himself against the goat's bulk. When he'd positioned the animal to his satisfaction, he turned to the crowd.

"Someone bring me my valise," he requested.

"Your what?" someone drunkenly responded.

"That satchel I got," he said.

Someone tossed him a cracked bag of brown leather, which landed at his feet. He bent down and reached inside, his hands shuffling through the bag, its contents clanking together noisily.

"You always carry around a satch of tools?" asked Loat.

"I do," the trucker said cheerily. His hands burrowed deeper into the bag until he brought out a long curved knife that looked like no knife anyone in the crowd had ever seen. The handle was titanium, but the blade stemming up was white steel, and bent at an odd angle. It appeared almost like a slender silvery trout. "Now see, it's no telling what the world will throw at you," he said. "I like to be ready for whatever it is." He leaned down beside the goat, lifted the animal's hind leg, and slid the knife across its groin. The crowd jawed and yammered as the animal's blood blackened the ground. "Now see, they say a man ain't got but two things to do and that's live and die, but I believe we are all of us better suited to the dying part than to the living." The trucker continued making angled cuts across the goat's gut. "There'a start and a finish to ever thing, but that finish is gone last lots longer than that beginning, ain't it? That makes a man wonder, is he supposed to live or is he supposed to die? Now see, a goat is carried about in the same rude form as any man." He paused and looked up at the crowd. "Or maybe man's form is ruder."

"All I'm seeing you do is butcher a goat," Loat said, "but you're talking about men. There's a difference."

The trucker cocked his head as if listening for something faint and distant, then slapped the goat's flank and went on with the knife, slicing away the peritoneum and the greater and lesser omentums before going further into the body cavity. After a few moments, he brought out the kidney, small, oblong and pale, about the size of a coin purse. He then knotted off the bladder tube and the blood vessels before producing from his coat pocket a spool of clean silver thread.

"Sheep gut," he announced. He threaded a needle and sewed the gash in the goat closed. When he was finished, he stood, dusted himself off, and carried the kidney over to Loat. "You wanted to know if I could do the job," he said. "Here's your evidence."

Loat leaned forward and poked the kidney with his finger. "Yeah," he said, "I see you've dug the thing out of that goat. But I ain't seen the goat come around just yet."

The trucker tucked the kidney into his pocket. "He's fine," he said. "Give him a spell and he'll wobble back to us."

Loat shook his head. "I don't think so," he grunted. He drew himself up from the lounge chair and teetered over to Samhill. He lifted the animal's hind leg and examined the newly stitched gash just below the inner thigh. A slick trickle of blood wept out.

"This goat here looks finished," he said, glaring back at the trucker. "You've killed Samhill Doug."

The crowd groaned. A few tossed away their drinks in disgust.

"He's not dead," the trucker declared. "Give him a rest and then tend his wound and let him have a good long drink of cold water once he comes around. You'll see."

"Yeah," Loat said doubtfully. "We'll see, won't we?"

Over the next hour, the wind increased, bailing the hay grass out in the field beyond the gravel lot and bringing in the sweet smell of rain. Except for Loat and Daryl, the crowd drifted away. Eventually, the trucker went over to Samhill. He knelt beside his bag and brought out a small vial of frosted glass. "Now see, this is a special kind of smelling salt," he said. "My own recipe." He bent over the goat, wafting the vial under its snout. At first, the billy only continued its long, labored breathing. Then it began to snort. Very shortly, it lifted its head and bellowed a throaty dolorous moan. The trucker then tugged gingerly at the leash and the goat staggered upright, still bawling, its head wagging groggily. "Here he is, gentlemen." He brought the animal over to Loat and handed him the leash.

Loat looked down at the animal as it gnawed a stem of clover at his feet. "Goddamn," he laughed.

"But there's one more thing," the trucker said. He reached into his pocket and took out the kidney. "The true test of any creature is to see what it will do with its own." He dropped the kidney in the grass beside Samhill. The goat nudged the organ with his snout, then quickly ate it.

"Now see," said the trucker. "He's his own being. Mastery over the self is proved through a defilement of the self." He said something else, but the sound of the rain surging out of the bottoms blurred his words, and soon the wind wove tresses of dust about the men as if they were corpses being bound in bedsheets.

"We best get inside," Daryl said. He and Loat retreated into the dry cavern of the Quonset hut. Loat led the goat back to the stage, tethering the leash to one of the bedposts.

The crowd milled about, jerking and spasming, yawing laughter out. Bottles clinked.

Daryl waddled up behind Loat and nudged his shoulder. "You aim to lay for Beam and draw a kidney out of him, don't you?" he said.

Loat turned and faced him. "That's what I plan to do."

"And you're satisfied that trucker can take it out of Beam and put it into you?"

"I don't aim to have him put it in me," Loat said. "I get that kidney out of Beam, I put it on ice and take it to one of these county doctors that's so fond of the whores out here. Put the squeeze on him that way. He won't ask where I got the sonuvabitching kidney from. So long as I don't go tell his wife about the whores, he'll do whatever I say." Loat wiped the sweat from his cheeks. "I thought all I had left to do was wait to die. Then Derna told me about Beam being mine and that changed things."

"You think she's telling the truth?"

"About Beam? Yes. I know she is. An old mama cat crawled in my window last night and said it was the truth."

Daryl folded his stumps together. "I've noticed it's a fair amount of old mama cats coming round you lately."

"It ain't nothing for you to worry over," said Loat. "I keep my own sort of company."

"I guess that's so."

Loat laughed. "Hell, Daryl. I didn't know better I'd think you were actually concerned for my wellbeing and not just riding out your last dollar-making days."

Daryl wiped his nose with a pink moist stump. "It don't make no nevermind to me," he said. "You go on and do what you see fit."

"I plan to," said Loat.

He turned away from the stage and went to the bar. The keep gave him a thermos of ice water and a clean washrag, which Loat took with him as he moved back into the hallway, walking down to the final door on the left. Inside the room, Ella lay awake on a king size bed, her hands and ankles roped to the corner posts so that she appeared splashed across the mattress. Loat shut the door behind him and brought a chair to the edge of the bed. He sat studying her quietly. Her face was swollen, but the blood had been toweled from her cheeks and her cuts doctored with ointment.

Loat uncapped the thermos and poured some water into the lid. He seemed to puzzle over something as the breath turned inside him in long grunts. He then bent forward, holding the water out to her.

"It's only water," he said. "You need to drink it."

He caught her face and she tried to twist away, but she soon quieted and let him pour the water down her throat. When she'd finished, he tipped the thermos and damped the washrag and began daubing her down, wiping the cool cloth over her cheeks, his eyes still and determined as if he sought to bring to her a fragile health.

Ella stared at the ceiling. The white plaster was stained with water so that it seemed like some dingy cartographic rendering of lands no longer extant, boundaries now gone and undone.

"Do you know who I am?" Loat asked.

Ella nodded.

"That's good," he said. "That way I don't have to waste no time explaining the kind of trouble you're in."

Ella remained silent. She didn't know if she'd spoken at all since waking in this bed, though she had some vague recollection of mumbling to strange visitors at her bedside, but those conversations that now had the slow drifty feel of dreams.

"I reckon you know your daddy's dead," said Loat. "And since you know that, I'm guessing you're thinking you might be dead yourself before too awful long." Loat shifted in the chair, the wooden floor creaking beneath him. "But that don't have to be the way things turn out. You can walk away from this once it's over. It's up to you. If you tell me where Beam went, I'll let you flap your wings and fly away home, little birdie."

"I don't know where he went," Ella said quietly.

"You'll have to do better than that, little birdie. I know he was out at Pete's. Otherwise, things wouldn't have turned into such a shit circus out there."

"If that's what you know, then you know as much I do."

Loat brushed his hands over his lap. "I think you got a pair of balls bigger than most menfolks I know. But that's nothing to be proud about. Biggest part of men are cowards. Boil them down and you get yellow bones and not much else." He leaned forward, close to her face. "I'd sure hate to have to boil you down and see what was inside, little birdie."

"You're going to do whatever it is you please so why don't you just go ahead and get it over with instead of sitting there jawing?"

"I was kindly enjoying the conversation. I'm sore pressed to find good talk these days."

"You want to know about Beam?" she said. "He ran when he had the chance. He left me. That's what I know about Beam."

"Is that so? Well, I think maybe you just proved my point about men." Loat reached out and touched her arm. She drew away, but the fetters held her in place and he grabbed her, his fingers brittle and dry against her skin. "So Beam ran. But you're not telling me where he ran off to."

"I don't have any idea about that. Ask me, I hope he's lying in a ditch with his neck broke."

"I don't believe that's likely."

"Well, it don't matter. And I sure don't see what you want with him."

"He's carrying something for me. Something I need."

Ella looked at him. His cheeks were washed out and ashen, his eyes jaundiced and runny as egg yolks. "You best find him soon, then," she said. "From the looks of it, you're about to fall over dead."

Loat pulled away from her. His eyes narrowed and he fixed his teeth together. "I'm finer than some folks I see," he said, nodding at Ella.

"I guess." She grimaced doubtfully.

Loat stood quickly, the chair clattering behind him, a rage unfurling in his eyes. "You know, I'm tired of your mouth," he spat. "I'm tired of you playing dumb with me. You think I'm 'most dead? Well, I believe I'll show you how much man is left in me." He began to unbuckle his belt, his cracked pale fingers rasping against the tarnished brass.

Ella shook her head slowly as a murmur of protest rose in her throat. "Stop," she whispered. "Don't do this."

"Not so tough now, little birdie," he said.

He tore at her clothes, his grunts coming loud and brash, his breath falling upon her thin and cool.

Ella closed her eyes as the world spun away in a crash of blinding light.

# XXIII

## MONDAY

Derna sat inside the cabin, guiding the ferry. She listened to the passengers chatter on deck, a woman and her two children, both fledgling boys amazed at the scooting of a boat through water. They had come down the landing in a clunking red Le Baron, and once they boarded the ferry and it began to move, the boys erupted from their seat to clutch at the railings and pitch wish-pennies into the river's brown foam.

Derna slackened the throttle and hoped for quiet. It was the one thing that seemed in ready supply around the river, and she had learned to covet the long petering days of silence, hoarding their memory like winter provender. She'd come to view her unaccompanied hours aboard the ferry as both pleasure and penance, a time to sift through all the wrong runs her life had made—the whoring, Loat, these last years with Clem beside the Gasping, bearing travelers between the shores.

She kept a Bible in the cabin. Though she hardly read from the book, she thought of how something so heavy made a good tool for discipline. Loat had beaten her once with a King James. She put her hand on it now. It didn't feel like much, just a book of ageless bound verses. It couldn't be much. But it was. Because it had to be. Because when there had been nothing left for a woman of her sort to clutch to, it had been there.

But then, those thoughts went away. There was a man on the landing. He stood beside the cleats where she wound the safety chains, his jeans crusted with dried blood. At first, she didn't believe it was him. It was only some trick of the morning, a phantom man standing above the current drumming the shores, the sheen of the water floating over him so that he seemed to walk toward her in disregard of the deeps of the river.

But then she did believe. And she knew. It would happen this way, she thought, as she cut the throttle and stepped onto the deck. It would be him returning again to the same crease of water he had always known and could never forget. It would have to be this way.

She stood watching him quietly as the ferry moored itself into the landing. The children had gone still. They clung to the boat railings, whispering. Derna never looked away from him as she wound the chains on, and when this was done, she walked up the landing and put her hands on her hips and said, "Well, it's you again."

Beam swayed a bit, and his hand trembled when he raised it to wipe a smear of mud from his cheek. "I smelled the river," he said.

Derna nodded. "It's strong."

She studied him. He was thinner and pale, and when he slid his hands over his hips, a soft dust rose from the denim. Long scratches marked his face, and his clothes were bloody and covered in dirt. He seemed about to speak, but remained silent as he looked beyond her to the ferry and its passengers, and then his eyes fluttered and rolled back into his head and when he spilled forward into her arms, she couldn't hold him and had to ease him carefully down to the warm wet concrete of the landing.

"Is everything all right?" The woman from the ferry had stepped onto the landing and stood half-bent, looking down at Derna and Beam, the blond streaks of her hair hanging into her eyes. Her children cowered behind her thighs.

"No," said Derna. "Help me get him to the boat."

They dragged him slowly aboard, his boots scraping the metal hull, and laid him on the deck.

"Who in the hell is this?" asked the woman. Her eyes gaped

and the wind wound the hair about her cheeks.

"I don't know him from Adam," Derna said, shaking her head.

The room smelled of rotten wood beams. Gray light crept down from a small window cobbed with spider webs. He made out the support posts and rafter joists and then the plumbing snaking overhead in rusted curls, the piping coated with verdigris. A corner shelf held jars of brinish green peas. Underneath the shelf slouched a recliner. There were other things. A push mower, gear sprockets hung on nails, damp cardboard boxes, shadows viscous and oily on the smooth concrete floor.

The cellar, he thought. She put me in the cellar.

Beam rolled onto his side and the mattress squeaked under him. He didn't know how long he'd slept, or even if sleep had come at all, though the bitter fuzz on his tongue seemed to suggest it had.

He sat up with some effort, the blankets falling from him. When he stood, his head felt like a weight tied to his neck. The bare concrete floor chilled his feet, and he shivered until he found his boots and slid them on. He walked slowly to the steps, rising up them carefully and quietly. When he entered the kitchen, his mother appeared startled and afraid at first, jerking back from the table, the chair legs grating on the linoleum, but after a moment she thumped her cigarette into the ashtray.

"Hungry?" she asked.

"I am, but I don't feel like eating right now." Beam crossed the floor and sat down, the bright kitchen bulbs making him squint.

Derna rose from the table and ran a glass for him at the faucet. She handed it to him and he drank it down slow, feeling the water's chill run the length of him, and then he held the glass against his chest and sat looking at his mother.

"I thought the worst," she said, sitting down beside him.

"Why'd you put me in the cellar?" he asked.

Derna tugged on her cigarette. "You walked there," she said.

"I did what?"

"You fell asleep on the landing but then came around enough to walk and where you went to was the cellar." She waved to the open door that showed the beginning descent of the wooden stairs.

Beam set the water glass on the table. "There's people after me," he said.

Derna stood up. Moving away from the table, she went to the sink and gazed out the window, keeping her back to him. She stubbed her cigarette out in the basin. "You know who it is already," she said.

"I want you to say it. And I want you tell me why."

Derna kept her back to him, and after a spell, he heard the soft patter of her breath.

"Do you even know your ownself what this is all about?" Beam asked.

A dish towel lay on the counter and she began daubing at the Formica top with it, smudging the coffee and jelly stains into bright smears. "I know Clem had to send you away."

Beam watched her hand circle over the counter. "You know that I killed somebody out on the river, then?"

The towel stopped. Derna's back stiffened and she drew a long breath and held it a time and then exhaled. "I know that's what happened," she said.

"I'm telling what happened, all right. For the first time, I'm saying it myself. What I did, it figures that people would be after me." Beam leaned forward in his chair. "But it should be the law looking for me. Not Presto Geary. Not Loat Duncan."

Derna turned to him, her eyes startled and sharp. "Why would Loat be after you?" she said. "Did he do you wrong? That's not what I asked him to do."

"Asked him to do?"

Derna's eyes turned far off, starry and dazed. She took her pack of Camels from the counter and lit a cigarette, the smoke lifting above her like a curtain, the gray drape of it lingering in the spacey kitchen light. "I shouldn't be surprised," she said faintly. "Why did I think it would be any other way?"

Beam lifted himself from the chair and crossed the floor to stand before her. He gripped her by the arms. "Mama," he said, "what are you talking about? You're not making any sense."

Derna shook her head. "None of this makes sense." She drew away from him and he let her go, her dress sighing as she rubbed her hips against the edge of the countertop. "I've tried to live right most of my days. But there's this world. It gets you so trapped and caught sometimes it feels like the things you do ain't really you. They're what somebody else would do." She threw her cigarette into the sink and ran water over it.

"Where's Daddy?" Beam asked.

She looked at him and then lifted the dishtowel from the counter, dried her hands, then dropped the cloth in the sink. "He's gone off."

"Gone off?"

"He's not here," she said.

"Where's he at then?"

"I don't know."

"What the hell is going on?" Beam demanded. "Start telling me all of it."

"I can't tell you anymore than you already know."

Beam raked his fingers along his cheeks and groaned. "Did you ever think what it might be like, killing somebody?" he said. "Think what that might mean for me? Knowing what I'd done caused some other poor bastard to not be around no more? How you reckon that is to think about all alone in the night somewhere?"

She turned to the window again, but he reached out and jerked her around and looked down into the pan of her face, the sun-cured cheeks hard and freckled, her glazed eyes like bobs of glass. "Think about that," he spat.

"I have," she said. "But what good does it do, one knowing this and the other knowing something else? The things you want told won't make nothing easy. Not you hearing them or me saying them. So why not leave them still?"

He let go of her arms. "I can't leave them still," he said. "Tell me why Loat Duncan is after me. Tell me what I did out on that river."

"It weren't you," she whispered. "It never could be you."

"The hell it weren't me," Beam said. "If it weren't me then who was it?"

"Not me," she said. "Not my boys. Never my boys. Somebody else, but not my boys."

Beam felt drowsy and he seemed to drift in the want of sleep. "You're crazy," he said, his speech a bit slurred. "I don't know what you mean saying 'boys'. It's just me. It's always been just me."

Derna put her hands on the table, her palms turned up as if waiting to catch some long expected gift. "Beam, you were my favorite. You got to know that. The other one, the one they found, I didn't even barely know him. I throwed him away. But I knew all along I'd throw my first one away. It was like something I couldn't help, like it was simple as taking air. I knew it, so my heart didn't break. But then you had to get took away too and that was more than I could stand. It was like somebody had just sucked my spirit dry. Because you were my favorite. Always. I'd put my hand on you and it'd feel no different than if I was touching my own skin. So when you left, I was just a ghost. I was somebody not even really there no more." She took hold of his hands. "You got to know it, Beam," she said. "I never did want anything like this to happen to you. That's why I never told you about Paul. I didn't want you to turn out anything like him."

Beam pulled his hands away from her. "Who's Paul?" he asked.

"Paul's the other one," Derna said. "The one I had before you. The one you killed out on the ferry." She kept her eyes on the

219

floor as her lashes glistened with tears. "We never did tell you you had a brother."

Beam remembered the night on the ferry, and the way the stranger he'd killed had muttered Loat's name. The swell of memory then rose to bear him back through the tumult of years to when he and his mother would drive into town to Wal-Mart to meet a man with a wide-brimmed straw hat and a thin drop of a nose, his shirtsleeves rolled to the elbows, his chin blackened by whiskers, a strange figment halting there in the aisle among the canned tomatoes and Ragu. Beam recollected the man's eyes, dark in his skull as they'd watched him.

*You keep good company,* he had said to Beam, winking. *But what about you, your own self?*

*Me?*

*Yeah. You. Are you good company?*

The man's laughter, like the cawing of crows.

*Loat,* his mother said. *We need to get on.*

So that was it, then. A name. So now it was said and the world would have it.

"I lived a way in my younger days that weren't nothing but wrong," Derna began. "I don't make no excuse for it. It was a way I come to live in the world and it don't hardly even seem like me when I look back on it now. But I had Loat and that seemed like all the everything I would ever need. And then I had Paul and it was all too much."

She seemed brittle now, browned and dried like some flower left pressed in a Bible. A revenant of an age now become only crumbling dust.

"I had to leave then. I had to go and Clem was the one to take me." She paused and lifted her wet eyes to look at Beam. "But I was already in the family way with you. And I knew you were another son. Another one that belonged to Loat."

Beam stepped away from her. All the Sheetmires had watered away and were gone now. Only a blank haze stood before him, as if all of his past were but a milky dream. He felt the sleep returning, his head gone sluggish and drunk, and as he backed slowly out of the kitchen, his mother receding before him, the murmur of deep waters filled his head, the long echo and purl of the river gliding over him. He turned as if to go out into whatever world remained for him, but the sound of the waters grew and he fell suddenly, as though drowning weights had been fastened to his legs, and a great flume of sleep bore him on into a yet thicker dark.

When he came to, he was on the sofa in the living room. The television droned and cast a green lathered light over the knitted afghan that covered his legs. A single lamp burned in a corner.

Derna was spraying Pledge over a pair of wooden bookends and scrubbing them with a cloth. She sat in a recliner beside his head and the bright lemony smell of furniture polish burned in his nose.

"You still got the sleeping sickness," she said when she saw that he was awake.

"Did you think maybe I'd found a cure out there in the woods?" he asked groggily.

Derna's hands worked at the bookends, her face marooned behind her hair. "No, I never thought no such thing. I was just talking."

Beam sat up and gazed at the floor, trying to draw the fatigue out. His neck was stiff, and his legs seemed jellied and worthless, and the weight of all his mother had told him perched on his shoulders so that he felt he could never rise from this place, but would remain in timeless supplication to the burden of knowing it and of having heard it spoken.

"I need to make a phone call," he said.

"Who you calling?"

"The sheriff. I'm going to turn myself in."

Derna sighed and stopped polishing the bookends. She

placed them on the carpet at her feet and looked at the window, the curtains standing like shrouded watchers at a tomb. "What I know is that you ain't the only one to blame for all this," she said. She wadded the polishing cloth in her hand, her fingers trembling. "I know that what is happening now is all part of a price for how we've lived. All of us. Me, I never was much good for being a mother, so I can't tell you what you should do. But I don't hate you for killing Paul because we had a hand in that, too. Me and Clem. I don't even hate Loat like I used to. Looking at you and knowing what we've all done together, I'm all chilled and clean with cold inside." She put her hand out and Beam took it. Her fingers were stiff and heavy against his own, icy to the touch. "You go on. Go on wherever is best and if you want to, in later years, you come see me." Then she left the room, coursing down the hallway in her pale green gown with the hem trailing behind.

Beam drew the afghan away and rose from the sofa and went to the kitchen where he dialed the sheriff. He then returned to the living room and waited until he heard the grind of tires on the gravel outside and saw the flash of headlights through the drapes, the light falling through the threadbare fabric like the light of morning on the river.

# XXIV

Other than a few terse commands grunted at Beam, Elvis and Filback didn't speak at all, showing little shock at the sight of this boy who had been the cause of so much trouble. They simply placed a pair of handcuffs on his wrists and then stowed him in the back of the cruiser as calmly as if they were loading groceries. Then they turned the cruiser around in the dry yard of the house and made the highway, heading back toward town which, this far out, was only a hazy fume of lights above the line of dark trees on the distant horizon.

They were perhaps three miles past the house when they met the Peterbilt on a corn-trimmed stretch of road. The rig sat idling in the oncoming lane. The blinding glare of its high beams struck them flush in the face.

"The fuck is this?" said Filback.

Elvis hit the cruiser bulbs and coasted to within twenty yards of the Peterbilt, the blue lights cycling over the truck and the road and the corn in plasmatic scatters.

"Think he's drunk?" said Filback.

"Or lost," Elvis added. He glanced into the backseat. Beam's eyes were wild in the thrust of the truck lights.

"Y'all sit tight," Elvis said. He took his hat off the center console and tucked it firmly onto his head, then picked up the cruiser's bullhorn and exited the car. The cool of the night licked his hands. He put the cruiser's spotlight on the rig and addressed the driver with the bullhorn.

At first, there came no response. Then one of the truck's

windows screeched down. "That you, Elvis?" someone said.

Elvis clicked the bullhorn again. "It is. Who we got out here in the middle of the highway?"

"We could ask you the same thing. Who you got in the cruiser with you?"

"That ain't no never mind," Elvis answered. "Why the hell are you stalled out here in the road? Did you run out of gas?"

Again, it was a spell before any answer came from the rig, and Elvis felt naked standing in the span of the truck's high beams. Finally, the voice from the rig came like a drifting cloud that choked out all other noise, even the grunting of the engines and the whine of frogs and crickets coming from the ditch water at the edge of the cornfield. "We got us a scanner in here, Elvis. You'd be surprised what you hear on it. You ain't got to tell us who's riding with you in the cruiser."

Elvis leaned down and popped his head into the cruiser. Behind the chickenwire grating in the back seat, the blood had drained from Beam's cheeks.

"Get that shotgun ready, Filback," Elvis said.

The deputy unbuckled his seatbelt. "Why?"

"Just do as I say."

Filback unlatched the Benelli from its cradle and fed several shells into the breech. He shucked one into the chamber and then held the gun against his chest.

"Just sit tight," Elvis said to him. The sheriff stood back up, squaring himself in the crook of the cruiser's open door. His mouth had gone dry, and he had to work some spit into it before he could speak again.

"Whoever it is in here ain't none of your concern," he barked through the horn. "Now I want you to come out of that rig showing nothing but hands."

The truck's fan clicked on. The belts sighed and whirred. "That won't work," said the voice from the truck. "We want to make an exchange. We got somebody in here with us worth a sight more than Beam. She ain't too pretty no more, but she's a woman at least. You could take her down to the station and tie her to a cot and give her a fuck whenever business is slow. Only, I guess you don't like pussy, do you, Elvis?"

Elvis ducked back into the cruiser. His hands were trembling now, and he had to grip the vinyl dash to still them. "Get on the radio," he told Filback. "Call some backup."

"Ain't but one other car on patrol right now besides us," Filback answered. "And it'd take them a half hour to get out here even if they was driving like a scalded ape."

"Do it anyway. Call every dogcatcher and constable in the county if you got to, but get some more badges out here."

Filback reached for the receiver and began signaling in, his voice coughing loud and palsied over the channels.

Elvis rose from the cruiser and squawked into the horn again. "I don't do exchanges," he said. "I want you to come out of that truck."

A span of silence followed as the truck blew its heat at him, until the voice from the rig said, "All right. You don't believe us, so we'll show you our goods." The passenger door of the Peterbilt swung open and two forms descended onto the ground. A Doberman hound followed them. The first figure was a woman. She was being coaxed forward by a man at her back and as both moved into the beam of the cruiser lights, they became clearer. The woman's face was bruised and swollen but clean, her clothes caked with dried blood. The man behind her was Loat Duncan. He held a pistol under the woman's chin and walked her to the front of the truck. The dog sat down in front of them.

"Here we are," Loat said. "What you going to do now, Elvis?"

Elvis dropped the bullhorn and it clattered on the roadway. He drew his revolver. "Let the woman go," he ordered, aiming the gun at Loat.

Loat shoved his pistol hard against the underside of the woman's jaw. "I'll do that when you give me Beam."

Sweat dropped into Elvis' left eye. He winked it away. "Let her go," he said.

"Not until Beam is sitting in this rig here. That's who I want."

"You don't get him," Elvis answered. "What you get to do is let the woman go and then drop your piece and lay down on the pavement. We got back-up coming."

Loat squeezed out a grin. "I don't hear no sirens," he said. "Look here, Elvis." Loat ran the gun barrel down the woman's neck tenderly. "I can blow this woman's brains all over the corn and then go home and eat a cold supper and get to sleep just fine. Who the fuck do you think I am? I ain't some redneck drunk on jar shine. You know me. I ain't some nightmare you can wash away with a cold shower."

Before he finished speaking, Filback swung out of the cruiser, bringing the Benelli to his shoulder and holding it on Loat.

"Steady," Elvis barked, holding a hand out toward Filback. "Just breathe."

Filback nodded, his cheek bulging against the shotgun's stock. "I'm right here," he said, his voice cool and certain.

"Y'all gonna have to do a sight more than just stand there and breathe." Loat shoved the pistol into the woman's neck and she mewled helplessly. "Give me Beam or things are fixing to get real messy."

Elvis braced himself against the side of the cruiser. He couldn't think straight. All he could do was hold his revolver on Loat and wait for Filback to get loose and nervous while the corn shook and rattled below the shoulder of the road.

Then the trucker stepped down from the rig. He walked into the cast of the headlights, dressed glossily in the tails of his fitted blazer, his white shirt collar wagging around his clean throat, the wind knocking his hair back. His shadow sloped over the pavement. "Evening, Sheriff," he said.

Elvis knew him at once as the man from the courthouse, the one he'd had the puzzling encounter with not three days before.

He aimed the revolver at his chest. "Lay down," he said. "Lay down on the road there and don't say anything."

The trucker put his hands on his hips, swinging his coattails out. "Now see, I can't do that. If I did, I wouldn't be able to help you. And I'm a man that's all about helping others." With the headlights at his back, the trucker was only a silhouette, and his voice seemed to emerge in a whirlwind out of the darkness. "Here is what you can do," he said, folding his hands in front of him. "You can give us Beam and then we'll let the woman go. Or you can stand there waving your little cap gun until one of us, me or Loat or your deputy there, loses his cool and gets jumpy. People get hurt when they get jumpy. You give us Beam and everybody can just drive away from all this. Now see, wouldn't that be fine?"

Elvis felt his head lighten. His vision blurred so that he couldn't clearly make out the corn or the road that stretched out before him. He felt as if he stood on the verge of a vast chasm of plummeting darkness and that he would surely soon plunge forever into that spinning emptiness. The sound of Beam kicking the cruiser's rear window brought him back. He stuck his head inside the car. Beam was lying on his back, looking up at him through the chickenwire.

"Let me out of here," he said. His eyes sparked with flinty light.

"They'll kill you."

"I don't care. I know that woman."

"I know who she is, too. She's Ella Daugherty. What difference does it make?"

"I know her," Beam repeated. "You've got to let me out. I want to go."

"They'll kill the both of you."

"I need to get out."

"Pete's dead," Elvis said. "You will be too if you go with Loat."

"I know Pete's dead. And I know what all will happen to me if I go with Loat. But this is something I need to fix. You just let me out and I'll go."

Elvis stared at Beam, who had a coldly adamant look on his face, and knew this was something he'd reasoned out and that there was no stopping him. He opened the door, and Beam stepped out of the car. He started walking toward the rig, but Elvis stayed him with a hand. "Hold up. I need to take the cuffs off you." Elvis fumbled with the keys.

"Just leave those binders on him, Elvis," Loat said. "Be easier for us that way."

"I'm not doing that," Elvis said. "These cuffs are county property."

"You need not to worry about what does or doesn't belong to the county right now, Elvis," Loat said. "You better just think about how you can get this whole shit mess cleaned up without nobody getting their brains blowed out."

"I won't do it," Elvis said. "You can have him, but you'll take him without the cuffs. That's the only deal you get."

Loat sighed and looked at the trucker.

"Do it," the trucker said.

Loat waved his hand and Elvis unlocked the cuffs and took them from Beam's wrists. "You ain't got to do this," he whispered.

Beam shook his head. "Yes I do."

"If we can stall, back-up will be here." But Beam was already walking into the lights of the rig.

"The fuck you doing, Elvis?" Filback asked.

"Shut up. This don't need any of your reckoning."

When Beam stood in front of Loat, close enough so the two men seemed to merge and become one, he said, "You can let her go now."

"Stand between me and the sheriff," Loat answered. "Anybody gets shot, it's going to be you."

Beam sidestepped into place.

"That's good," Loat said. "Now move on up here until you're close enough to breathe on this bitch." The trucker returned to the rig, stowing himself behind the wheel.

Beam shuffled forward, his boots dragging on the gritty pavement. He saw Ella clearly now. Her clothes looked as if they'd been glued to her in haste. Wrinkled blouse. Hair a woven mess. Eyes swollen, blood crusted on the same denim shorts she'd been wearing when Beam first met her. He remembered their night on the sofa. It was all dizzy in its distance now, and he wondered how he had ever been there, naked with a strange woman as the moonlight slid through the window blinds.

"Turn around," Loat said. Beam did as he was told. He could see Elvis now. He'd cocked his gun and was holding it at arm's length. The blue cruiser lights slid over him in deep currents. Then Beam heard Ella's breathing at his back. A warm wheeze. When Loat released her, she ran forward, then slumped onto her knees, catching herself with her palms on the pavement. A small choked sob rose from her throat, but Beam could do nothing to help her.

"Walk back with me," Loat told him, jabbing the gun into his spine.

They went to the truck. Beam climbed up the running board first and got into the rig, seating himself beside the trucker, who held a Heckler pistol in his lap.

Loat whistled and the dog bounded up into the cab. Then he raised himself onto the running board.

"You won't come looking for me, Elvis," he yelled. "You want Beam to go on living you won't come looking. I see squad cars anywhere near me and I'll put a slug in him. I won't ask questions. I'll just do it. That clear?"

Elvis confirmed no understanding. He kept his gun on Loat, gauging the distance, the wind. He considered angles. The control of formulaic velocity.

When he pulled the trigger, the shot went high and ricocheted off the truck's roof with a whine. Loat dumped into the cab and swung the door closed and then Filback let go on the windshield with the Benelli, the glass turning frosty. Elvis fired again and one of the rig's tires blew. Then the gears ground and the Peterbilt leapt forward. Elvis and Filback jumped away as the rig smashed into the cruiser, sweeping it down into the road ditch in a smatter of windows and headlamps.

Elvis ran to Ella and dragged her into the soft grass of the ditch. She moaned in pain when he touched her. He squatted and covered her with himself, his face shoved into the mud. Pistol rounds slapped the corn behind him, then the Benelli roared again and buckshot splatted against the truck before it turned and slurred off down the highway, the steel belt of the blown tire flapping and then flinging off with a shudder, a rage of sparks scattering out in a bright swarm from the wheel as the noise and light of the rig slowly shrank away into the blackness.

Elvis pulled himself off the ground. The cruiser steamed in the ditch. Its roof lights spun on in blue shivers. Filback staggered up to him, holding his shotgun limply. Gray smoke grew from the gun's barrel, and slicks of dark blood draped his left arm. He'd taken one just above the elbow and the wound bled profusely.

"Easy Filback." Elvis took the gun from him and laid it on the ground. "Sit down," he said.

Filback crumpled to the pavement. His face was clear and still, not a flicker of agony or movement crossing it. He laid his head back on the road. "It don't hurt," he mumbled. "It don't hurt at all."

Elvis went to the cruiser. He tried to radio an ambulance, but the channels were only hot spray. He let the remote dangle and searched the car. Under the driver's seat, he found a medical kit. He opened it and pilfered through the gauze and stitching equipment, the poultice bandaging. Ibuprofen in a bottle. Morphine syringes. Scissors. Antivenin for snakebites. A tourniquet. He closed the kit and carried it back to Filback. His cheeks were shaking now as shock took him. Elvis laid the kit beside him. He brought the tourniquet out and fixed it around Filback's arm, wrapping the banding rubber tightly above the wound and then cinching it with his teeth and knotting it off as the blood slipped warmly between his fingers.

"It don't hurt," Filback repeated.

"It will," Elvis said. He punched a morphine syringe into Filback's arm.

When he'd done all he could for Filback, Elvis sat down on the pavement. He closed his eyes. Far off, sirens. A red shriek in the night. He knew he should get up and go to Ella, that he should comfort her in some way, put a hand on her and remove whatever nightmares flushed through her mind, but he only sat there with his eyes shut, hearing the sirens and waiting for some kind of dream to come out of the night and the corn to take him away from all this.

# XXV

The smell of blood was thick inside the rig. Loat leaned against the passenger side door, gritting his teeth. A few pellets from Filback's shotgun had glanced his neck, and he kept a hand over the wound as it bled between his fingers. Enoch, the Doberman, tried to lick at the blood until Loat slapped the dog away and it slunk into the floorboards.

"Good that you can do that," said the trucker.

Loat looked at him. "Do what?"

"Hit the dog. Means your spine is okay. The shot either nicked you or only wedged in the muscle." The trucker grinned. "No worries so long as you don't bleed to death."

Loat put his head against the cold window and watched the dark runnel by. More corn. Trailers. A tin warehouse haloed by a security light. The glow of a soda machine. Corn again.

"Don't talk to me," he said.

"Why?"

"Because I don't want to have to answer you because it fucking hurts to talk."

The trucker laughed softly. "I'll just talk to Beam, then."

Beam sat between the two men, staring ahead at the road. If he so much as shifted his weight the Doberman muttered a low growl, so he remained motionless.

"I guess you thought you and me was done, hey?" the trucker asked him. "But here you are." The trucker slapped Beam's knee. "Right back with me riding in the wild country."

Beam wadded his hands together in his lap and did not speak.

Loat lifted his head. "We all need to just shut the fuck up and ride and not talk until we get to where we're going," he said. The blood dripped like the beads of a rosary.

"He'll be okay," the trucker said. "But I don't guess you're too worried about that, are you?"

Beam shook his head. "No," he said. "I ain't."

"Now see, you're probably just curious about why we've been so eager to get a hold of you. I mean, Christ, I shot a deputy back there. Feller don't act that way less he got reason to."

"I know why you been after me," Beam said. His voice surprised him in its steadiness.

"Do you, now?"

"Yes." He nodded and pushed himself hard against the seat, holding his breath. All the while, he'd been smelling Loat's blood and he knew now it was his own blood and that it flashed inside him with a heat and a power stronger than any prayer he might have offered to the quick and silent dark.

"Well, then you know you did your own brother in. But where are we taking you and why do we want to take you there?"

"I don't know." Beam shrugged. "Maybe you're going to kill me."

The road dipped suddenly and the tires whined as the rig staggered through a curve.

"Now see," said the trucker, "that just might be the case. I got a mite of a bone to pick with you and maybe killing is the only way that bone gets picked." He turned onto an unmarked highway hedged by weedy banks of thin sumac and mimosa. The headlights of the truck flared against rain puddled in the dip of a bend. Vagrant moon fluxing bright and dim through the tree limbs, the road granular beneath. The sky coarsened by stars. No houses. Distant barns rising on the hillsides. "I can't abide anyone calling me a thief," he continued. "Now see, it's true that I took that money off you while you was sleeping in my truck. But I didn't steal it."

"You don't call that stealing?"

"No sir. I give you a ride, so the money was just a payment for services rendered. Hell, you're a businessman yourself, running that ferry. You ought to understand a fair price for fair work."

"I usually say upfront what a job costs before I lay a hand to it."

"Now see, I knew you'd say something like that. But here's the way it is, see. I give you this ride and we're rolling down the highway and all of the sudden you start to sleeping. Right there in my cab. Now see, a sleeping man ain't shit for company. Way I figure, I'm owed at least a small dollar for driving your lazy ass around." The trucker waved his arm through the cab. "I can't be giving rides to lazy folk and not expect to get paid. And expect to get paid without having my good name run through the mud and be called a thief and all manner of unpopular and outright untruthful things. Don't you see what I'm talking about here?"

Beam flexed his hands in his lap. At his feet, Enoch had begun to snooze. Loat remained slouched against the passenger window. His breath cast erratic glazes on the cold glass while the road seemed to slip and dive through a country of strange sleep.

As the road came on, bearing him toward whatever place he'd finally be done in forever, the thought of his death jolted through him like a polished blade and in one motion he reached over and jerked the wheel so the rig surged from the road into the bank and a long howl boiled up from the gutworks of the machine as it rolled from the roadway and plunged into a ravine, felling cedars and sapling hickory as it flumed downward with a wavy surge of black soil rising in its wake until it turned upright again and stalled against a girthy oak. Then, nothing but a trickle of noises. Fluids. Gear oil. Antifreeze. Diesel. The drip slithery in the dark. A hiss of water slapping hot metal.

Beam was sprawled on his back across the dash. The windshield had broken free and the glass had scraped his arms, but his injuries felt slight and he managed to raise his head. Loat lay wedged against the passenger side door. His eyes were open and for a moment, Beam believed him dead until he blinked and then worked his jaw, twisting it open and closed. He leaned forward and spat a bloody clot onto his lap.

"The fuck you do?" he slurred.

"Wrecked us," Beam said.

"The fuck for?"

"So you wouldn't kill me."

Loat choked and spat again, his lips reddened with blood. He wiped his mouth with his wrist. A pistol gleamed in his fist.

"How bad you hurt?" Loat asked.

Beam lifted a hand to his face and scraped a seam of blood away. "I don't know," he said. "Maybe not too bad."

"I think I made it out all right myself. Might have knocked a few of my fillings loose, though." Loat closed his mouth and slowly worked his jaw some more. "We got to get out of here," he said. "They'll be looking for us."

Beam shifted his hips and a hot shank of pain slid through him, all the way down to his heels. "Go on then," he managed to say.

"You're coming with me. And anyway, that windshield's the only way out. Driver's door looks stove in and mine over here is blocked by this oak tree. So we're both going to have to crawl out." Loat swept the pistol through the air. "Go on ahead."

Beam rolled onto his side. The frame of the windshield was torn, and bits of glass clung to it like jagged teeth. Beam struggled through the opening, the glass cutting his hands and belly, and then slid down the hood into a soft nest of black dirt. He nearly passed out, but he steadied himself and walked from the rig to rest against a fallen hackberry log.

"Now, that's lots better, ain't it?" Loat's voice swam to him through the dark as he staggered toward Beam through the dead leaves and broken limbs. He held his wounded neck with one hand and the pistol in the other, and the blood draped over his shoulders like a stole so that he appeared sanctified and holy in the silver moonlight. "That fucking rig ain't worth pissing on." Loat arched his back, then leaned forward and spat blood on the ground. "Where is everybody else?" he coughed. "You didn't see that trucker or my dog anywheres?"

"There weren't nobody else that I saw."

Loat pushed two fingers under his tongue and whistled. When the dog didn't appear, Loat whistled again and waited and listened. Only the wind spun and chattered in the leaves. "Enoch," he called into the night, but the dog didn't emerge. Loat spat and shook his head. "Fucking dog," he said. He lifted his eyes and stared through the trees at the ravine where the saplings were broken and the earth gouged and rutted. "Come on." He waved the pistol. "We got to get up to the road."

"Why?"

"Because we got to get the fuck out of here. Don't tell me you want to stand out here in the woods and bleed all night."

Beam gripped the hackberry log under him. "I guess that depends on what you aim to do once we get up to the road," he said.

"You ain't got no say in this," Loat said. His voice moved through the night with a reedy hiss. "You come along and follow me now."

"What if I don't?"

"I'll kill you."

Beam squished his hands into the damp moss that grew on the hackberry log. "I don't believe so," he said.

"Don't, do you?"

"No. If you aimed to just kill me you'd already done it."

Loat drew the slide back on the pistol and shucked a round into the chamber. He aimed the gun at Beam's chest. "Go on and talk then if you think I'm all bluff."

The wind slid off the top of the ridge and into the ravine to cool the sweat on Beam's cheeks, and he felt suddenly chilled to the core, staring at the bore of the pistol, but he shook his head slow and easily. "I'm your blood," he said.

Loat stood poised before him, his breath labored and ragged through the tiny vents of his nostrils.

"I'm your blood," Beam repeated.

Loat lowered the pistol. "More than that," he said. "I'm your daddy."

"That's right." Beam said. "And you're the daddy of that one I killed."

The night clicked and chimed around them so that it seemed as if they were standing in the belly of a ponderous clock, the hours timed not of this world and measured not by its ways.

"I'm sick," Loat said. "I'm dying. The doctors say my kidneys are ruined. So I need one from you. I was aiming to get it out of Paul, but you damn sure put a stop to that."

"You want one of my kidneys?" Beam asked. "That's what all this had been about? All this killing had been on account of you not wanting to die?"

"What other reason is there for doing anything?" said Loat. "It's why people steal, cheat, and rob. It's why they fuck. Anything to make a stand against not being alive. When it comes your time, don't act like you won't be doing your damnedest to keep yourself in the world."

"You think I'm just going to give you one of my kidneys?" Beam said.

Loat snorted. "I don't think," he said, "that you've got much of any say in it."

"It's my kidney. I reckon I say where it does or doesn't go."

"You just ain't as quick as you ought to be." Loat raised the gun. "This here is what does the only kind of saying that needs to get heard."

"You shoot me and you won't get any kidney."

"That's true. And don't think I ain't seen the itch in your step. You're wanting to run. But if you do that, you better think of what I already done and what I can do to them you leave behind." Loat ran his tongue over his lips. "You better think what I can do to Derna."

The trees shook and waved like brooms that would sweep the sky clear of stars and make of this a blacker night yet. Beam planted his feet in the firm dirt. He could go if he wanted. The woods were open. The thick and shadow-tangled world would hide him. But what world was there that could keep him for more than the respite of a few days? His body ached and his mind staggered dizzy with the thought of the horror his life had become, a horror so certain and absolute that it stood within him like the very frame of his bones. He saw how it was and how it would be. There was no earthly way to run. No earthly place worth running to. And there was Derna. She was old and worn and deserved whatever measure of peace he could give her in whatever hours remained to him.

Beam lifted himself from the hackberry log. He moved forward and Loat fell in behind him. They went slow under the trees, the moon dusting them with gray shadows as the elm saplings and sawbriers ripped at their clothes. They climbed through scrub brush and the surf of foam flowers and sedge and more Johnson grass until finally the crumbled shoulder of the road appeared where the trucker sat perched on a stray tire waiting for them with a wry and scant smile. Between his thighs sat Enoch. The trucker stroked the dog's ears. "Now see, some take less time to climb a hill than others," he announced. "But it's not any trouble. I don't mind waiting."

Beam and Loat stared at him incredulously. "How'd you come out of that wreck so clean?" Loat asked. He and Beam were crooked and stove to varying degrees, yet the trucker seemed polished and showered.

"Just lucky, I guess."

"Well, it don't matter," Loat said. "Let's just walk." He whistled and Enoch sprang from the trucker's grasp and followed at a trot as they all began to walk along the shoulder.

"Did you think you'd kill us all by wrecking my rig?" the trucker said to Beam.

"I think it's a wonder somebody ain't never loaded you with double-ought and throwed you down a hole somewhere. That's what I think," Beam answered.

"It wouldn't work."

"What wouldn't?"

"Shooting me and throwing me down a hole." The trucker shook his head. "It's been tried before."

"Whatever," Beam said. "I don't care one way or the other."

They walked a little while longer in silence until a pair of headlights shone on them and a long, white Buick pulled up. The driver's face flared pale in the window. A cigarette seeped orange light over his lips. He wore glasses and a blue cotton shirt, the collar smudged with lipstick, his salt-colored hair wafting in and out of the gusting wind. He was older, but not so old that he seemed feeble. A slight beery smell rose off him. "You boys having trouble?" he asked.

Loat bowed, squinting into the car. He took a few steps forward and examined the backseat. It was empty, save for a throw rug piled on the vinyl. "You might could say that," he said.

The driver took the cigarette from his lips and coughed into a wadded fist of brown fingers. "You look it," he said. "What'd y'all do, wreck?"

"What are you doing out here?" Loat asked.

"Me? Hell, I'm just driving around in the fresh air. Got done taking my old lady home and now I'm riding back to my place." The driver waved a hand. "What are y'all doing out here?" He thumped the cigarette and it shattered in the road.

Loat put a hand into the small of his back and winced. "We need a ride," he said.

The man in the car coughed again. "Yeah," he said. "And from the looks of it, I guess you need to go to a hospital."

"Not to no hospital." Loat shook his head. "We need a ride

to a cemetery."

The driver put both hands on the steering wheel. "A cemetery? Who's dead out there?"

"Nobody's dead," said Loat.

"Then why you want to go to a cemetery?"

"It don't matter why. You just need to take us."

"Well, I never heard of nobody wanting to go to a cemetery just for the hell of it. Are you sure there ain't nobody dead out there?"

Loat shook his head. "We're all alive. Now take us to a cemetery."

"Oh, I don't think I can be a party to that," said the driver. "There's some strange folks around these days. I ain't saying you're some of them. But then again, you might be. You know what I read in the paper the other day? They was a man up in Ohio got caught fucking his dead wife. Dug her up from the ground and just went to hunching on her right there in the dirt." The driver narrowed his eyes. "You sure you ain't got a dead girl out there with you?"

Loat spat onto the road. "Take us to the cemetery," he said.

"I can't do that," the man said.

"You're gonna take us to a cemetery."

A match snickered. The flame curled brightly as the driver lit another cigarette. "I ain't going to no graveyard," he said.

Loat leaned against the car, like a hawker pushing his wares. "Whatever it is you want that don't matter none. We are going and you're going to take us."

The man hung his arm out the car window and flicked ash into the road. "I ain't," he said. The moonlight fell off his glasses and slid murkily down his cheeks. "I don't even know who y'all are."

"We're getting in," Loat said. He pulled the pistol from his jeans, and the shot splashed blue flame over the car and lit the interior. The top of the driver's head tore away. Blood washed

over the dash and windshield. The man slumped forward over
the wheel and the horn blared. Between his fingers dangling out
the window, the cigarette still smoldered, a small red dot in the
middle of the night.

Loat opened the door and grabbed the man's shirt collar and
yanked him into the road. "Grab his feet," he said to Beam. "Pull
him into the woods." He motioned toward the trees with the
pistol, but Beam didn't move. "Now," Loat commanded.

Beam went to the body. Where the man's face had been there
was now only a squashed damp black hole. Somehow, it was odd
to think of the body as being a man, or even what was left of one.
But it was a man. The shirt with its cotton collar smudged with
lipstick, the jeans—all of this was what a man would wear. And
now Beam would have to pick up his legs and drag him off the
highway into the woods. And, in some dim time yet to come,
there would only be a cage of sun-washed bones in the ditch and
then that would be all.

He lifted the man's legs, struggling with the weight as he
wheelbarrowed him toward the forest. The man's watch scraped
on the pavement until Beam reached the edge of the woods.

"That's good enough," Loat said. "Now get your ass in the
car."

Beam wiped his hands against his thighs and quickly returned
to the car and placed himself in the passenger seat. The trucker
sat behind the wheel. In the back, Loat had laid himself out on
the seat while Enoch panted on the floorboards.

"Take note of what just happened, Beam," said the trucker.
He yanked the gearshift into drive and they rolled out, the car's
bald tires squelching on the pavement. "Loat will speak a blunt
tongue if the moment calls for it."

Beam put his head against the window and the cool glass
stung his skin. All he had done—the killing on the ferry and the
days and nights of running—whirled about him in a cloud until
he became lightheaded and sick. He tried to sit straight in the

seat, but his movements seemed hindered and sluggish, and he felt the slow drown of sleep coming on.

"Stop," he whispered. "I need to get out. I'm not supposed to be here."

"Now see," said the trucker, "there just ain't no time to stop. There ain't no time at all."

Beam swallowed the bile down and shook his head. "You got to let me out," he said.

"No, we ain't letting you out," Loat said from the backseat. "We're taking you to a real special place and we got some real special plans for you."

Beam dizzied and coughed and his head stirred with a frenzied light as they drove on, the trees knotty and arthritic as they traveled down the corridors of a night provoked to forever vortex by those at large within the darkness.

# XXVI

Beam didn't know at first if he was awake or if he had somehow trespassed into the realm of nightmare. The latter thought gave him some comfort. He was only an interloper ranging into the mind's far wilds, traipsing through the weedy bottom ground of a country strange and hostile, but it was only a dream country that would water away in the day's breaking. But then a clear pain burned at the back of his eyeballs, and he knew that he was awake.

The sound of water troubling stones brought him round to a dim consciousness. He lay on cold marble. There was a smell of bat guano and damp earth. He tried to raise himself, but his hands and feet were hobbled by coarse hemp ropes and he could only lift his head. A lantern burned at his feet, a pallid fire curled inside a bowl of glass like a sprout of swamp grass. Voices and footsteps scuffled together in the darkness, perhaps the clopping of hooves, the quick broken nicker of a goat. In the cast of the lantern's flame, he saw that he was naked.

He let his head down. The heat of the pain burned off and then slid through him coldly. The voices muttered, then melded with the sound of the water as it slipped over the marble until neither was distinguishable from the other. Shadows reared and then died on the walls about him like the guttering light of a furnace that burned only murk.

He turned his head to his right. Someone was beside him, sprawled in a posture of sleep, their mouth gaped open.

"Hey," Beam whispered. "Hey, you awake?" It was agony to speak.

Only the echo of water answered.

"Where are we?" Beam asked.

"Don't ask that." Someone spoke from the other side of the room. Beam turned his head and a form rose from the wall. It came and lifted the lantern, and the trucker appeared suddenly, his eyes fixed and steady orbs, no different than the clean blank eyes of marble cherubim. "You know where you are," he said, his voice a slither.

Beam tried to raise himself again, but the ropes held him and the pain thundered in his head. He pulled and struggled, but it was useless and he soon slumped breathless against the stone. "Where am I?" he whispered.

Turning again to the figure lying beside him, he saw in the span of withered lantern light that there was no one there at all, only a blanched and empty skull.

# EPILOGUE

The days grew wizened and then the frosts came. Elvis noticed the change as it arrived in slow intervals—the leaves dropping their green and flashing to fire and then to mute brown and falling in vast endless clutters and sweeping over lawns and streets and pastures, the corn in the river bottoms grown rickety and skeletal, the slight glaze of ice appearing in a lacey veil on his windows each morning, the world aging into a pale fragility, and when the wind shook the grasses and empty winter trees they seemed to tremble with the burden of knowing something weighty and awful. Clans of robins moved south. Jaybirds and grackles as well. All things in flight from this place, seeking a warmer clime innocent of cold.

He kept to his appointed routes. In the cruiser, with the heater blowing and the radio squawking its bored talk, he drove and drove, knocking miles of roadway down until the distance seemed to accrue into a kind of sleep, a travel-bartered reprieve from thought and dream.

On occasion, he went to a bluff overlooking the Gasping River, a pull-off of gray dirt scattered with beer bottles and spent condoms. From there, he would sit and look out over the water. Now that the trees had shed their leaves, he could see the Sheetmire ferry, Derna prowling the platform, gathering her fares, six days a week, twelve hours a day. At this distance she was only a speck, a sexless mote driven perhaps by the same forces that drew the river on to its inevitable confluence with the Ohio. At times, he thought of driving down to the landing and crossing. But he never did. There were no more words to pass. He'd spoken enough of them already, in her living room, at the courthouse, in diners and at country gas stations when he happened to cross paths with her. He'd spoken too much, had gone beyond acceptable talk, even sputtering apologies to her one blustery October afternoon at the Micadoo post office. Derna, her bent fingers clutching a pile of envelopes, only lifted the blue lid of the mailbox, deposited her bills, and left. No cursing. No tears. No shake of the head. Only a brief glance, her eyes like the fire-hollowed burls of a tree that had been struck by lightning.

Often, when he pulled away from the gray bluff that overlooked the river, Elvis would drive to a small aluminum trailer yarded with pinwheels and birdbaths. Ella always let him in and they would drink coffee together in her kitchen while the television played in the living room.

"When I get ready," she told him one afternoon, "I'm going to leave this place. Save my money. Maybe move south. I got a brother lives in Springfield, Tennessee. I can stay with him and his wife. Find a job. Lord knows, there ain't none here."

Her arms were thin. Her hands steady. She lifted the cup and sipped. Already, her belly was beginning to show, and the color in her cheeks had flushed.

"I guess you're set on keeping it," Elvis said, nodding to the bulge above her waistline.

Ella's hand fell across her belly. "What kind of question is that?" she asked.

"I don't know. It's not too late. I could take you up to one of those clinics in Louisville."

Ella looked at him as if he'd lost his mind. "Who does something like that?"

Elvis scooted the placemat away from him on the tabletop. "Things like that happen every day, Ella."

She shook her head. "I'm keeping it," she said. "For once in my life I'm going to do what's right. I don't care what happens every day in this world. I'm not like this world. Not anymore."

Elvis sighed. He lifted his hat up and scooted the hair back on his scalp and then replaced the hat. "So you're leaving town?"

Ella nodded. "I'd tell you to do the same thing, Elvis," she said. "Get out. This ain't no kind of place. Everything is dried out and empty. The kind of people in it…Jesus."

"There's bad all over," he replied.

"I'm aware. But the trouble around here, it gets to know you well enough where it thinks it can own you. I'm through with all that." She tossed her hand through the air. "So I'd tell you to leave, but I know you won't go."

"I got reelected, so I can't go."

"Sure, you can. Just pack up and be gone. It ain't hard."

Elvis ran his thumb over the leather of his gun belt. "I figure if I ever left they'd haul me back."

"Only if you let them."

"You act like I got some kind of say in it." He stood and refilled his cup from the pot and lingered at the sink.

Ella balanced her cup in her lap. She smiled. "Well, I've said all I can. It won't help, me talking anymore." The winter light falling through the curtains gilded her cheeks. "Best of luck to you," she said.

One day in early December, Elvis clocked off his shift early and drove out to Daryl's. The parking lot was full of the usual old vessels—redundant trucks and station wagons. A primered green Javelin slouched on racing slicks. A starved red hound gnawed hamburger foil beside the grease-spattered dumpster. Dust whirled and eddied. Faint snow drifted across the gravel.

Elvis waited in the car for a long while, feeling the wind rock the cruiser. Then he put his hat on and walked into the Quonset hut. Inside, the buffed floors shone polished and slick, dancers scooting together as they crossed back and forth over the shine. The jukebox played Merle Haggard's *I Am A Lonesome Fugitive*. He'd long become used to being stared at—the uniform, the gun and badge, it made people look, you couldn't blame them—so when the drinkers at the bar turned he made no acknowledgement but only pulled himself onto a stool and rested his elbows on the damp mahogany.

The tender walked down to him.

"Old Milwaukee," Elvis said.

The tender dragged a can from the icebox. He popped it with a filet knife and placed it in front of Elvis.

Elvis took two long sips. The beer tasted germy, like moldy bread, but it was cold.

"It's two dollars. Start a tab?" the tender asked.

Elvis swallowed and shook his head. He reached in his pocket and took out eight quarters, placing them in a careful stack on the bar.

The tender scooted the money into his palm and knocked the register open and slid the coins inside. The tin sale bell chimed when he slammed the cash drawer closed.

"Strange for somebody to pay in quarters."

Elvis turned. Daryl stood before him. He'd lost weight and his eyes were sunken. Elvis scooted a stool out with his boot. He waited for Daryl to stow himself down, but he just stood there, armless and strange in a camo vest and t-shirt and pleated khakis. The tops of his loafers gleamed like fresh tar.

"I'm all pocket change," Elvis said. He tapped the stool with his boot. "Sit down."

Daryl lowered himself onto the red cracked vinyl seat. The tender brought him a bottle of Jax with a bendy straw. He sipped and turned his head and wiped his mouth against his shoulder. "What do you want?" he asked. "You come in here like this, I know you want something so you best go ahead and say what it is."

"Why? You in a hurry?"

"No. But the way you're dressed don't make anybody want to dance."

Elvis leaned over his beer and ran his thumbnail over the sharp aluminum edge of the mouth of the can.

"I ain't seen Loat," Daryl said. "It's the same today like it's always going to be. I ain't seen him."

Elvis lifted the can and took a pull. "What about Beam?"

Daryl shook his head. "My guess, he's probably taking turns with Chicago whores and eating rainbow pie." He drew himself closer to Elvis. "My advice would be to stop your looking. I can tell right now it ain't helping your age none."

"Maybe you're right," Elvis said. "But you don't mind me coming in here once a week and having a brew. Long as I'm paying, I can drink my beer, right?"

Daryl stiffened. He rose straight and pulled away from Elvis, then leaned down over the straw sprouting from the bottle of Jax and slurped. "I don't guess I got any say in that, do I?" he said.

Elvis wrapped his fingers around his can of Old Milwaukee. "What about that trucker," he asked. "Where's he gone off to?"

Daryl squinted. "There's a lot of truckers in the world."

"You know the one I mean."

Daryl tilted his head back. The whiskers on his throat were silver. "If you mean that one that you had a run in with then I can't say. I guess he had to head out for another run somewhere. You know how truckers are. They ain't got no place."

"Well, if he lit out he didn't go in the rig he come in. You know that. We found the wreck. Matter of fact, I'd be willing to bet that you know exactly what become of him. Matter of fact, I'd say he had a good portion of help from you in getting wherever it is he's gone to."

Daryl lowered himself over the straw again and sipped. "You know how those folks are," he said, shaking his head. "The whole world's their home."

Elvis chewed his lower lip. The bar noise groaned around him, a thick toneless scuffle of glasses and juke music and laughter and gnawed bits of drunken talk. Dusky light bled from the light bulbs in the ceiling and the shadows of the dancers withered over the bright polished floor, the smoke buckling and settling in their wake.

"The whole world and nowhere," he said.

"Don't worry about it," Daryl continued, in mock comfort. "Folks like you and me, we're lucky. We got our places. We ain't like the trucker. We notched us out a groove a long time ago and now all we got to do is sit in it. You realize that and I'd say you'll sleep lots better."

Elvis tugged the last of his beer down. He sat the can on the bar and turned to Daryl. "Don't you ever think I'm like you," he said. "Me and you, we don't come from the same place at all."

Daryl grinned. "Tell yourself that then," he said. "If that's what keeps your nightmares away."

"Nightmares." Elvis grunted. "You're looking at your nightmare right here." He scooted closer and grabbed the front of Daryl's vest, bunching the lapels in his fists. "I know you had a hand in all that mess with Beam," he said. "I can't prove it, but I know it. So you can sit up here the rest of your life sipping beer and playing at being some kind of country kingpin and I'll be in here once a week to drink my Old Milwaukee and ask my questions. So you best be about finding your own way of getting to sleep and not worry about how I get mine."

He let go of Daryl's vest and made for the door.

"Where you going?" Daryl called after him.

"To look for Beam."

"You ain't gonna find him."

Elvis paused with his hand on the door handle. Then he shook his head and stepped outside into the gusting winter air. He let his eyes adjust to the gray light and then walked to the cruiser. He took his hat off and laid it on the seat beside him and cranked the engine and drove away.

A wet snow began to spit. He clicked the wipers on. The country he drove through was a dingy worn trouble of hollers junked with burned trailers and washing machines and wrecked vehicles, chambers of jagged black trees and wide pasture where snow jotted in the fescue a strange haunted script of ghosts. Elvis thought of the word *lazaretto*. He'd heard it on the vocabulary tape his sister had sent him. Another useless hobby, something she'd hoped would use his time. He remembered the sentence, the tape's narrator breathing it out long and coolly, as if he spoke in a plush library amidst towers of leather bound books: *Those with cholera were taken to the lazaretto.* The word seemed to fit the land. Trees darkened by winter, the hills slinking down to the soggy bottom country—these were wards where the people were afflicted with night-mired souls, where the derelict and bereft were quarantined. It was a keep.

He drove on. On a blank stretch of road, he came to a green highway sign that marked the end of the county. There was a grimed turn-off and he pulled in, the tires snarling in the gravel. He shut the cruiser down. Sided by rearing hills, this was a place where the light slid down in short dim wisps the color of suturing thread, but he could not say what wounds the light mended, what flows it hoped to stanch. There were only hills and road, yawning out and going off into the further wilds. He could not imagine anyone coming to this place. There were only those being kept and those that left, either in flight or exile. He did not know which one he was, or even which he hoped to be, and he could not have said if there was less courage in being kept in a place, bound to a bitter soil and a bitter people, than in leaving it.

He rolled the window down and the cold bit his face. A fence ran alongside the road and the wind twanged the strands of rusted wire. A kestrel had perched itself on one of the locust posts, the wind ruffling its feathers. It sat in complete stillness, like a hawk fashioned from substances older than blood and flesh, its polished black eyes watching him with a stillness that was beyond the mere absence of motion, but seemed to contain all the fixed clarity of the end of time's long unfurling, a stillness that was depthless and unreadable and without governor. Elvis did not know what seeing a hawk in such weather meant, but he knew that it did mean something. Or, at least that it had once meant something. He tried hard to recollect his grandmother's naming of birdly omens, but couldn't. There was no knowledge to the thing at all anymore. No wisdom. Only the kestrel, sitting quiet on a locust post while the snow lay down in silence against the cold waiting earth.

He ran his hand through his hair. The rearview mirror was there for him to look into, but he did not look.

When he turned the ignition, the kestrel rose and swam up through the graying winter light. A thing that could not be kept. What the world could not ensnare.

"Best of luck to you," Elvis whispered.

But the bird had already flown and he might as well have spoken only to the air.

## ACKNOWLEDGMENTS

The author wishes to acknowledge the expertise of Robert Lasner and Elizabeth Clementson of Ig Publishing, and as well as the dedication of his agent Terra Chalberg.

T